Everyone loves books

"A laugh-cry book from first page to last."

—Milly Johnson

"Simply brilliant."

—Jane Linfoot

"A proper heart-burster."

—Laura Kemp

"Moving, beautiful, and heart-wrenching."

—Cathy Bramley

"Witty, beautifully characterized, life-affirming—and I shed an actual tear at the beauty and perfection of the ending."

—*My Weekly*

"A heartwarming read, with pure love at its core."

—*Woman*

"Humor, tears, and, above all, hope. Bring tissues."

—Catherine Isaac

"An emotional, wise, bighearted gem of a novel—if you need your faith restored in the world, this is the perfect read!"

—Miranda Dickinson

"This book will tug on your heartstrings. . . . It's clever and wise, brimming with warmth and poignancy."

—Carmel Harrington

"Funny and poignant—a celebration of life and the enduring power of love."

—Carys Bray

The
MOMENT
I Met
YOU

Also by Debbie Johnson

A Wedding at the Comfort Food Café
A Gift from the Comfort Food Café
Sunshine at the Comfort Food Café
Coming Home to the Comfort Food Café
The A–Z of Everything
Christmas at the Comfort Food Café
Summer at the Comfort Food Café
Pippa's Cornish Dream
The Birthday That Changed Everything
Cold Feet at Christmas
Never Kiss a Man in a Christmas Jumper
Maybe One Day

The
MOMENT
I Met
YOU

A NOVEL

DEBBIE JOHNSON

ωm

WILLIAM MORROW

An Imprint of HarperCollins*Publishers*

P.S.™ is a trademark of HarperCollins Publishers.

THE MOMENT I MET YOU. Copyright © 2021 by Debbie Johnson. Excerpt from MAYBE ONE DAY © 2020 by Debbie Johnson. All rights reserved. Printed in the United States of America. No part of this book may be used or reproduced in any manner whatsoever without written permission except in the case of brief quotations embodied in critical articles and reviews. For information, address HarperCollins Publishers, 195 Broadway, New York, NY 10007.

HarperCollins books may be purchased for educational, business, or sales promotional use. For information, please email the Special Markets Department at SPsales@harpercollins.com.

Originally published in the United Kingdom in 2021 by Orion.

FIRST U.S. EDITION

Library of Congress Cataloging-in-Publication Data has been applied for.

ISBN 978-0-06-300369-9

22 23 24 25 26 LSC 10 9 8 7 6 5 4 3 2 1

For Sandra Shennan,
the best apocalypse buddy a girl could have x

The
MOMENT
I Met
YOU

Prologue

Four months ago, Cornwall

My name is Elena Godwin. I live an ordinary life in an ordinary place, and the greatest joys I feel are the simple ones—the ones so easy to miss.

I laugh at terrible jokes. I stop and stare at rainbows. I cry without embarrassment at happy endings. I try to appreciate every single good thing that this life has to offer.

We all have our own versions of "good things," I suppose, depending on our tastes: one person's Marmite is another person's Nutella. The bright spots that shine in a sometimes gray world.

I don't have an actual physical list of these good things—but maybe I should. Maybe it would be a wonderful form of mindfulness, to jot them down in a notepad, or start a spreadsheet, or get them tattooed on my back in Sanskrit (kidding—that would hurt way too much).

But my mental list is long, and ever-evolving. At the moment, it includes—but is not limited to—the following: a cold glass of water after a long walk on a midsummer's day; a solitary train journey with a good book; the bread-and-beans smell of a coffee shop; a sleeping dog wagging its tail; the silken smoothness of a rose petal between my fingertips.

That first moment after winter when you notice blossom buds curving on branches and feel the sun on your face and know that spring is miraculously coming, yet again. Anything to do with the sun, really: its rising, its setting, its light, and its shade. The way it sinks into the sea-lined horizon at the end of the day, as though it is putting itself to bed.

Some of my favorite things admittedly make me sound like I'm a hundred years old, not thirty-five, but I don't care. I cherish them. The simple joy of settling into a comfy chair when your legs are aching. Taking your bra off at the end of the day. The feeling of complete luxury when you've changed your bedding and are stretched out alone beneath a duvet cover that still smells of fabric softener.

Sometimes, the simple joys belong to someone else. Like the small swoosh of the heart you feel when you see young lovers kiss.

A group of women giggling together in a café. Drunk people dancing. An elderly couple waiting at a bus stop, holding each other's hands.

Kids at the side of a flooded road, hoping that passing cars might race through the puddles and drench them. A baby asleep in its mother's arms. The squeals and shouts as you walk past a school playground. Anything to do with children, really, even though it can feel bittersweet to a childless woman. The key, as with so many things, is to concentrate on the sweet.

I do my very best. I make sure that I appreciate these everyday pleasures, these mundane treasures, and I relish the normal routines of daily existence that allow me to experience them.

Daily existence, in all its tarnished glory, is full of small miracles if we pay close enough attention. Sometimes, we don't even notice them happening—the moments that change everything, or the moments that change nothing. The moment you meet someone who will alter the way you view your life. The moment you stand at a hidden crossroads and make a choice that feels as unimportant as a snowflake, that becomes a snowball, that becomes an avalanche.

These days, I do pay attention. I notice as many of those moments as I can, and I don't take any of it for granted—because I know what it feels like to almost lose it all. To be afraid in the dark, unsure if you'll ever feel the clean caress of fresh air or drink that cold glass of water. Ever hear the sound of laughter again. Ever be able to stretch your limbs and fill your lungs and feel the space of the world around you.

When I was twenty-six years old my world was turned upside down and inside out, like a coat pocket being excavated for loose change. It was terrible and frightening, and it taught me a lot of things I never wanted to know.

It taught me that the ground we walk upon isn't as solid as we think. It taught me that our feet skim the surface of hidden uncertainty every single day. It taught me that we can all fall, no matter how carefully you step or how strong your legs. It taught me that we can survive so much—but at a cost, always.

I learned about frailty, and strength, and the way that we are all made up of both. I discovered that the human body combines amazing resilience and amazing delicacy, one minute as robust and present as an ancient tree trunk, the next clinging on with the fragile tenacity of a dragonfly hovering above a sunlit pond.

We are made of bone and muscle and tissue, like the earth is made of a core and mantle and crust. Imperfect designs, with unpredictable flaws and unimaginable complexity.

On the night it all happened, I was still under the misguided belief that my destiny was in my own hands. That I could make my own choices.

Now I know differently, and in some ways that has been a blessing. It has made me value those small miracles so much more. But I also know that safety and stability are illusions, fairy tales we tell ourselves.

Change is all around us, even when we can't see it. Cells mutating, valves straining, friction building, all hidden beneath the surface. Nothing stays the same, even when you want it to. That's the thing about these moments that make up our lives—they all pass, no matter how hard we try to hold on to them. The moments become memories, and the memories become stories, things that happened to someone else—the person we used to be, long ago.

I recovered from that night, the night the world turned upside down—or at least I appeared to. Sometimes I wonder if I ever even left that place, or if in some alternate universe, a different Elena stayed: shattered, broken, buried in the earth. A distant memory.

Sometimes, I wonder if I think too much.

Now, almost ten years later, I can feel the subtle vibrations and internal creaks that tell me that things are about to change again. That the small miracles may be overwhelmed by larger events, and I will soon be yet another version of myself. I have agreed to do something that scares me, that could change me, that could divert the flow of my life. Point me in a different direction. It was one of those moments: the ones that leave you altered.

Today, I sense the tectonic plates of my life shifting, the unseen fault lines spreading. Subtle cracks are appearing where my truth is pulling away from other people's truths, where there is a separating of realities, the intrusion of a never-quelled past into a never-whole present. A change that I have hidden from for too long.

I lie in bed at night, awake, next to him as he slumbers—a man-shaped shadow in a shroud of sheets, one arm slung over his head, hair tousled. Small snores puff from his lips, endearing or irritating, depending on my mood. He is apparently untouched by the tremors I am feeling, the sensation that everything we have together is built on sand.

I am amazed and envious of his peace, of his lack of fear. This is his story too, you see. It is a story that belongs to many people. In particular, in my personal universe, it belongs to me, to Alex, to Harry. The three of us, twined together like plaited rope. I know the beginning of our story. I know the middle. But I have no idea how it ends . . .

He dreams gently, and I stare at the ceiling, sleep a distant land. I am resigned to the sore eyes and fatigued mind, and I lie there waiting for daylight to bleed into the night sky and tell me it's all beginning again. I stare, and I wait, and I wonder: What will the landscape of my world look like once the dust has settled?

I

Nine years ago,
Western Mexico

Chapter 1

We are sitting behind Jorge, the coach driver, as he pulls into the car park. Well, I say car park—it's actually just a piece of pockmarked concrete on top of a hill. Everything, it seems, is on top of a hill around here. Even the hills.

An excited gaggle of little boys is running beside the chugging coach, waving at us through the dusty windows. One of them is holding a football; all of them are laughing and smiling. It's infectious, and I stick my tongue out in response. They look shocked then delighted, and all start pulling faces at me. I am lowering the tone already, and I haven't even got off the bus. My mum always says you need to be a bit of a kid to work with kids, and I suspect she's right.

Harry shakes his head at my antics, in an amused but mildly exasperated way. I stick my tongue out at him as well. That'll teach him.

"Hope Jorge's hand brake is good . . ." he murmurs, as he starts to stretch out his arms, pressing his palms against the luggage rack and gazing at his own biceps. They are good biceps, to be fair, but the view outside is

9

even better. The forested slopes, the red rooftops of the village, the heat that seems to shimmer in the air.

This part of Mexico is exotic and enticing and a million miles from our normal lives in London. Even a million miles from the hotel we've been staying at, really. I am excited to be here, in this place, and excited to be getting off the coach and breathing in the late-afternoon mountain air.

The engine of the bus seems to sigh and belch as it shudders to a stop. I feel it jarring through me, my bones rattling and settling after hours on the road.

I glance at Jorge and see that he is also sighing, just like the bus. Though not, as yet, belching. He is a lovely man, Jorge—physically he is made entirely of circles, a round face on top of rounded shoulders that hulk down to a round belly. I see him reach out to touch the Saint Christopher medallion he has hanging around the mirror, before leaning back against his seat, which has a T-shirt tied around it bearing the logo of a football team I don't know.

It's been a heck of a journey, the longest and scariest stretch of driving we've done as part of our mini-tour. All hairpin bends and jaw-dropping scenery and frankly terrifying heights. This little bus has been our only protection against the wild world, keeping us safe on narrow roads and cool in the searing heat.

That heat has taken its toll, though, and the wind-screen is coated with a patina of red dust and stray flower petals and flattened insects. There's been a mini-beast massacre.

I can tell that Harry is itching to get off, and I can't really blame him. He's a lot taller than me, and a lot less patient, and a lot less interested in scenery. He didn't even want to come on this trip—he'd have been far happier in our posh hotel, sitting by the pool sipping cocktails or lounging on a pool float. He came only to please me, which was either sweet or another sign that we have nothing in common—I'm not really sure yet.

Our tour guide, Sofia, gets up to speak. She turns first to Jorge, and they give each other an enthusiastic high five. If I was driving these roads every day, I'd celebrate too.

I know Jorge has grandchildren; there are photos of them tacked onto his dashboard, from babes in arms and toddlers through to teens. He talks with great affection about his wife, Maria, and is always very amused when we all ooh and aah about whitewashed adobe buildings— he says he prefers his air-conditioned apartment with all the modern conveniences.

He must be in his sixties, and he holds his round body with a lot of dignity—but every now and then he winks playfully or puffs with laughter, and a much younger, much more mischievous man peeks out.

Sofia comes to face us all. She is in her thirties some-where, with deep laughter lines at the corners of her eyes, and accented but perfect English.

She has kept us entertained and informed for the whole of the trip, speaking into her crackling micro-phone, all the way out of our resort in Puerto Vallarta, through the Sierra Madres and the old mines and the forests and the magical places that are sprinkled across the hills and valleys.

We had an overnight stay in what I called "rustic" accommodations, which Harry called "a shithole," and was maybe a bit of both depending on your perspective. We've seen astonishing wildflower meadows and abandoned haciendas left behind as strange time capsules, and the most picturesque places imaginable.

We've seen so many different types of birds and animals and met so many people, and I've loved it. Harry has endured it as graciously as he could manage, so I can't hold that against him.

When he suggested this holiday, I hoped that it would bring us closer together. Heal some of the rifts I've started to feel developing between us. Instead, I am starting to think that it is actually only highlighting our differences.

That makes me feel sad and confused—I have been with Harry for what feels like forever—so I set it aside to worry about later. I don't want to spoil the present worrying too much about the future.

It is late afternoon, and we are here in Santa Maria de Alto for our dinner before we set off again. We are scheduled to arrive back at our hotel sometime around midnight, and then we will be back in the modern world, and all of this faded grandeur will feel like a dream. I can't lie—I'm with Harry and Jorge on the air-conditioning—but there is something wild and free about these remote corners of the world that calls to me.

Sofia tells us about the history of this particular

village, about its isolation, many hours from any other tourist destination. She tells us about the way it reflects the wider history of the region, and how visitors like us are making an important contribution to the micro-economy. She encourages us to visit the church, to talk to the locals, to eat, to laugh, and to drink tequila. Everyone laughs at the last point, especially the gaggle of Aussie backpacking girls who have brought a near-feral sense of fun to the whole trip.

"Jorge and I will be there with you," she says, "at our friend Luis's bar. We'll be here for a few hours, and if you need us, please just come and find us."

"No tequila for Jorge, is very sad!" adds Jorge, rubbing away fake tears. His English isn't as good as Sofia's, but he makes his point, and I laugh again.

He opens the door to the coach and it makes a familiar hissing noise. Jorge will do what he always does—wait until we are off before he tries to move. It's a complex maneuver, squeezing his bulk from behind the steering-wheel column.

I wait while the other passengers troop past. I like people-watching. I like making up stories to match everyone, creating fictional lives for them, assigning them nicknames. I have always enjoyed doing this, ever since I was little.

In my mind, my teacher was a fairy-tale princess, and the man in the sweet shop was Willy Wonka, and the old gent who lived in the bungalow on the corner of our road was actually a mysterious time traveler. There were some harsh realities in my childhood, and

I think all the tall tales helped me cope. These days, I am less fantastical with my imaginings. I realized that real people can be just as interesting.

Those Aussie girls, for example. They're so loud, and vivid, and completely confident in their own skin. They're the first off the coach, a tangle of long limbs and short shorts and sun-kissed skin and flip-flops. I see Harry's gaze linger as they prance past in a flurry of laughter and see Jorge watch them wistfully as they jump down the steps. I get it, I really do—they're not just hot, they're happy, carefree.

Next past is the one family group on the trip. There's a tired-looking mum and dad, a young boy who constantly asks questions, and a teenage daughter who looks professionally bored as she slouches along behind them. She has bright red hair and pale skin and is clutching a fancy phone. There is no signal here, but she still clutches it, like an empty oxygen tank that might have one last puff of air left inside it. She's been like this for the whole journey, and every time I look at her I have to bite my lips so I don't laugh out loud. If I laughed out loud, she might stab me.

I remember that phase—that deeply rooted conviction that the world sucks and that nobody will ever understand you. It's funny in hindsight—but deadly serious at the time.

The elderly couple goes past next. I don't like to ponder the intimate details of other couples' lives, but they must be in their eighties and I saw them snogging in the back seat yesterday. Life goals. He—I think his name is

Donald—goes first, then holds up his hand to help his wife down the steps.

Next there's a much younger couple, maybe in their thirties, who are at the other end of the relationship spectrum, at least from the outside looking in. They've been bickering for the whole trip and, from the look on her face, I wouldn't bet on a romantic dinner for two. She pushes past him to get out of the coach first, jumping down onto the graveled concrete instead of using the steps. She hits the ground so hard dust flies up, her face angry and resentful behind it as she strides off.

Others pass, everyone bright and happy, making their way into the next stage of our adventure.

Last off, after politely offering to let us go first and me equally politely declining, is the Mystery Man. The Man in Black. He of the Big Boots and Backpack.

Of all the stories, of all the people-watching-inspired fictions, his is possibly the most interesting. Even Harry—who has a strict policy of only ever reading sports autobiographies—has joined in.

All we actually know is that he is traveling alone, that he is European, and that he takes a lot of photographs. He doesn't talk much to any of us, and because of this seems extremely fascinating. Harry's theories thus far are that he is either an eccentric tech billionaire looking for anonymity or a serial killer who has several women locked in his basement.

Mine have included him being on the run from a drug cartel; on the run from an ex-wife; or on the run from the FBI. He's definitely, somehow, on the run—but not from any of the above, I suspect. He is distant but courteous, silent but not rude, and carries with him an air of deep-frosted melancholy that makes me think he is on the run from something altogether less interesting, and altogether more sad.

He's not very chatty, though, so we'll probably never find out. He will remain as the Mystery Man forever, I think, as I watch him set off into the distance, alone as usual.

"Okay. Can we actually leave the coach now?" Harry asks, not unreasonably.

I laugh and nod, and he climbs out of the cushioned seat and stretches, his T-shirt riding up to expose a scattering of dark hair pluming a gym-toned stomach.

I wonder, as Jorge nods at me, smiling, what people make of us. What stories do they make up to match us? People-watching, I know, goes both ways.

On the surface we must look perfectly normal, perfectly happy—a young couple off on a dream holiday together. Harry is handsome and athletic-looking; I am adequate if not at all extraordinary. He has a well-paid job and all the trappings. I work as a teacher and love it. We have been together for eight years, having met and fallen in love in our first week at university.

We are edging toward the age when people start to ask about wedding bells ringing, where parents start to make small comments about grandchildren, where friends are throwing engagement parties or looking to move from the city to a bigger house in the suburbs.

We are at the age where people see us as solid, united,

committed. As the kind of couple who will take the next steps expected of them.

I wish we were that kind of couple. I wish I was that kind of woman. In all honesty, I'm not sure what I want anymore. There's been something simmering inside me this year: a tiny seed of discontent that is making me question this well-trodden path. Whether it's the right one for me.

Whether, truth be told, Harry is the right one for me. I came on this holiday in the hope that it would heal us. That I would feel that magical spark again—that I would look at Harry and feel more than affection; that we would be bound together by more than history. That a different future—one I'm more than half considering—would be the wrong choice.

He jumps down the steps and immediately launches himself into an impromptu game of football with the little boys who were running alongside the coach. One of them kicks up a high ball, and Harry heads it so far away they all chase after it. Harry himself throws his arms up in the air and does a victory dance, like he's just scored the winning penalty in the World Cup.

I smile and follow him out into the sultry air of Santa Maria de Alto.

It's hard not to like Harry. But is that enough?

Chapter 2

The village is small but perfectly formed. It is pretty, all soft yellows and golds as the setting sun casts its last rays across the red rooftops and mellow stone. Birds and insects loop and swoop through the sky, and my feet kick up little clouds of red earth as we walk. The air is still deliciously warm and, even as the light fades, I feel like I am being bathed in gentle heat. This is, I have learned, my favorite time of day in Mexico.

I look around at the small central plaza, dominated by a fountain that is lined with blue tiles. The square is edged by small homes, by a taverna that has set up tables and chairs outside, and by a strangely ornate church that casts a welcome shadow. The building seems far too grand for the village, a hint of a long-gone and more imposing past.

Today, the locals have organized a whole cottage industry to make the most of our visit. There are make-shift stalls set up selling leather bags and glazed pottery and jewelry that glints in the sun. There's a tequila stand, lined up with glasses of liquor and rompope, and a large fridge stocked with soft drinks being manned by two teenage boys.

A young woman with a baby beside her in a stroller has a stall selling everything from touristy fans, cigarette lighters, and fridge magnets to teddy bears and giant sombreros, as well as bowls of fresh fruit, pomegranates and strawberries glistening.

A group of women has set up a large open-air grill, and the smell is incredible. I didn't even realize I was hungry until it hits me: garlic and spices and roasting meats. My mouth waters in response, and I wonder how long it is until dinner. Music is playing, and it feels like a good time is about to be had by all.

Harry takes my hand, the action so natural we don't even think about it, and together we wander the streets of the village. There's not much to it really—several small and winding passages that lead off from the square, pretty but lived in, with washing hanging from lines and air-conditioning units and terra-cotta pots full of plants and herbs.

I enjoy the shade and the quiet as we stroll, listening to Harry's commentary as we go. Never knowingly caught without an opinion, Harry—but even he only has favorable ones so far. I can tell he's enjoying it more than he expected.

"Why does everyone in Mexico seem to support Chelsea?" he asks, peering through a window and pointing out a club banner.

"Why does anyone support Chelsea?" I ask. "In fact why does anybody watch sport at all?"

I don't really mean it, but Harry is a slave to anything involving grown men chasing balls and it's fun to poke the bear. He fakes a horrified look and replies, "I shall ignore you said that, Elena. Like religion and politics, it's something we just shouldn't discuss."

We walk on and find ourselves emerging from the tangle of streets back out into the square. I drink in the sound of laughter and the bright colors and the flower-drenched trellises and the sun-scorched stone, and decide that I am a little bit in love with the place. I have been feeling the tug of wanderlust recently, and this is only adding to it. London seems light-years away, and I think perhaps I'd like to keep it that way. I've enjoyed my time in the big city, but I feel the need for change.

Everywhere around us we see smiling faces, busy people. Kids are milling around, either helping their parents or dashing in and out of the bustle, some smiling shyly, others waving and giggling. The footballers are still kicking around near the coach, and we are greeted with welcoming cries by everyone we see, in Spanish, English, a mix of the two.

I see Jorge and Sofia inside the taverna and the various members of our coach party scattered about, shopping and drinking and taking photos.

"It's a hive of capitalist activity, this place," says Harry, as he looks around. "Bet it's dead as a doornail until the coach gets in."

"Probably," I reply, distracted by a pair of purple butterflies dancing around the gentle splash of water in the fountain. The fine spray makes them look like their wings are patterned in gold lace, and it is mesmerizing.

"Am I right in assuming," says Harry, apparently not as mesmerized, "that you're going to want to look inside that church?"

I have to laugh at the expression on his face. I think he'd be happier if I suggested he should give Jorge a donkey ride around the village instead. It has become very clear on this trip that my love of "rotting old buildings," as he puts it, is something he cannot understand. It just does not compute—a bit like my views on football, I suppose.

He has tried hard to go with the flow, and managed to fake it through the first two or three, but by this stage he is so transparent that he's incapable of hiding his dread.

I know he was quite happy in Puerto Vallarta, at the hotel. So was I—at least for some of the time. But what can I say? That wanderlust again. I just couldn't see the point of coming to the other side of the world and only doing the same things we'd be able to do in Benidorm.

So I dragged him away from the piped music and daily games of water polo, and into the big, wild world. The world that doesn't always come with air con and a minibar.

For me, it's been a glimpse of another side of Mexico, another side of life—and possibly a taste of what my world could look like in an alternate reality. I have half-formed plans, ideas that are right now just tiny seeds, tentative shoots into a different future.

But for now I am here, in a beautiful village in a

beautiful place, with my boyfriend, who is dancing impatiently by my side and eyeing up the tequila stand with a lustful gaze.

"Of course I want to go into the church!" I reply, widening my eyes at him. "Why wouldn't I? And I know there's nothing you love more than an intricately carved baptismal font . . ."

He blinks rapidly, trying to formulate a positive-sounding response, and I can't torture him anymore.

"Well, let's look at the stalls, shall we? Maybe have a drink? Then see where we end up . . ."

Truth be told, I'm not feeling brilliant myself—I have a tummy ache that is probably the forerunner of starting an inconvenient period, and I'm pretty tired. I'm happy to stroll around and then sit still for a while.

"Good idea, Batman," he says quickly, leaning forward to kiss me on the forehead. He has had a last-minute pardon from enforced culture, and he is happy about it.

He is more relaxed here, on holiday, than he has been for ages. Mainly, I suspect, because he is away from his job. It's not my job, so I have no right to feel so strongly about it, but I do—over the years I've seen how it's changed him, how it's started to dominate his life. How it's sucked so much of the fun out of him—the carefree, kind Harry I fell in love with.

I don't want to sound hypocritical, because it's his work that pays for our fancy flat and our nice car and these holidays. My teaching salary certainly wouldn't. The thing is, I've never cared about stuff—I'd be just as happy living in a tiny studio and having picnics in the park instead of trips to Mexico as long as we were happy together.

Harry cares, though. Harry is a man of immense charm and immense determination—he is able to talk most people into most things, and often leaves them thinking it was all their idea in the first place. He'd probably make a great politician, which isn't necessarily a compliment, is it?

It also makes him great at his job, working for a management consultancy firm that specializes in making businesses "leaner and more efficient." I think he has persuaded himself that it's a force for good, his work— that it's allowing companies to function better and longer, that it is securing economic longevity, building a solid future for generations to come. If that all sounds like it's out of a marketing brochure, then it probably is—but Harry can actually talk like that and make it seem convincing.

Over the last year, though, I have started to want different things. To wonder if we fit as well as we once did. If it is even natural to expect two people who fitted at eighteen to fit years later. Most teenage relationships don't last, and there's a reason for that—we are ever-changing, especially at that age.

He's never understood why I'd want to work in a school for children with special needs. He's never understood how I could be satisfied with so little money. I'm not saying that one of us is right and one of us is wrong—but maybe we have simply grown apart and want different things from our futures.

Perhaps I am too aware of how our life together seems predictable, mapped out. How mine is getting sucked into his. I go to work events and parties with Harry, where I am always the least glamorous of partners, and I hate them. I hate the conversations, the braying laughter, the competitive edge.

I hate the way they compare their cars and holiday homes and investments. Every time I hear it, every time I see Harry joining in, I can't help thinking about the reality of "lean and efficient" for the people on the receiving end of it.

Money, as Harry once told me, isn't the only point of work, but it is a way of keeping score. And Harry is scoring well. He is a rising star, on track for greatness—I'm just not sure I want to be on that track with him. Not sure I want to see all that charm, all that intelligence, used in a way that makes me cringe. Of course, it's not up to me to decide Harry's future, but it is up to me to decide mine.

Harry's not stupid, and he's not emotionally blind, much as he pretends to be when it suits him. I'm sure he's noticed the distance opening up between us, sensed me edging away. So far, it's only been in little ways— saying no to nights out with his colleagues; getting the bus to work instead of a lift. Sending off for a brochure for a language course at the local community college; looking at volunteering opportunities in places that Harry wouldn't want to even visit, never mind live.

I suppose I've been, without even noticing it that much, making myself more self-sufficient. A subtle withdrawal rather than a drama. Drama doesn't work with Harry—whenever we have argued, which has been rare, he has always convinced me he was right. Fighting with him is like running up a down escalator—it's exhausting.

If I squint and only look at us from the corner of my eye, we are happy. The holiday has been a success. I enjoy his company and I cannot deny that he is gorgeous, with his thick floppy hair and athletic body. He is funny and strong and alpha in a way that makes me feel safe.

But if I open my eyes wide, and look more deeply, I still find myself wondering why we are still together at all, brutal as it sounds.

I have been lost in thought as we stroll, admiring the stalls, Harry grabbing a quick tequila on the way. I have held bowls, and patted bags, and run my fingertips along the sparkling silver jewelry. The topaz rings are especially beautiful, and I find myself placing one in my palm, holding it up to the sun, trying it on, but ultimately deciding instead to buy some bracelets as gifts.

I keep one in my pocket and show the other to Harry.

"It's for Olivia," I say.

Olivia is my much younger sister—or she's my half sister to be exact. My own dad died when I was young, and Mum married later in life. I love Olivia to bits, but as far as Harry is concerned she is demon spawn. She's only eight years old but she's never been a member of the Harry Fan Club. She seemed to despise him from birth.

"That's nice," he replies. "Shall we take it to the church and see if we can get it blessed with some holy water?"

I snort out a laugh and punch him on the arm before putting the gift into my bag

"You're right," he adds, rubbing his biceps as though I've actually hurt him. "Holy water alone wouldn't help. I think we need a priest and a personal letter of recommendation from the Archangel Michael. Maybe we could call in at the Vatican on the way home?"

"I bought you a present too," I say, grinning and fishing in my pocket for the other bracelet. His face lights up, and he claps his hands together like he's five at his birthday party.

"Hold out your wrist," I say.

He obeys and I fasten the bracelet around it. It only just fits, a string of black-and-white yin-yang symbols chasing each other around.

"To help you find light and shade," I comment, patting his hand. He examines it from all angles, pretending to be delighted. He's not a jewelry man, Harry, but he keeps it on.

"I shall wear it forever," he announces somberly. He turns to the stall, surveys its many items, and picks up a neon-pink straw sombrero. He perches it on his head, hands on hips, and strikes a modelesque pose, pouting as both I and the lady running the stall laugh.

"I'm not sure," I say, pretending to give it some serious consideration. "I think maybe it's a bit too macho for you?"

He fakes a hurt look and places the towering hat on my head instead. It totters on my high ponytail, then falls over my eyes and halfway down my face.

"Perfect," he says. "We'll take it!"

He haggles with the stallholder—just for fun, it's not like he can't afford it—and we become the proud owners of one undeniably horrible keepsake.

"I feel like one of those girls at a fairground," I say as we walk away, the hat dangling against my thighs. "Like my big, strong man has just won me a stuffed panda and now I have to carry it around all night."

"Yep. You're one lucky lady," he replies. "Play your cards right and you might get a goldfish in a bag as well."

He slips his arm around my shoulders, and as I nestle into him I remind myself of my earlier vow to try to enjoy the present. To feel the soft warmth of the breeze on my skin, to soak up the sights and sounds of a magical dusk in a magical place, to simply relax and enjoy the company of a man I have loved for a very long time.

"You still looked beautiful, even in a pink sombrero," he says as we walk. "When you smile like that, it always makes the world feel like a better place."

This is, from Harry, an unusually deep statement. I can't tell if he's being serious.

"I mean it," he says, stopping and holding me back so we are standing still, facing each other. "Anyone who talks to you falls a little bit in love with you. One look into those green eyes and all is lost . . . honest, I'm not even being sarcastic! You have this way of making people feel warm inside. Like you're actually listening to them, and actually interested in them."

"I am listening, I am interested! Unless they're talking about football . . ."

"Ha! Well, nobody's perfect, I don't suppose . . ."

We have reached the shadow of the church, its towers hovering over us, the broad dark wood door open and calling to me.

He follows my gaze and says, "Do you really want to go in there? It looks like the kind of place they keep donkeys on cold nights."

I grin, but also shake my head in exasperation. Clearly, Harry has seen enough "crappy old churches," as he calls them, to last a lifetime. I need to let him off the hook—and frankly, I need a bit of time alone as well. It looks cool and shady and silent inside, and like a good place to let my whirlpool of a brain calm down for a few minutes. There is a strong chance I will enjoy it more without him.

"Tell you what," I reply. "Why don't you go and get a drink? I'll explore the church, and you can have a deeply spiritual experience with a pint of lager. Diff'rent strokes and all that. I'll meet you back here after—don't get lost!"

I point toward the taverna tables with their red-checked cloths and unlit candles, and he acknowledges me with a relieved smile and a jaunty salute.

"Aye aye, Captain!" he says, leaning forward to kiss me and to take the sombrero from my hand. "I'll take that. You won't need it when you're talking to God."

I watch him walk away, wait until he is seated at one of the shaded tables, and turn my attention back to the building in front of me.

The church is old, yes, and a little on the crumbling

side, but it's also decorated with ornate stone carvings, has at some stage been painted bright and vibrant colors, and has two tall towers on either corner. It looks like something from a fairy tale.

I walk up the steps, a mild aroma of wax and old incense already noticeable. It's dark inside, the only light coming from flickering candles and the setting sun slanting down through the bell towers, stripes of dusty yellow that break up the gloom. I catch the glimmer of gold paint and carved stone and the shine of a crucifix.

The change in temperature gives me a slight chill, and I stand still, letting my eyes adjust to the dimness. Gradually I make out more, like you do in the early morning in a curtained room, and I see that I am not alone in here.

A woman, wrapped in a black shawl, sits silently in one of the wooden pews, rosary beads clutched in her hands, mouth moving as she prays. And off to one side is the man from the coach—the one who's here on his own. The one who Harry insists is a serial killer.

He's probably not a serial killer, but he is dressed all in black and would fade entirely into the diffused light if not for his hair—blond, thick, slightly too long. He's reading an inscription on a stone tablet set into the wall, and I wonder if he can understand it. My Spanish extends only to ordering beer and saying please and thank you, which I should rectify.

One of my alternate futures involves travel, maybe working abroad, and I'll need a lot more than "*dos cervezas, por favor*" if I follow that thread. Even if I don't, it will be useful—there's nothing to be lost by going to a night class, after all.

I don't want to intrude on either the man from the coach or the woman praying so fervently, so I simply sit, in the calm and the peace and the cool, and try to switch off the chaos inside my mind.

Try as I might, though, I cannot find any internal serenity to match the external. I spend five minutes trying not to fidget before I realize that I am not going to achieve any state of Zen, and then I become weirdly worried that I will somehow infect that place with my mood—my viral load of doubt and uncertainty—and decide to leave.

I stop first to drop a few coins into a metal lockbox and to light a candle in memory of my dad. I can never resist—whenever I'm in a church, I have to do it, even though I wasn't raised in a religious way at all. It just seems like a simple way of showing some respect, or showing some grief, or showing some gratitude. One other candle is already lit, the flame dancing, and I light mine next to it so they can take strength in each other.

I close my eyes and whisper my usual mantra: "Hello, Dad—still love you. Still miss you."

As I emerge back outside, the sun has faded even more, and the candles on the tables are being lit by a teenager holding a long taper.

I see the grill is now working overtime, flames licking and spitting, and that a trestle table has been set up next to it, laden with bowls of guacamole and salsa, bread, tortillas, and salad.

Music is being played from speakers I can't see, and the Aussie girls are dancing around the fountain, all of them holding tall glasses of beer, looking like they're having a blast. I might not be able to achieve a state of Zen, but maybe I can just have a fun night.

I glance over at Harry sitting at a table, one of a small row set up at the side of the taverna, in the shadow of the church towers. He's sipping his own beer, looking on as one of the Australians starts twerking while her pal takes photos with one of those disposable cameras you get on the table at weddings.

"Are you lusting over antipodean goddesses in short shorts?" I say, smiling as I sit opposite him. He's ordered a bottle of wine, which has been delivered with two glasses.

"Of course not," he replies too quickly, dragging his eyes away. "Merely enjoying the sight of someone living their best life. Also, really impressed at how she can dance like that and not spill a drop of her pint."

"Australian," I say, shrugging. "Probably learned to do that at nursery."

He smiles and pushes a glass toward me. "How was it? The church? Any major karmic revelations, or just a load of candle stumps and a faint smell of decay?"

"It was lovely, thank you very much. We can't all be culturally defunct."

"I'm not . . . defunct. I just know what I like. Hotels that have five stars after their names. A guy came around a minute ago, said the dinner will be ready soon. We just pay a set fee and help ourselves. Smells pretty good, and I've got my Imodium just in case."

"Why are you so obsessed with that? Not everyone who goes to a foreign country gets food poisoning."

"From your ears to my arse, darling. And you've not been feeling so good yourself, have you?"

"I think that's just all the travel, or impending lady times, not being poisoned by guacamole."

"Who knows? Better safe than sorry. Anyway. Do you mind if I go and have a wander?"

"No," I reply quickly. "Go. Fill your mind. Run free, little one."

He grins and heads off back to the center of the plaza. The Aussie girls are still dancing like nobody's watching, all easygoing giggles and wriggles. One of them—a tall blonde in a neon-pink cut-off T-shirt—makes a grab for Harry as he passes, trying to persuade him to boogie with her. He laughs, and breaks out one of his very best smiles, as he jumps out of the girl's grasp and heads for one of the other little bars that has opened up on the square.

"Aw, come back and play, Hugh Grant!" the blonde shouts after him, and I know he'll be secretly delighted with that comparison.

He does look a bit like Hugh Grant. That's not a bad thing, but real life isn't a rom-com—even if it felt that way when I first met him, during freshman week at Liverpool University.

Harry was studying economics; I was doing English. It was my first time away from home, and with hindsight it shouldn't have been. I needed to experience a bit more of life—to travel, to work, to try different things.

But my domestic situation never really allowed me a lot of freedom when I was younger, and even going away to college in England felt as though I was shirking responsibility.

I think that's one of the reasons I fell for him so fast and so hard. It wasn't just that he was dishy, it was that he somehow brought out a deeply hidden sense of recklessness in me. He made me forget responsibility and led me astray in the best ways possible.

He had a way of giving me confidence, of seeing the wild side I didn't even know I possessed. He was always leading the charge into new nightclubs, and persuading me to rappel down buildings, and convincing me it was absolutely a great idea to make love in shadowy urban graveyards as crowds of bachelors and bachelorette partyers staggered past on the other side of low walls.

It all seemed so exciting—like he knew me in a way that nobody else did.

But that was then, and this is now, and I feel like we are on different paths, trying to cling on to each other as life pulls us apart. I'm not even quite sure why we're still clinging—is it out of habit, out of insecurity, fear? Or is it that we still have too much love for each other to be quite willing to give it up?

All I know is that now, I sometimes find his charm annoying. I find the way he styles his hair annoying. I find the amount of time he spends in front of the bathroom mirror annoying.

I lean back in my chair, and my hand goes to my mouth in horror. I am shocked at how vitriolic all of that sounded in my own mind. Shocked, and a little bit ashamed. A little bit disgusted at the judgmental way that train of thought hurtled off the tracks.

It's not even remotely fair to be irritated with Harry for just being Harry. He is who he is, and there is a lot to like about him. A lot to love. He isn't perfect, and neither am I. Far from it.

For me, I think the turning point came at New Year. We were at a party thrown by his boss. I just remember watching him through the eyes of a stranger, seeing the way he worked the room, flirted with everyone, pretended to be tipsy even though I knew he'd been sipping the same drink for over an hour.

By the time he came over to grab me for the midnight countdown, I felt like part of me was detaching from him, from us as a couple. Watching, weighing, wondering—distant and apart.

He danced me around in his arms, kissed me amid a drunken "Auld Lang Syne," whispered something about this "being our year." For a split second I thought he was going to propose, and was shocked at how strongly I didn't want that.

I tried to forget it afterward, to write it off as a blip, but that feeling has just built since then. It's as though a door was unlocked that I can't quite slam shut again.

It's also, I think, pouring some wine with shaking hands, nothing to do with him. Clichéd as it sounds, it's also me, not him. Even if he offered to come with me and volunteer abroad, I'm not sure I'd want him to. I am yearning for adventure, to open my mind—not to spend another trip being asked if I've packed a jumbo box of antidiarrheal pills.

When I look back, I see so many simple things I've never done. I've never lived alone, or traveled alone, or even spent more than a few nights in our home alone. I've never been free of the expectations and needs of others, no matter how benign. First it was Mum, then Harry—and that was my choice. A choice I made willingly, because at the time it was what I wanted.

Now, though, I'm not totally sure what I want, but feeling more content when I'm on my own probably isn't a good sign. It's not fair to me, and not fair to him, to stay with someone out of habit, out of convenience, out of a sense of shared history.

We need to talk about it, but even the thought of making this real feels terrifying. What if I change my mind? What if I'm just going through a phase? What if I'm making a terrible mistake?

What if I'm not even capable of ending it? Telling Harry anything he doesn't want to hear is almost impossible. He can be so persuasive. This time, though, I need to find more resolve. I need for us both to stop pretending that everything is fine and have a grown-up conversation about what happens next.

Or, of course, be a total coward. Maybe I could just move out one day while he's at work and leave him a Post-it note on his hair gel. Or send an email. Or scrawl the words *Goodbye forever!* in the frost on the windscreen of the car one morning.

I love him, in my own way, and I am scared of leaving

him. But I'm also scared of staying—scared of getting trapped in a land of company dinners and charity functions where nobody cares about the charity, and luxury holidays where you never leave the compound, and a house in a gated community that keeps the poor people so far away they can't even breathe the same air as you.

A life that would leave me feeling embalmed. Entombed. Pinned to a board like one of those butterflies in museum collections, their color fading, all life gone. A faded remnant of what they could have been if they'd only escaped the net.

Perhaps I just need a break, I think. Perhaps I could roam free for a year and come back and be delighted with Harry and our life together. Maybe it doesn't have to end completely.

Maybe I just need to get drunk.

I finish my glass and let myself get distracted by the brightly decorated paper lanterns arranged along the rooftops. As the sun has set, they flicker into magical neon light, wavering rows of brightness against the dusk.

The tables in the courtyard are filling up now, as though the dangling lanterns glinting into life have acted as some kind of visual dinner bell.

I see the older couple strolling toward the square, holding hands as usual. I see Sofia laughing at some tale Jorge is weaving. I see the girl from the coach—the teenager with the angry red hair and the angry red face—sitting with her family.

She's slumped with her head flat against her backpack on the table, using it as a pillow. She's pretending to be asleep so she doesn't have to talk to anyone, but from this angle I can see her eyes are open and alert. The sight makes me laugh inside, remembering that age—all spit and vinegar, furious with a world that can't possibly understand.

I feel calmer as I do this, as I look around me. It's far more interesting—and restful—looking into other people's lives than contemplating my own right now. And this seat, here at the side of the square, is quiet and cool, like a private booth at the theater where I can sit and watch the show from a distance.

A shadow falls over me, and I look up to see the man from the church approaching. The European man, who may or may not have a stash of abducted girls locked in his cellar back home.

He's wearing black Levi's and big boots and a black T-shirt that looks as though it's been washed many times over. He's tall and lean, like someone who runs long distances. He's been a mystery on this trip, pleasant but reserved, perfectly polite and casually chivalrous—one of those men who can open doors for you without it seeming forced or patronizing.

He's looking along the small row of tables, and our eyes meet.

I don't know why I do it. I don't know what possesses me—other than the fact that I am still disturbed by the image of myself being pinned to a butterfly board. Perhaps it's the prospect of being trapped that makes me act on impulse, and I wave to him. Frankly I am sick of sitting here thinking thoughts that are making me feel physically nauseated, and any company other than my own would be welcome—even if he is a serial killer.

"Please," I say, gesturing to the table. "Join us. Join me."

He hesitates, and I immediately regret saying anything. This is a man who has deliberately kept his distance from all of us for the entire trip. A man who sits alone, walks alone, eats alone. Why the heck did I think it was a reasonable idea to invite him to join me? I feel like the world's biggest idiot.

But then he smiles back and walks over, sliding into the opposite chair that Harry has left vacant.

We stare at each other, and my nervous grin feels stuck to my face. I want to apologize, which is weird—I have nothing to apologize for, apart from perhaps disturbing him.

He seems as taken aback as me, surprised that he is sitting opposite me, both of us vaguely embarrassed.

"So . . . how is the wine?" he asks.

"It's surprisingly good," I say. "Or maybe I'm just hot, and it's not, so it automatically becomes the best wine in the world. Do you know what I mean? Like when you've been on a diet for months and then you eat a jam doughnut, and even though you know it's not, it tastes like the best food ever invented? Well . . . you probably don't know. Anyway. Drink some wine so I stop gabbling. *Please.*"

He does at least look amused now, rather than worried. His eyes are a striking shade of icy blue, but his whole face softens when a smile creeps up on him. He reaches out for the glass and takes an experimental sip. I can't help noticing the plain white-gold wedding band on his ring finger, and immediately tell myself off for noticing.

"Well, I wouldn't describe it as the best wine in the world," he says eventually. "But I've had worse. Thank you."

"You're welcome. Did you like the church? I saw you in there."

"It's beautiful," he replies, smiling, glancing back at the solid form of the building looming over us.

"I'm never sure what I really believe, you know, about God and religion," I say. "But I do believe in the power of human emotion, and maybe churches gather that up somehow. Soak it up into their walls, keep it for future visitors—all of that hope and pain and devotion. All the peaks and troughs of life—the births and marriages and deaths."

He has lapsed back into silence, though to be fair he may just be thinking. Something I seem to have lost the knack of.

"That must have sounded totally mad . . ." I add.

His eyes meet mine and he shakes his head.

"No, not at all. I think something similar. I've always believed that buildings are more than they seem. That they have their own secret lives, stored in memory cells made of plaster and brick. Sometimes, there's even too much in them. I went to this church a few hours outside of Stockholm once, early morning when it was completely empty. Tiny place, but ancient, you know? One of those structures that was probably built on a pagan site, been a place of worship for over a thousand years . . . It was still, and silent, and simple, but almost overwhelming, the way you could close your eyes and imagine all of the life that passed through it.

"See—you don't sound so mad now, do you?"

It's my turn to stop and stare and stay silent. That speech pretty much echoes an experience I had once, which I've never even told anybody about because it makes me sound like a fruitcake.

"The same happened to me once in Salisbury Cathedral," I reply. "I was on a school trip, and the place was packed, but I could still feel it—like if I hid myself away in a corner, I could probably time travel. Follow the threads back through the decades, like I was part of some huge tapestry. Obviously I didn't tell anyone I thought that—I was fifteen. It wouldn't have been cool. Is that where you're from, then, Stockholm?"

"It is, yes. You?"

"Originally from Cornwall, now London. What do you do, in Stockholm?"

"I'm an architect."

"Oh! How wonderful! You create buildings—the future keepers of all that magic!"

"Not really," he says, but looks a teensy bit delighted. "Mainly it's social housing—finding ways to build affordable communities for people to live well in."

"Well, that's just as magical," I insist. "I'm sure there's as much power in a communal playground as there is in a cathedral. I work in a school. I love it, but . . . well. I'm thinking of making a few changes."

I drift off a little, my eyes searching the plaza to find

Harry's familiar form. I don't know why. I feel marginally guilty for talking to a stranger, for no good reason. Maybe I actually feel guilty because I'm enjoying it so much.

"What kind of changes?" he asks, drawing my attention back.

I stare into my glass, hoping it contains some of the secrets of the universe. Sadly it's just white wine and it provides me with no new answers.

"I don't know for sure," I say. "But I want to travel. I love my job, as a teacher, but I feel like I've gone straight from home to uni to work, and I . . . it sounds like a cliché, but I want to see more of the world, you know? It's so big, and so beautiful, and I've seen hardly any of it! So travel, yes, but maybe not just that . . . My work in England matters, it really does, but I feel like I could do more. Give more. Experience more . . . I've applied to work as a volunteer at a school in Guatemala. I don't know if I'll get it, or if I'll take it even if I do—but I need to shake things up. At the moment I'm too settled. My life feels too planned out. Too fixed."

"Like all of eternity is stretching out before you, every day the same, onward and onward forever?"

"Yes! Exactly like that. I need to stretch my legs. Unfurl my wings. Escape from the bloody butterfly board."

"I'm not quite sure what you mean about the butterflies, but I do understand what it's like to be trapped in your own life. It sucks, to use a technical term."

I laugh and realize that this is the first time I have said any of this out loud. I have thought it, vaguely, but never discussed it with Harry—the timing has never seemed right.

"Why is it that it's sometimes easier to speak to someone you don't know than to your family and friends?" I ask.

"I don't know. I find it difficult to speak to anyone. I can only apologize for my lack of social skills, and if I made you feel awkward earlier."

"Don't be silly," I reply, pouring a little more wine for us both. "I ambushed you. It was a totally selfish move, anyway, I just didn't want to sit here talking to myself. Mentally at least. Anyway, it might work in my favor—I haven't told my boyfriend any of this, so please don't start getting all chatty."

"It seems unlikely. You might not have noticed this, but I'm not one of life's great talkers."

"Ha! I had noticed that, yes. Very much the strong and silent type, aren't you?"

"Definitely silent. Still working on the strong. But don't worry—what happens in Santa Maria de Alto stays in Santa Maria de Alto . . . That sounds much better with just 'Vegas,' doesn't it?"

"It does, but you work with what you've got," I reply, smiling. His English is fluid, but his accent underlies it.

"So—the boyfriend. Is he one of the things you want to escape?"

I want to deny it, even to myself, but I need to stop lying. He is looking at me so searchingly, so honestly, that I don't even want to anymore.

"Maybe," I say. "I don't know. We've been together

since we were eighteen. Harry and I, well, we wear each other like comfy old sweaters. Everyone falls in love with him, he's so easygoing, so charming. But something has changed. It's not his fault, or mine. It's just that I don't . . . I don't . . ."

"Love him anymore?" he suggests.

"I think you might be right," I whisper. "Though I'm struggling to even say it, never mind accept it. Maybe I'm expecting too much? Don't all couples reach a stage where they're more like friends than lovers? Where they . . . I don't know, settle for what works, rather than what fairy tales tell us relationships should be? Isn't it normal for some of that fire to fade?"

He seems to ponder this deeply, and is, probably without knowing, twisting that wedding ring around on his finger.

"I'd like to say yes," he says, "to make you feel better. But in my experience? No. You don't have to settle for anything. And that fire? It doesn't have to fade. It can burn even brighter with time, with the right person. With someone who ignites your passion, who inspires you, who challenges you. Who argues with you but makes you feel safe. Someone who makes you feel . . . more alive. It's not just about finding someone you can get along with—it's about finding someone who makes your whole world better."

I am momentarily stunned by this small speech, by the raw emotion in his voice, by his sheer conviction. I feel an unexpected sting of tears in my eyes and reply, "You're very lucky, to be married to someone like that."

"I was," he says quietly.

I register the past tense and wait. He will tell me if he wants to—and if he doesn't? Well, I'll probably ask anyway.

"She died," he adds, staring at his wedding band. "Two years ago last Monday. We'd always planned to come here together, and I didn't want to be at home, in our home, on the anniversary of the day I lost her . . . I almost didn't get through it the first time. So here I am, in a place about as different from Stockholm as I could possibly find. Still missing her."

I reach out, take hold of his hand, cradle it in mine. He looks up, shocked, as though he hasn't been touched for all that time. Perhaps he hasn't.

"That's terrible," I say. "I'm so sorry. What was her name?"

"Anna," he replies, frowning. "And that's not the usual response when people find out . . . to ask her name. Thank you."

"What is the usual response?"

"Oh, you know, sympathy, nice words, but underneath it all? Fear. Once you drop the D-word into a conversation it dominates everything. Within seconds people are trying to find out how she died, if it was a car accident or suicide, if she had any underlying health conditions, what the symptoms were . . . was she a smoker or a drinker, or did she come from a long line of hemophiliacs? It's like people think it could be contagious. They're scared by the proximity of death, fear on some animalistic level that it might be catching, a fatal bug they can't clean off with hand-sanitizing gel.

"I become the Grim Reaper by association, and even though people want to be kind, they back off. I probably don't help. I'm not exactly encouraging."

"Because you want to avoid conversations like this, where you have to talk about it?"

"A little bit, to be honest. Every time I say Anna is dead, it becomes a bit more real—another step away from her. And every time I see that look of horror on someone's face, it makes me feel worse. I started working from home, to avoid my colleagues. And usually, if I'm asked about it when I'm away, I lie. I just say she's at home with the kids, or on a business trip, or some other pretty fiction. It seems . . . easier."

"I can imagine it would," I say, still holding his hand in mine. "You must miss her so much. You must feel so lonely."

He nods, avoiding my eyes, and stares instead at our entwined fingers.

"Sometimes I do," he says, tugging his hand gently away from mine. "No, that's a lie actually. I feel lonely all the time. This is probably the longest conversation I've had in a year, and you holding my hand is the first time anyone has done that for even longer . . . I miss that, you know? The contact. I mean, obviously, I miss all kinds of things—but it's surprised me, how much you take that casual stuff for granted. Hugs, hand-holding, waking up next to her, her hair tickling my nose when I held her, kissing each other goodbye in the morning and assuming we'd be able to do that every day, and . . . and I have no idea why I'm telling you all of this."

I smile. I know exactly what he means—we are strangers.

"Maybe it's the church," I say. "Maybe we're close enough to feel like we're in a confessional? I mean, we're complete strangers. We only really met a few moments ago, and here we are sharing our secrets like old friends."

He nods, and we are silent for a moment. I have the strangest feeling that we are caught out of time, in our own bubble, like the sounds of the music and the laughter of the dancing Australians and the aromas of freshly cooked food exist in a parallel universe. That we are here, but not here.

"Who did you light the candle for?" he asks. "In the church?"

He has clearly reached the limit of his conversational boundaries, and I am caught slightly unawares by the question.

"Oh! You saw that? My father . . . he died when I was young. Heart disease. I don't remember too much about him, to be honest—I was only seven. But whenever I do think about him, I feel warm and safe, you know? Like I might not remember specifics, but I remember how he made me *feel*. Ancient history. My mum remarried about ten years ago, to a really nice man called Ian, and I have a half sister, Olivia. She's eight and what people kindly refer to as 'spirited.' In other words, a bit of a nightmare."

"You sound very proud of that."

"I suppose I am—I think it's good for a girl to be spirited, don't you? Women need that. They need to shout and be awkward and not do as they're told and not want to please all the time. I wish I had more of that myself. Have you seen that bird?"

I whisper the last few words, gesturing behind him with one finger. He looks confused, but turns his head and sees it: a hummingbird, hovering within a mass of purple and orange flowers that are growing on vines along the wall. Its feathers are a startling shade of iridescence, a riot of emerald green and flecks of gold, its long beak wavering as it hovers. It looks like something from a fantasy story.

He reaches quietly for his phone and takes a few shots. The bird pauses, perfectly still, its minuscule head cocked to one side as though listening to something. Then in a bright flap of wings it leaves us, disappearing off into the gathering dusk. I notice a few other birds take to the sky at the same time; a small flurry of squawks, chirps, and feathers, disturbed by some sound our human ears can't discern.

"They must be off to some crazy bird party. Did you get a picture?" I ask, leaning across the table to look at the screen. "Oh, you did! That's so nice. Well done."

I look up, realizing that I have a very silly grin on my face.

"I look like a ten-year-old, don't I?" I ask, laughing. "I've been told that's what happens when I'm excited about something."

"You do a bit," he answers, sounding amused. "But

it's good to have a sense of childlike wonder. It's even making me smile, which as you can imagine is a small miracle for Mr. Grumpy."

"You're not grumpy," I reply dismissively. "You're just . . . well, you're Swedish, aren't you? You can't help it."

He laughs out loud and puts his phone back down on the tabletop. We are both smiling, and it is a nice moment. It feels like neither of us needs to talk. Like if we just try hard enough, we could even communicate telepathically.

It is only a moment, though. A moment that is shattered by the weirdest sensation—like the ground suddenly rolling to the side, chair legs twisting beneath me enough to make me slap my hands down on the table to steady myself. There's a low rumbling sound, the shaking and clinking of glassware and plates being pushed around by invisible diners.

The table vibrates, his phone bunny-hopping across the gingham cloth, the wine bottle falling onto its side and rolling off the edge.

He reaches out, grabs my hands, our eyes meeting in primal panic as the world seems to shimmer around us, alien and terrifying. I grip his fingers way too hard, as the wineglasses join the bottle on the ground.

As quickly as it starts, it stops again. I blink, hard and fast, still frozen in place. There is a stunned silence, the ominous rumbling gone, the tables still, the crowds too shocked to speak. I know I am.

Within seconds, though, the communal tension is

released with a loud whoosh of laughter that circulates around the plaza. Like all at once, we breathe out together. The music restarts, and the night goes on as though the temporary glitch never even happened.

"What was that?" I say, trying not to sound as freaked out as I am.

"A tremor," he replies calmly. "They're common enough in Mexico. Nothing to worry about."

"Are you actually as relaxed as you seem about it, or are you faking it to reassure me?"

"Both. It's a good thing I have you to impress, or I'd be hiding under the table and crying like a schoolgirl."

"Ha! Feel free; I won't think any less of you . . . that was scary. Anyway. I'm glad it's over . . . what a relief . . ."

I look down at our hands, still clinging on to each other. Somehow it surprises me. I know I should let go. I know I should laugh it off. I know that Harry is here, and he will be back soon, and that whatever faults there are in our relationship, I shouldn't be getting so close to another man. Hand-holding after an earth tremor is forgivable—enjoying it so much is not.

He is staring at me intensely, and I wonder if he is having some kind of internal monologue about it as well, whether he is telling himself to back off, to let go, to retreat.

If he is, he takes about as much notice of it as me. We leave our hands where they are, skin against skin, the excuse of adrenaline fading into something different now.

It is so perfect, so right, that I simply stare at him as he starts to speak.

"We should probably—"

I never find out what we should probably do. It could have been anything. We should probably stop holding hands. We should probably go our separate ways. We should probably run away together, off into the hills, to live in splendid isolation amid the hummingbirds and the wildflowers and the sun-soaked mesas.

I never find out, because the world explodes.

Chapter 3

He leaps from his chair and shouts something at me. I see his lips moving and the frantic hand gestures, but I can't hear what he is saying. All I can hear is the deafening roar that seems to be coming from the ground, the air, the buildings, from everything. Like a thousand storms howling through my ears all at once.

I stare at him, lost, confused, terrified. The noise is horrendous, the sound of the earth eating itself.

He staggers toward me, wobbling and unsteady, like he is walking across a bouncy castle, and yells into my face, "Get under the table! Now!"

He grabs hold of me, pulls me down, tugs me beneath the table. I wonder what use it will be, a few slats of wood against whatever is about to be thrown at us. I'm aware of my knees crunching into the ground as I am pushed down, of clanging and banging and screaming, of him, climbing beneath with me.

I've instinctively curled into as small a ball as I can, and he has wound his long body around mine, cocooning me. He wraps his arms around my head, clutching it to his chest, whispering words that are probably reassuring but are in Swedish. We huddle together, fragile and human in the face of what is being unleashed around us.

I glance up at him, see him looking around, a strangely analytical look on his face. I realize that he is staring at the church, at the taverna walls; that even while he tries to comfort and protect me, he is assessing the structures around us. His architect's brain is working away, and he will know even better than I do that these buildings are old. They won't have earthquake-proof foundations. They won't have the same precautions as more modern buildings. They won't survive if this carries on—and neither will we.

I narrow my eyes against the dust that is starting to fly up and hear a terrible tearing sound from somewhere close by. It's a scraping, a grinding, a slow, deep groan. I can tell from his reaction that it is bad, and he grips me more tightly.

All around us, people are screaming, glass is shattering, stalls collapsing. The noise is indescribable. The grill that was being used to cook our meal whooshes into a ball of fire as the gas tank ruptures and ignites, the neon lanterns strung along the walls fall and dangle, and clouds of red and brown dust and earth are billowing into the air, like the ground is coughing them up.

Shouting, crying, yelling in different languages. It's a Tower of Babel of panic and terror. The piped pop music finally stops, and I hear the thud and tumble of a nearby building coming down, swallowed by its own foundations.

The fountain in the center of the square cracks and folds in on itself, water pouring through its rent tiles, gushing along the red earth. An electrical wire is ripped free, whipping in the turmoil, sparking and twisting like a luminous snake.

Shards of glass and pottery and snapped wood are flying around us, and through my squinting eyes, I see a child running through it all, a football crushed to his chest, shouting for his mama. He stumbles as the earth moves beneath his feet, falls, disappears. The fountain follows him, swallowed into a sudden void where no void should exist. It is horrifying, and fast, and unreal.

The man is trying to turn my face away, trying to shield me, to shelter me from seeing it all, but I resist his gentle pressure. I need to see.

Even if I couldn't, I can hear, and I can smell. I can smell fire and blood and gas and old stone reduced to rubble, the clogging dust of the collapse clinging to my nostrils, invading my eyeballs, coating my tongue.

I see a young boy, the family from our coach trip. He is crouched under a table like us, his sister next to him. They are clinging on to each other in terror, the teenage girl's long red hair whipping around both their faces. Their mother is trying to wrap her arms around both of them at once, their father has laid himself across the tabletop in a bid to anchor it down above them. His hair is matted with dust and blood as rubble rains down onto him, a human shield.

The pretty adobe houses with their whitewashed walls and red tile roofs are coming down, bottom first, tumbling as though pulled and tugged by an invisible hand, Jenga blocks crashing. A car alarm goes off, bleating a low repetitive note, a counterpoint to the awful screech and whine of twisting metal.

The table above us shakes and judders, wracked by intermittent loud slams of scattered debris as bricks and stonework fall. Our backpacks are long gone, the glasses and wine bottle shattered nearby, glinting in the reflected glow of the fires. A lone plastic water bottle rolls past, and I reach out to grab it in a strange moment of clarity.

I am choking on the foul air, compressed beneath the protective body of a man I barely know, witnessing what feels like the end of the world. Harry is out there somewhere, and I have a sharp pang of panic as I think of him.

"I can't breathe!" I shout, my voice muffled as I turn my face into the chest of the man above me.

"It's okay, it'll be all right . . . it'll stop soon . . ." he says, stroking my hair, trying to calm me. Trying to calm himself maybe, his voice shaking.

The screams around us continue, people who were only minutes ago having a normal night now in pain and misery. Children are crying; parents are running in a desperate attempt to find them, braving falling chunks of their former homes, their arms held over their heads, inadequate flesh umbrellas.

The rumbling sound from deep below continues, the stomach-turning churn throwing everything off-balance. I wipe my eyes, peek out at the insanity. I look at the church, at its looming towers, its already decaying brickwork. I have lost all sense of time, no idea how long we have been enduring this.

The church is quaking and shimmering, its once-solid form now flickering, as though I'm seeing it through a heat haze. When it starts to fall, it seems to come in slow motion, inevitable and deadly, mocking the flimsy protection of a single restaurant table.

The man shoves me firmly down against the ground, twists his body even more completely around mine, bends his head and tucks it next to mine. The sound is awful, unnatural, drowning out everything else. All I can do is hold on to him, sobbing. I realize I don't even know his name as I shelter within his arms. The last thing I remember seeing is that father, stretched across the table as his family cowers beneath. His limbs are limp and dangling, his eyes glazed and empty, staring unseeing into the chaos.

Chapter 4

I have that weird sense you have when you are dreaming, and you know you're dreaming, but you can't find a way out. When you let out a scream that is smothered to a whisper. When the urgent thrash of your limbs becomes a twitch of a finger. When you are trapped inside a hellscape of your own making.

In this one, someone is holding me facedown into a pit filled with grainy sludge. I am trying to struggle free, but my body isn't responding. I feel paralyzed, and no matter how hard I try to kick and fight, wicked hands hold me still. I know I need to break free so I can become a hummingbird—that being, of course, entirely possible in a dream—and fly away.

The dream me tries to shout out, but every time she opens her mouth to bawl for help, it fills even more with thick, oozing mud, choking out all sound and sliding down her throat to solidify into brick in her windpipe.

I can't breathe, or move, or make a sound. I am terrified.

I tell myself over and over again that it's just a dream. That if I can force myself to speak, to wake myself up, then the nightmare will be over and I will open my eyes and everything will be fine. The curse will be broken.

I make one last, desperate attempt to cry out, and eventually I manage one ragged murmur. It is not loud, but even that sigh seems to be enough, and I wake up.

I wake up, but the nightmare doesn't end. The curse is not broken. It is still dark. I still cannot move. I can still barely breathe, and although no hands are holding me down, neither do I have hummingbird wings.

I blink my eyes over and over again, waiting for that rush of relief I know will come soon, when I am properly awake, when I know I am safe in bed, heart still racing with panic but able to laugh at it all in the cold light of day.

No matter how much I blink, though, nothing changes. I concentrate on the simple things first—inhale, exhale, do it all over again. The air is stuffy and dusty, and each time I suck in a breath, I seem to take a mouthful of grit with it. My lips are dry and coated in the stuff, my eyes sore.

I force myself to keep breathing, telling myself to stay calm, and as I do, I start to remember. Remembering is not good. Remembering brings the panic back, as my bruised mind catches up with my bruised body and reacts to this new reality. One that I cannot wake up from.

I was with the Swedish man. In the square, in Santa Maria de Alto. We were drinking wine, talking, finding an unexpected connection. There was . . . what? A landslide? An earthquake? Yes, definitely, I think, as the terrible images come back to me: an earthquake.

The ground trembling. The world breaking. The screaming and the wailing and the splintering. The table above us, shaking and creaking as the collapse went on, the hiss of gas and the boom of fire. Children crying. The man from the coach, lying across his family, trying to protect them.

The Swedish man dragging me down to my knees. Talking to me, holding me, telling me it was all going to be fine. His arms around me, his cries of pain as the church came thundering down. And then . . . then there was this.

This, here, in the dark, sucking in dust.

The fear starts to invade me again and I push it down. Fear is the enemy right now. I decide to carry out a self-applied triage and move my head slowly from side to side, relieved that I can. I do the same with my arms and legs, testing how much it hurts, what I can feel and what I can't.

My legs are trapped, by what I don't know. It's heavy, but not agonizing, and I can still wriggle my toes. My extensive medical training—watching TV shows set in hospitals—tells me that this is a good thing at least.

My left arm is sore but all right. My right arm is, I think, broken, or at least badly damaged. Any movement, from the tips of my fingers to my shoulder, results in the kind of searing pain I've never experienced before. We're not used to pain, are we? We take ibuprofen the minute a headache makes itself known, we have anesthetic at the dentist, we have pills and potions that take the edge off most things. I'm not used to pain—not pain like this—and I like it about as much as I'd have expected to.

I try to ignore it and carry on with my assessment. My tummy is off, like it's been punched, and there is a dull humming in my ears. My whole body feels battered and compressed.

There is moisture on my face, and I use my good hand to wipe it away. It's sticky and gunky, and I think it must be blood, so I can add some kind of head wound to the list.

There is more room around me than there was in my nightmare, but not a lot. I can raise my head, maybe roll to one side or another. I can't see much, though; not even the slightest chink of light is coming through into this dank cave.

I reach out and grope tentatively around, feeling chunks of rubble and moist soil beneath my fingertips, under my nails. Above I can stretch my arm mostly straight, before my hand encounters a smooth, flat surface. I pull away quickly—it feels too much like the lid of a coffin for me to bear. It sets off a primal panic that takes me what feels like an age to control.

It is, I think, as I lie there with my eyeballs rolling, forgivable to feel scared. It does not make me a wuss. I am alone, in the dark, breathing air that is clogging my lungs, trapped. I have a broken arm and blood all over my face and no idea what to do next. Can I find a way out? Can I dig myself back to the surface, with a broken arm? Is there even still a surface to dig my way back to?

How much longer can I breathe this air in before

I suffocate? How long can I go without water? How much blood can I lose?

All of these thoughts shout loudly in my mind, competing to see which one can freak me out the most. I am immediately filled with shame and anguish, and I tell them to shut up and back off. I am alive. I have survived, and I know so many others probably didn't. I don't know what became of the man I was with, and I have no idea where Harry even was when it all happened.

The last thing I felt about Harry was a sense of relief when he left me alone, and then I sat and told a complete stranger that I wasn't in love with him anymore—and now I don't even know if he's alive or dead.

My breath starts to come in panting gusts, and I know I have to stop myself from spiraling into a panic attack and concentrate on what I can do to get out of this. On finding out what happened to Harry—because if I am alive, then he could be too. Knowing Harry, he'll be fine. He won't have a scratch on him, I tell myself.

And the man . . . the man who held me. Who tried to protect me. I don't know if he has survived as well—but if he has, I need to find him too.

Having a goal helps to calm me again, and I swallow, licking dry lips with an even dryer tongue. I try to speak, and at first my voice is a near-silent croak, a fumbled echo of what I usually sound like. I swallow again, even though there is nothing to swallow but grit, and manage one weak word. "Hello?"

Pathetic, I think, and try again, as loud as I can. I am a teacher, I remind myself. I am a master of making myself heard.

"Hello?" I say again. "Is anyone here?"

I strain my ears and wait for a moment. No reply, but vague noises starting to coalesce beyond the background hum of my damaged hearing. Please, I think, let it be the sound of rescue teams, of blessed heroes with hard hats and heavy machinery and morphine and foil blankets.

I have literally no idea how long I've been out of action, how long I've been down here. It could be minutes. It could be days. I have no clue what is unfolding out there—or if there even will be a rescue. The village is in the middle of nowhere, and it all happened so quickly. Maybe nobody even knows.

I try to move my legs again, shifting them gently, inch by inch. I don't know what's weighing on them, and for all I know the slightest displacement might bring everything that is above down below, which would be a very bad thing indeed.

As I poke and prod with my toes, the sensations tell me that one of my sandals has come off.

I curl my bare toes and investigate the mass that is covering me from the knees down. It feels warm, firm but malleable. Not brick or mud or stone, I don't think. It's like being on some strange TV show, trying to identify the substance with my big toe.

I carry on exploring as much as I can, wondering if there is a way I can slither free without causing any disruption. After a few seconds I hear a noise. A quiet moan, so delicate it might not even be real. I stop moving, lie completely still, straining to hear.

Again, a dull groan.

"Hello?" I call out. "Is there someone there? Please! If there's anyone there, please speak!"

I feel the slightest tremble of movement around my legs, a subtle shifting, then a voice, as hoarse and broken as mine. "Yes! I'm here! Are you okay?"

I recognize the voice. I recognize the accent. It's him—the man from the coach. I don't even know his name, but the rush of pure relief I feel is overwhelming. I know it's ridiculously selfish to be glad that someone else is trapped down here with me, but I can't help it—I'm not alone, and that makes everything more bearable. It gives me hope, which right now is probably just as important as water and air.

"I think so," I reply, swiping blood from my eyes, "but I'm stuck. Something heavy is on top of my legs . . ."

He replies with a low grunt of pain, then says, "Ugh. I think that's me. Can you stop poking me?"

"Oh no! I'm so sorry! Are you all right? Can you move?"

"I'm going to try—hang on."

It takes an age, but slowly and carefully he inches himself up and away from my legs. I feel the sensation rush back into them, and a warm fizzing in my veins as the blood flows again. It's not just physical—the mental relief of not being trapped is huge.

I listen to more grunting while he tries to shuffle himself around, tense as he does it. This fragile retreat of ours is small, and he is a tall man, and he's obviously injured so it's a long and fraught process. I whisper encouragement, while also hoping he doesn't bring the roof in.

Eventually, I feel him moving toward me, the touch of his hand on my face, warm breath against my cheek. He is lying next to me, coming to rest by my side. I reach out and trace his outline, finding him contorted onto his side, one arm coming across me.

"You're bleeding," he says, his fingers gently exploring my forehead. "It doesn't feel too bad, though. What about the rest of you? Are you in one piece?"

"My arm's broken. I feel completely battered, and something's wrong with my stomach, but I'm basically fine. You?"

"My ankle, I think. Maybe a rib. Both broken."

"Ouch . . . I'm sorry. And thank you."

"What for?"

"For what you did out there. For putting yourself between me and . . . everything. Thank you. And also, you know, thank you for being alive—I'm sure you'd prefer to be elsewhere, but not being alone down here is stopping me from going mad."

"You're welcome. It was all part of my master plan . . . How long have you been conscious? And have you heard anything from . . . up there?"

"Only a few minutes, and no. What do you think is happening? How long do you think it'll take them to find us?"

"I have no idea. I don't know how long we've been

down here. I don't think my backpack and phone are around. How about you?"

As soon as he asks, I feel like the world's biggest idiot. I wonder why on earth I didn't think of that myself. Okay, so I've been a bit distracted with the whole earthquake thing, but still.

"My jeans pocket," I mutter, wriggling my hips to check that I can still feel its outline. "I can't reach, I'm kind of stuck here. Can you try? On my right side."

He reaches across me, sucking in a shocked breath as he does. Broken rib kicking some ass. It's awkward, having a stranger crushed against me, rooting around in my pocket, and he is mumbling apologies as he does it.

"It's all right," I reply. "I think the etiquette book goes out the window in a situation like this."

He nods, his thick hair in my face, and then finally manages to tug it clear. He lies back, breathing heavily, before offering it to me.

"You do it," I say. "Broken arm and all."

His fingers fumble along the edge of the phone, turning it this way and that until he finds the on switch. The screensaver bursts into life; even that low level of light dazzles my eyes. The glass is crisscrossed with a spiderweb of cracks, but it seems to be working.

We both study the screen and let out a joint sigh of disappointment. No bars. He tries to dial anyway, in case the telephonic gods are smiling on us. They are not.

"No signal," he says, sounding frustrated. "Which I suppose is to be expected when you're buried alive."

"Don't say that! We're not buried! We'll be all right . . . we'll get out . . ."

I hear the terror in my voice, as though it belongs to somebody else. He has unintentionally pressed a panic button, painted a picture that has triggered borderline hysteria. I feel my heart rate zoom up, my skin go moist and clammy, my breath fast and shallow. Buried alive. Trapped here, until we starve or dehydrate or run out of oxygen or get obliterated by falling earth . . .

"No," he says quickly, his fingertips touching mine. "You're right. It was just a silly expression. I'm sorry. We need to focus on the alive bit. We've had one miracle, I'm sure we'll get more. Let's see . . . at least we have some light now . . ."

"There's a flashlight thingy on it," I say, glad to have something else to focus on, trying to steady myself by thinking about practicalities. "See if you can find that."

It's a flashy phone, one of the new ones that is basically like a little computer and uses the internet, and way more than I need. It was a gift from Harry, who is always quick to adopt a new gadget. Right now I'm super-thankful for it. As soon as he turns on the flashlight, I feel better.

He holds up the phone and moves it around us. There's not a lot to see, but at least we can see it—dirt and bricks and random bits of smashed pottery, and a gnarled fork sticking out of it all. There are tangled tree roots and a chair leg and a mishmash of crumbled plasterwork.

The gap we're lying in is as small as it felt, and above us is a smooth slab of stone that's forming a kind of roof.

I refuse to let my mind go where it wants to—to the word "tomb"—and instead look at the man holding the phone. A man I've never really spoken to before tonight, and now a man I might be spending my last moments with.

His blond hair is tangled, streaked with earth and dust, and his face is filthy with both. He senses my stare and turns toward me, so close our noses are almost touching.

"You have lovely eyes," I say. "I especially like the black streaks around them. Makes you look a bit like a panda. Ha. I'm buried alive beneath a Mexican village with a Swedish panda."

"Well," he replies, an echo of amusement in his voice, "you said you wanted to expand your horizons. And I didn't want to be alone. So I guess in a very weird way we both got what we wanted. One day you can look back on all of this and it'll seem funny."

"It seems pretty funny right now, to be honest, which is worrying. Maybe I've got oxygen deprivation. And I'd kill for a drink of water. Or Guinness. I'd quite like a Guinness, strangely enough."

"I tried Guinness once, on a trip to Dublin with Anna. I wasn't quite sure. But we do need water . . ."

"I grabbed some," I say, remembering. "Before we fell. I don't know why, I just saw it rolling past and snaffled it. But I don't know where it is—maybe nearby?"

He twists around to search, and I see him wince and

bite his lip, his pain illuminated by the phone. I also see the skin of his shoulders, where his T-shirt has torn, raw with scrapes and cuts.

"Oh God!" I say, once I notice. "You look like you've been . . . grated! Are you all right?"

"I'm fine," he says. "Don't worry about it."

Of course, I do—because the reason he was grated is because he was shielding me from the worst of the debris that was tumbling around us. Every cut, every graze, every bloody scratch on his skin, is one that could have been mine. I am awash with awe at his simple bravery, but know he won't welcome me saying it.

He shines the phone around in a searching sweep and finally makes an aha noise.

"How good are you with your toes?" he asks.

"At what?" I reply, following the ray of light downward. "Ah. I see. Another miracle."

Down near our feet, crumpled but hopefully intact, lies the plastic water bottle.

"I don't want to risk moving around too much," he explains. "I'm not sure why, but I think we're in some kind of void here. Maybe because of the mining nearby, maybe just dumb luck, but instead of getting crushed, we fell into this hole—and that stone above us is keeping us safe. I can't risk dislodging it. I have a less than cooperative ankle and big boots. You, though, seem to be barefoot, or at least semi-barefoot. Do you think you could snag it?"

I nod and concentrate as I twist and turn my feet, kicking off the other sandal. It's awkward, and every movement sends another jolt of agony up through my arm.

"Okay?" he asks. "Not too painful?"

"It's not good," I reply, inching close enough to prod the bottle with a toe, "but at least I don't have a broken rib. I had one of those once. I fell off a trampoline—long story, involving alcohol—and it hurt like a bastard whenever I laughed or coughed or took a deep breath . . ."

I'm talking to distract myself from my own discomfort, but I also want to acknowledge his. He is clearly not the kind of man to complain, but he has got to be in misery with all those injuries. We're both in a bad state, and both pretending we're not for the sake of the other. A mutually beneficial deception.

After a few attempts and a bit of swearing, I finally manage to get the water bottle balanced between the soles of my feet. I raise my legs up carefully, tugging my knees toward my torso, until it's close enough that he can reach down and grab it. The plastic crinkles in his grip, and he sloshes it around to show it is still full. He raises it in the air and cheers.

"Yay! We did it!" I say, legs flopping back down in relief. "I think that was probably a yoga move . . . If it wasn't, I'm going to invent it. I'll call it the Cheeky Tortoise. What do you think?"

"Perfect. Would madame care to celebrate with a drink? Finest vintage bottled *agua*?"

"God, yes. You first, though. Your breathing sounds funny. I can't have you dying on me; it'd be gross."

He smiles and takes a small sip before passing it to me.

"Don't drink too much," he warns, helping me lift

my head enough to put the bottle to my lips. "We don't know how long we're going to have to make it last."

"That's a cheery thought," I reply, giving it back to him after a quick glug. "What about food?"

"We can go a long time without food," he says. "But as a matter of fact, we're in luck."

He carefully maneuvers his arm so that he can delve into his own jeans pocket and produces a small handful of treasure—four cellophane-wrapped boiled sweets.

"I had them in there from the plane journey, for my ears? No idea if it actually works, but I always remember my mother giving them to me when I was little, when we flew anywhere. The habit stuck, I suppose. Orange or strawberry?"

"Goodness. You are spoiling me. Strawberry, please."

He unwraps the sweet for me, and we both lie as flat as we can, silently sucking.

"Funny, isn't it?" I say, after a few moments. "How your concept of luxury can change? This morning it would have meant being back at my hotel room, lounging by the Jacuzzi on our terrace. Now, it means this—being alive, with a bottle of warm water and some boiled sweets."

He nods, but stays silent. He looks thoughtful, full of focus and concentration.

I suspect he is aware of the same harsh realities as me. That we need to ration that precious water. Turn off the light to protect the phone battery. That his rib could interfere with his breathing, or my disgusting head wound could get infected. That we could run out of air before anybody can help us.

But for now, I think, lacing my fingers into his and holding them firmly, we can allow ourselves this. Five minutes of peace and rest before those realities take center stage.

Chapter 5

"What's your name, by the way?" I ask, once the euphoria of the boiled sweet has faded.

"I'm not going to tell you yet," he replies. "And I don't want to know yours either."

"Rude. I thought we were friends."

"We are. Survival buddies. But I think we need something to look forward to. So we can officially introduce ourselves once we're out. When we are next sitting together in a beautiful sunset, and neither of us is in pain. Anyway, I have good news."

"Excellent—go for it."

"You know how I've been holding those sweet wrappers up and waving them around?"

I nod. I did notice but didn't comment—I thought perhaps he was just stretching. We have turned off the flashlight to save power, and now everything is cast with strange shades of half-light and random spots of color.

"I did a scientific experiment," he announces, deliberately making his voice pompous. "The results were conclusive. There is air coming into our cave."

"Okay, Dr. Evil, that is good news—but how do you know? I don't see much lab equipment around here . . ."

He grins and holds up the sliver of cellophane that one of the sweets was wrapped in. He grips the end between his thumb and fingertip, and I watch as it delicately twists and lifts in an unseen air current. It's not exactly a breeze, but it's oxygen. Delicious, nutritious oxygen. I hold my fingers to the same spot and can just about feel it.

"That is brilliant," I say, grinning. "I didn't even know how worried I'd been until then."

He nods and screws the wrapper up in his palm. I am guessing that he also doesn't want me to know if that precious air supply dwindles.

The two of us are crammed closely together, side by side, with about forty centimeters above us to the solid rock shelf and maybe twice that on each side. He can stretch his arms out to the left and reach over me to the right. I'm curled into a twisted fetal position, cradling my broken arm, leaning toward his chest.

Both of us are coated in grime and blood, and both of us are trying to hide how much pain we are in.

"How are you?" I ask, reaching out to tuck his hair behind his ears. He has the kind of hair that always needs tucking behind ears, but I realize as soon as I touch him that it is an intimate gesture, and I feel him tense beneath my fingertips.

I pull away and say, "I'm sorry."

He smiles sadly. "No, I'm sorry. I'm just not used to . . . company, shall we say? And I'm all right, thank you. I've been thinking about how long we've been down here—looking at your phone, I'd say maybe an hour, something like that? Did you say you heard movements earlier? I'm trying to figure out what stage they might be at up there . . ."

"I thought I heard something, but my ears are still a bit weird. Plus I could well have dreamed it. Are you sure you're all right? You have so many cuts . . . I know you don't want to show it because you're worried about upsetting me, but I can tell it's bad."

Now that we have air, I feel a lot calmer—which seems to free up some mind space for being concerned about him. I can see the shock of pain that washes over his face every time he moves. We're both hurt, and we're both scared, and I don't want him to pretend not to be for my sake.

"It will all heal," he responds gently. "I promise."
Subject closed.

"So," I ask. "Do you think we should try and dig our way out? Or bang and shout to attract attention?"

"Definitely not dig," he replies firmly. "We could bang, but carefully perhaps?"

"Well, yes. Careless banging can get you into all kinds of trouble."

He half grins and says, "Please don't make me laugh. Comedy is the enemy of broken ribs."

He sits up as far as he can and slowly runs his fingers around the surfaces that surround us. He comes up with a chunk of old masonry he can just about grasp in one palm and taps it softly against the rock above us.

It barely makes a sound, just a kind of dull thud. He pauses, waits and watches to see if it has had any effect on the stability of our refuge, and tries again, slightly harder. This time there is a small but steady trickle of loose debris from one side of the ledge, a slurry of soil and crushed brick and thick dust.

We both look on in horror, only breathing again when it stutters, slows, and finally stops. He very carefully presses his fingers against the flat surface, testing for any signs that it's about to come down, then murmurs that it seems okay.

"All right then," I say, wiping my eyes. "Well, we've got a new layer of crap on our faces, but at least we've still got faces. Let's look on the bright side."

"You were right about the careless banging." He offers me the water bottle. "Better not try that again. I don't know how solid the layer above us is. It's not been long, and it'll take a while for a proper rescue response to start up. We're a long way from civilization."

I take a small sip, wishing I could splash it over my face and wash some of the filth away, and say, "Yep. I am choosing to believe that there were survivors, and that they'll have raised the alarm, and that someone will be looking for us. Jorge and Sofia will know who was on the coach, or someone will anyway, and they'll be looking for us. Plus Harry . . ." I trail off as I say his name, assaulted again by a strange mix of worry and guilt. "Harry will be fine," I continue firmly. "He's that kind of guy. He's too lucky to be hurt. At least I hope he is . . ."

"I'm sure he will be," comes his response. "There's no reason to expect the worst. We have to work on the basis that people will search for us, and we will be fine, and Harry will be out there waiting for you. Then you two can sort everything out—I'm guessing this kind of experience will definitely help clarify a few issues."

"Well, as couples therapy goes, it's definitely original," I reply, trying to scrunch up my top enough to clean my face. Harder than it sounds in a confined space when one arm is a screeching beacon of pain.

"Close your eyes," he says, seeing my dilemma. Seconds later I feel the gentle touch of his fingers, wrapped in the soft fabric of his own T-shirt, clearing the worst of the grit and dirt from my skin. It's an odd sensation, and if I keep my reality sensors set on low, it's actually enjoyable. Like having the world's weirdest facial.

He smooths stray strands of hair away from my face and lies down again, one hand on my waist. I'm glad of it; we both need the reassurance.

"Thank you," I say. "That feels a lot better. And as for our issues, I don't think I've ever felt clearer, bizarrely. I desperately want Harry to be all right—because I do love him, of course I do. We've been together for so long, and we know each other so well, that he'll always be part of me.

"I think I was using this holiday as a final chance really, a way to see what was really left between us. And you know what? This is a pretty life-changing event, right here—nothing like facing death to make you reassess life . . . and, well, if I get out of here—"

"When," he interjects firmly.

"When I get out of here, I need to make some changes. It'll be hard, ending something that's been so important for so long, but . . . well, not as hard as this, eh? Not as hard as everything else people have gone through tonight."

"No. Not that hard," he replies. We are silent for a while, lost in our own thoughts, remembering the horrors we have seen. He did his best to save me from seeing the worst of them, and I am grateful that I ended up in this truly terrible situation with a truly good man.

"I don't know a lot about these things," he says eventually. "But I'd say we have a while to wait before anyone finds us. We have air, and some water, and we need to be patient. There are ways they can look for us when they get here, ways they can find us—they'll have lifting equipment, and cameras, and thermal imaging, and . . ."

"Magic wands?"

"Yes. Those too. So for now . . . we need to stay positive. Keep breathing. Take it in turns to stop each other from panicking."

"You don't seem to be panicking at all," I say. "It's actually embarrassing how calm you are in comparison to me."

"That's just because I'm being all Nordic and chill. Inside I'm absolutely freaking out."

"Nordic and chill . . . Harry thought you might be a serial killer, or have girls locked in your basement."

His eyebrows raise in a "WTF" way before he calmly replies, "I can assure you I'm not. For a start I don't even have a basement. I live in a two-bedroom apartment in Stockholm."

"What's it like?" I ask, genuinely curious. "Stockholm? Your place? Your life? We have time to fill, and all this spare oxygen. Go crazy. Tell me your whole life story."

Chapter 6

We are, finally, discussing Anna. It has taken him a long time to get here, and I am listening intently as he begins.

"You actually remind me of her a little," he says. "Anna. Not in the way you look. She was a lion."

"A lion?"

"Yes, you know, how everybody resembles an animal?"

"I didn't, no. Silly me."

Even as he says it, though, I am wondering what he might be. A slender polar bear? A kindly wolf?

"Well, her father was Nigerian," he continues, "and her mother was a classic Swedish ice princess. So she had this beautiful dark skin, and brown eyes, and incredible hair—blond corkscrew curls. So, she was a lion. She was an explosion of a woman, all texture and vivacity. You're a . . . fox, I think. Or maybe a hare."

"I'll take that," I reply. "You could have said I was a walrus or a warthog. So how do I remind you of her?"

"I think it's . . . the warmth. The fact that you actually seem to like people, seem so open, so curious."

"And you're not?"

"Well, I am curious, always—but there's also a part of me that is more of a hermit. There always was, even before I met her, even when I was a child. I didn't lack confidence, either when I was a kid or now—I just . . . often prefer to be on the edge of things. Anna was the one who'd organize dinner parties, drag us out to concerts, convince me to go dancing at the Christmas markets. She pulled me into her social maelstrom. Except now she's gone, and a maelstrom leaves quite a gap. Now, I feel like . . . like I'm invisible. Like I can't reach out. Like I'll never feel that kind of connection again . . ."

I twist myself carefully onto my side and lay my head on the right side of his chest, the side with intact ribs. I can't put my arm around him, it would make me scream, so I do the best I can.

"You're not invisible," I say quietly. "I see you."

I feel him clench slightly, then he sighs and lays a hand on the back of my head, his fingers splayed across my hair. "So, what happened?" I ask. "If you can talk about it. No pressure."

"No, that's okay. I feel strangely comfortable talking to you. I did from the moment I sat down with you, back in the real world. I felt like I could trust you. And now . . . well, now it's as though these crazy circumstances have taken us from being virtual strangers to confidants in a few hours."

It's been more than a few hours now—over twelve, at least. I don't say anything, though—neither of us needs reminding of that.

"I know exactly what you mean. Like we've been in fast-forward. I can honestly say that if I had to fall into a deathly underground chasm with anyone, I'm glad it was you."

"Thank you. Likewise."

His voice is strained, and I think he might be crying. I fight the urge to look up and check. I'm sure he wouldn't want me to see it if he is. Anyway, if I did, then I'd start crying too, and then we'd both be in floods, and we can't spare the liquid apart from anything else.

We both know we probably should be resting, conserving our strength and our air supply, but I think we both also need this connection. Both need to communicate, to share, to laugh, to feel human—to avoid the panic that will result in us trying to claw our way out of the ground like characters in a gothic novel.

The water bottle is now only a third full, and we are still lying in the same space, unable to move more than a few inches. The fullest range of movement that either of us has is turning onto one side and back, bending our knees, stretching fingertips into the air, and contorting into a strange half-sitting position.

The minute I allow myself to think about how trapped we are, how we can't get up or walk away or even sit completely upright, my breath speeds up and my heart booms with palpitations.

It feels like we have told each other everything—and now, finally, we are here. Anna.

"I don't talk about her a lot," he continues. "And that is unfair. She deserves to be talked about. She deserves to have her name said out loud. It's like . . . like I've hoarded her memory somehow. I've cut myself off from the friends we did have. I work from home. I've kept her to myself. But here we are . . . in this insane predicament. And there is so much about her that I don't want to leave unsaid.

"At first, she was feeling bloated, and tired," he says, "and she had to pee all the time. We thought she was pregnant, and we were delighted. She was young . . . she was healthy . . . we'd been trying for a while. With all those signs, we assumed it was going to be the very best of news, not the worst. A beginning, not an end."

He pauses, and I feel him shudder.

"It was very early; we were hopeful but she hadn't taken a test yet. Then I came home from work one day, and she was wrapped up in a blanket on the sofa, looking sad. She didn't often look sad, my Anna. I wish I could show you a picture of her . . . she was full of energy. She viewed living as one giant adventure. But not that day—she just looked deflated, like something had gone out of her. She'd done a pregnancy test, while I was out. She'd been planning to wrap it up and give it to me as a present. But instead, it was negative, and she was so disappointed. I remember sitting next to her and wrapping the blanket around both of us, and her crying so much it soaked through my shirt."

"Oh, how horrible, for both of you."

"I told her we could do another test, later—that it might be a false negative. That even if she wasn't pregnant, we had lots of time. I just wanted her to feel happy again. But for the next month or so, she carried on feeling sick. Her appetite went. Her tummy was sore. She did about three more tests, but they were all negative, and eventually I persuaded her to go and see the doctor."

He pauses again, and I don't push him.

"She had some tests, and it was ovarian cancer, not a baby. In fact we were warned the whole baby thing might not happen, and that the priority now needed to be keeping her alive. The next couple of years was a blur really—she had surgery, she had chemo, then she had more surgery, and more chemo. She was brave, and determined, and incredibly positive all the time . . . until she wasn't.

"Until she couldn't do it anymore. Until the doctors told us that she needed to be moved to a hospice, that it was the end of the road. Honestly, I think even then, she was more worried about me and how I was going to cope without her. She was probably right—she knew I would fall apart without her. Wouldn't know how to go on."

"But you have gone on," I say firmly. "You're still here. Still living. You lost the love of your life, your companion, your soul mate—but you're still here. Still trying. You've not done so badly. She'd be proud of you."

He doesn't reply immediately, then says, "Maybe. It's a nice thought. I do sometimes wonder what she'd think of me now. Mainly I think she'd want to give me a kick. I often feel like I'm floating, detached from the world, not really engaging with everything around me. The exact opposite of what she'd have wanted me to do."

"I'm sure she'd understand. I'm sure she knew you better than anyone else."

"She did, and that's why she was worried about leaving me behind . . . she knew I'd be lost without her.

"She even told me to make sure I found someone else. Although she did say it couldn't be anyone as good as her— and not too quickly, or she'd come back to haunt me."

He chuckles lightly, but stops himself, clearly in pain from his ribs. "As if I could ever forget about her. I knew Anna better than I know myself. Coming on this trip was my attempt to give myself that kick to start living again."

"Well, I know it didn't go as planned," I say, "and that you probably didn't expect to end up trapped with a weird English girl, but here we are . . ."

"She'd laugh her head off at this. The irony of it all would be too much for her—I come on holiday to find some meaning to a life without her and I end up in an earthquake. Although, I think in a strange way, it has helped. I thought I'd had enough, that nothing was worth it—but now I know I'm wrong. I want more. I want to live."

"Well, that is definitely a silver lining. Maybe there's been a smidgen of good in all the bad?"

"I've never heard that word before—'smidgen'? What does it mean?"

"It means a tiny, teeny bit. Like, we have a smidgen of water left. We have a smidgen of room. We have a smidgen of everything. Which is definitely better than having no smidgens. And now that thing's happened, where you say a word over and over again and it suddenly sounds ridiculous? Although with the word 'smidgen,' it probably always sounded ridiculous . . ."

I trail off, realizing I'm doing that thing where I just keep on talking again—and that nothing I say will ever be able to capture the pain he's been through. The loss he's been through.

"I lost my dad when I was young," I say. "Just a little girl, really. I felt very lonely. My mum didn't cope well, and I . . . well, I suppose I became the grown-up, way too soon. I looked after her, and the house, and pretended everything was fine at school because I was scared of losing her as well. Even when she met Ian, got her life back on track, I felt tense, worried about her . . . It was only later, when I met Harry, that I realized how much I needed other people. How much I'd closed myself off from everyone. Harry . . . he helped me open up again. Showed me how to relax, to live. I'll always be grateful to him for that."

"I'm sorry you went through that," he says. "Grief is . . . well. You know what it is."

We are both silent for a few moments. The kind of silence that does not feel uncomfortable.

"Anna always planned for us to move out of the city," he says, completely changing the subject. "Once we had kids. She used to describe her dream house to me and make me draw up plans for it—then every time I had it done, she'd change her mind. She had too many dreams to commit to paper. What about you—if you could live anywhere, where would it be? And what would your home be like?"

"Why? Will you design me my dream house if we get out of here?"

"Of course I will—*when* we get out of here. Whatever you want. A yurt. A mansion. A hobbit hole. You just tell me what you like, and I'll do the rest . . ."

"It doesn't need to be big," I say eventually. "I like things that are cozy, you know? Somewhere I'd feel safe, like I had my own little nest. I'd like a garden, and windows that open out over the garden so I'd have birds to look at while I cook, and green fields and maybe the sea . . . just a hint would do, because even if it's just a hint, it always gives me a sense of freedom, knowing I'm near the sea . . . Nothing too posh, nothing too perfect, nothing where I'd feel out of place if I was wearing odd socks . . . though I'd be lying if I said I'd object to a Jacuzzi bath . . ."

I continue to talk, amazed at how many ideas I actually have for my nonexistent dream house, and he asks me technical questions that engage his mind, and eventually, we both settle. We settle, and are still, and I feel the warm, even breath against my forehead that tells me he is asleep.

I close my eyes, knowing I shouldn't but unable to resist. I let my mind drift to gardens and the coastline of home, and to big blue skies and freedom. I try to ignore the dull and constant ache in my arm, the tenderness of my stomach, and allow myself to drift. Just for a second or two.

Chapter 7

A noise wakes me up, rousing me from a sleep I didn't even notice I fell into.

I lie still, hoping it is real, that noise, not just the remnant of a disturbed dream. I glance across, see that he is somehow sleeping as well. His breath is coming in painful gusts, and his lips are moving, talking with the mute button on. I move his thick fringe of hair from a forehead that feels too warm.

I strain my ears, and am about to give up when I hear it again: muffled human voices, and the shrill background bleat of a whistle being blown. People. I use my good hand to shake him slightly, saying, "Wake up! Wake up! There's someone out there!"

He shifts his position, groaning as he moves his foot, then silently listens. "I hear them," he finally says, after a few moments.

"Thank God," I reply. "If you didn't, I'd start to think I was going mad. Madder, anyway. What do you think's going on out there?"

"I don't know," he answers. "Have you heard anything else? Any machinery or sounds of digging?"

"No, nothing like that—but just because I haven't

heard it doesn't mean it hasn't happened. I think we both might have dozed off there. Isn't that bonkers, that we can sleep?"

"I don't think it's quite as restful as sleeping, is it? It's more like going unconscious because our bodies and minds need to switch off. But . . . yeah. It's been a while since we last checked anything."

I glance at the cracked screen of the phone and see that there is still no signal. That we have been down here for almost twenty hours.

"We need to try and let them know we're here," he says, unscrewing the plastic lid of the water bottle and passing it to me. "Drink this. You'll need it for your shouting voice."

I save him half of the tiny amount that is left, even though he didn't ask for it, and savor the sensation of the now warm liquid in my dry mouth. By the time I've squished it around my gums and lips, there's hardly any left, and what there is does nothing to quench my thirst. It's been a long time with too little of everything.

I notice that he is speaking in a croaky whisper, and suspect I am too. I'm not sure how long either of us will be able to shout for. He is staring at the stone slab above us, and I know he is worried. That stone slab has kept us safe for all this time. Any attempt to free us could dislodge it, and if that happens, it would all be over very quickly.

He has kept the phone on, and I am grateful for the light. My corneas feel scrubbed raw by grit, and his once bright blue eyes are now bloodshot and crusted with smeared dirt, his blond hair matted in dust-gray clumps.

"You look really hot right now," I say, laughing.

"You too—I've never been trapped in an underground hole with anyone sexier. Ready?"

I nod, and we try to shout. We are both so dry, so exhausted, that we don't make anywhere near as much noise as we'd like. We've tried this before, obviously—shouting just in case—and managed a lot more volume before the dehydration and dust took their toll. Still, we do the best we can, then lie and wait for a response that simply doesn't come.

I feel the desperation and disappointment rise up inside me. I don't know how long we can go on like this. I need to get out. I need to taste fresh air. I need to feel the sun on my face and get out of these filthy clothes. I need to drink and drink and drink, and eat pizza, and lie on a soft mattress in a big room with the windows open.

I need to find Harry, to know he is all right. I need to see Mum and Ian and tell them that I am all right. I need to see Olivia, and watch her grow up and become the amazing woman I know she will be.

I need all of these things, but I am suddenly crushed by the certainty that I will never get any of them.

"It's okay," he says, squeezing my waist to attract my attention. "Look at me. Don't give up. Don't start thinking it's over. I have to build you that dream house, remember?"

I stare at him, trying to focus.

"Just breathe," he murmurs. "Just breathe in, and breathe out, and don't think beyond that . . ."

He holds my hand in both of his, and together we breathe.

I will not give up.

It is not over.

"Damn right," I whisper, my voice a hoarse rasp. "If I get nothing else out of this, I'm going to get my very own architect. Shout again?"

He nods, and we both start yelling once more. We don't last as long this time, barely making ourselves heard to each other, never mind the world outside.

We fall silent, and listen again, on the verge of defeat. It's feeling hot now, stifling and stuffy, as though the gentle breeze that's kept us alive this far is objecting to the sudden bursts of activity.

Both our eyes go wide as we hear the voices again.

"We need to let them know we're here, but I don't know how," he says, staring at the top of our cave–jail, his fists clenched and banging against his own thighs in frustration. He adds something that sounds like an unintelligible mishmash of angry vowels.

"Did you just swear in Swedish?" I ask.

"I did," he replies. "Sorry."

"That's okay. It seems an appropriate time. I'm not sure I have much more shouting left in me. We've been talking in whispers, and now it feels like my throat has closed up."

"I know. Mine too. And we can't bang around too

much, in case we bring the whole thing down on us . . . We need to send out some kind of SOS."

I stare at him, and at the phone, my eyes bouncing from one to the other. Something about him swearing in Swedish, and the glowing screen, and the need for an SOS, has jogged a train of thought in my fatigued mind.

"The phone!" I say eventually. "The phone has no signal, so we can't call anyone, but it has a speaker—and music. We can play music!"

He doesn't reply at first, just fixes his gaze on me and frowns. I'm starting to wonder if I've suggested something incredibly stupid, or if he's doing some complicated mental equation about sound waves and earth displacement. He holds my face in both his hands and gives me a quick but triumphant kiss on the lips. I barely feel it, they're so dry.

"You're a genius!" he says. "Now tell me how to find it . . ."

"Hardly a genius." I smile. "It's my phone, after all. I just hope it works."

I tell him how to find my playlists, and his eyes flicker over them. I wonder what music he likes. Down here, in this weird subterranean world of ours, we have been friends. In the real world, maybe he only listens to Rachmaninoff, or death metal, or obscure improvisational jazz. Maybe in the real world, we'll have nothing in common.

"Okay," he says, sounding amused. "It's between Madonna's *Like a Prayer* album, Adele, or—for the sake of my national pride—*ABBA Gold*."

"Go for ABBA," I reply quickly. "If there's a rescue team up there and they hear 'Mamma Mia,' they'll definitely start singing along . . ."

"Good point. I think I'll start it with 'S.O.S.,' though—it seems more relevant."

As he says it I realize that's probably what triggered this whole idea. He was talking about needing to send an SOS earlier, and my subconscious picked up on it for me. Good old subconscious. I should have thought of it earlier, but I am not exactly firing on all cylinders.

He puts the song on and turns the speakers as high as they will go. The dramatic piano intro kicks in and then Agnetha—I think it's Agnetha, definitely the blond one—starts singing. Even here, like this, it's infectious, and I'd love to join in.

The chorus gets going and I see he has his eyes closed, his mouth moving as he sings silently along. I settle down onto my back, lowering my damaged arm to the ground, taking hold of his hand with my good one. He twines his fingers into mine in a way that is now so familiar I can't remember a time when I didn't hold hands with this man. He leans his head sideways so it's resting against mine, and I smile.

I can't sing. I can barely speak. I'm half crazy with fear and thirst, and the discomfort in my tummy has graduated to full-on pain. Yet somehow, ABBA can still make me smile.

"S.O.S." fades away, but the songs keep coming. All the classics. "Super Trouper," "Dancing Queen." "Voulez-Vous." The greatest disco that never happened.

Both of us are crossing in and out of reality now, the music only adding to the surreal quality of our enclosed world. It's in the middle of "The Winner Takes It All" that things start to change. At first it's just a small flurry of loose dirt coming down from the ledge above us.

He leans over me protectively, just in case any more follows. I appreciate the instinct, but know it won't do any good if the flurry turns into anything more severe. I smooth down his hair and peer over his shoulder.

"There's something there," I say. "Coming through."

A thin tube has been pushed through the earth above us. It's narrow and looks like it's made of some kind of flexible wire that can twist and snake through small spaces. On the end of the cable is a small glass blob, like an eye that's staring right at us.

We both stare back and he says, "It's a camera!"

Someone is looking at us. Someone knows we are here. Someone is trying to find us!

I wave my arm frantically above my head, grinning, croaking, "We're here! Hello!"

He joins in, and the two of us ride the crest of a new wave of energy, yelling and gesticulating. The tiny camera remains impassive and inscrutable, but moves up and down, as though it is taking a survey of our surroundings. Or nodding.

He flicks on the flashlight on the phone and moves it all around the place, illuminating it for the electronic eye. It moves too, following the light.

"What do you think they'll do?" I say, waving my hand in front of that tiny eyeball again. "Have they seen us?"

"I'm sure they have," he replies. "And I suppose we have to be patient now, and try to stay awake and strong. It'll be complicated, getting us out—I know we're both desperate, but it's better they don't rush it. They'll have to survey the ground, use hydraulics, whatever else they need—and they'll have to do it in a way that doesn't . . ."

He pauses, seeming unsure of what words to choose next.

"Make everything collapse and crush us to death?" I suggest.

"That. Yes. All we can do now is wait."

Chapter 8

We are trapped underground for another four hours, and it is a terrible four hours, even by my current low standards.

I feel so helpless, lying there, aware that while every move up above brings us closer to escape, it could also bring us closer to death. All it would take is one false move. They are clearing space around the stone ledge, which they have hooked up to grapple lines and pulleys, and bit by bit we are emerging back into the surface of the world.

The last hour is especially hard, with voices shouting down at us in Spanish and English, the grinding sound of heavy machinery, the smell of burning, the clouds of dust and displaced earth whooshing around our faces in toxic clouds. We lie there, immobilized, a strange mix of hope and fear.

There are moments of absolute joy. Our first glimpse of the sky above us. Touching fingertips with the gloved hand of a rescuer as he passes down a bottle of water. The sounds of life, of people, of the world.

But there are also the other moments, as they work to safely remove the heavy stone ledge that was our savior and is now the greatest threat. Moments of absolute terror.

I keep my eyes closed for the last few minutes, my face turned into his chest, his arms wrapped around me. He is murmuring soothing words and stroking my hair, and I have one leg hooked around his hips. We are curled together like a strange double embryo, ready to be reborn into the world.

I open my eyes and look up at his face. He is watching me, smiling. It is almost over.

I say, "I can't wait to get out—but in a very weird way I am going to miss being trapped in a cave with you."

"I know what you mean," he replies. "But don't worry—I'll see you in the real world too."

I nod and close my eyes again. We've given the rescue team our names, and I hope they've told my mum, so she can stop having a nervous breakdown. I've shouted up questions about Harry, but nobody has answered. I am choosing to believe it is because of the language barrier, not anything more sinister.

"Get ready!" yells someone from up above. There is a flurry of falling soil and pulverized brickwork and dust so thick it coats our mouths in gray sludge, and finally, finally, the stone ledge is fully hauled away.

We are exposed, broken and helpless, the whole world above us. The sudden rush of light is dazzling, and for a moment I feel utterly vulnerable.

I shield my eyes and see a small crowd of men peering down on us. They are dressed in jeans and flannels and high-vis vests and hard hats, their faces covered by white masks. I give them a small wave and they break out in cheers and laughter, celebrating with high fives and fist bumps.

It makes me smile, their joy infectious. I can only imagine how hard their work has been.

As my eyes calibrate, I realize we are about six feet under, which is ironic. The men above start to insert metal poles into the sides of the void, presumably stabilizing it while they get us out.

It takes a while, between his broken ankle and my broken arm and our chronic state of exhaustion, but eventually, we are free. Strong hands grasp us and pull us upward, into fresh air and more space than seems humanly possible.

I stand on shaky feet, cradling my arm, and take one moment to let the relief wash over me. He is sitting next to me, his leg extended before him, looking around with the same sense of wonder as me. I put a hand on his shoulder, and he leans his head against it.

"It's a beautiful day," he says, gazing at the setting sun, at the golden blanket it casts on the hills, at the sky that is caught between shades of blue and purple.

"The most beautiful ever," I reply.

We are surrounded by chaos, by carnage, but for that one moment, we both choose to only see the sunset, and each other.

I am greeted by a nurse, walked slowly to an ambulance, asked to sit on a stretcher. I slump down, wrapped in a tinfoil blanket while they check me over.

I finally look around me, as the sun sinks and artificial lights are switched on, hoisted into the sky on mobile gantries.

People are still digging in small scattered teams, occasionally calling for silence with a raised fist in the air. Smartly dressed men and women are talking into microphones in front of cameras. A child is crying somewhere, the noise somehow piercing through the machinery and the chatter.

There is a haphazard collection of vehicles—ambulances, fire trucks, vans with satellite dishes on top of them, massive jeeps, flatbeds with shadowed machines lurking in their bellies. As the natural light darkens, headlights tunnel into the shade.

The world that those crisscrossed, glowing yellow tunnels show is very different from the world we left behind. The beautiful church has gone. Most of the houses are gone. The plaza and its pretty fountain have been churned up, left in furrows of rubble.

There are fires still burning, electric cables still dangling, the smell of dust and destruction.

I make out the shapes of human bodies, broken and abandoned. At first my brain doesn't register what I'm seeing, but logic forces me to accept that I am looking at people who didn't make it. They can't possibly be alive—they're too twisted, too taut, too still. I can't see any faces, and I'm glad.

I see smashed tables, shattered glass everywhere, trees and plants mashed up into the earth. I see a mangled baby's stroller, upside down, wheels pointing skyward. I remember that baby, chubby-cheeked and sleeping, and it takes my breath away.

The machinery is thudding and hissing, and the fires are smoking, but other than that it is eerily quiet.

I look up, unable to keep my eyes on the destruction. Thick clouds of dust float in the air, motes dancing in the electric light, but higher than that, right up in the heavens, the sky has faded to a deep blue. It is clear and beautiful and perfect, the just-emerging stars looking down on this desecrated patch of earth.

I try to stand, wanting to find him, find my friend whose name I still don't know, wanting to tell him to look up at those incredible stars.

A woman in green scrubs places a firm hand on my shoulder, pushing me back down. I feel the sharp sting of a needle and look on as she hooks me up to a drip. Worried that it might be some kind of drug that will knock me out, I am filled with a need to know about Harry. I need to know that he is not out there, alone in the dark.

"Where are the others?" I ask the medic, desperately. "There must be others? Please? I'm looking for Harry?"

"Is okay," she replies soothingly. "Go to the hospital now. Others are there. Okay?"

"Is Harry there? At the hospital?"

The medic shrugs, obviously not sure who Harry is, and adds, "Many people are there. Maybe this Harry."

They're simple words, but they feel magical. There are others at the hospital. Many others.

Harry will be at the hospital, I tell myself. Harry will be fine. Harry will not be one of those crumpled shadow people discarded in the rubble, battered and empty shells where people used to live.

I'm told to lie down, and I do, even though I have spent way too much time lying down recently. I let my head fall back onto the stretcher and feel the pain in my arm start to fade. Morphine. Must be. Excellent stuff. I've lived with that pain for so long now it feels odd to be without it.

The medic carries out a few other checks, asking me to look at lights and follow fingers and answer questions, then the stretcher is lifted and pushed into the back of the ambulance. I lie there, staring at the brightly lit roof of the vehicle, blinking rapidly, trying to stay awake.

There is a clatter as another stretcher is pushed inside the ambulance. I turn my head and see him lying next to me.

I study him and realize how battered he is. They have cut away his shredded black T-shirt, and he is covered in cuts and grazes and streaks of blood. Some gashes look deeper than others, and one side of his torso is painted with violet bruising.

I put my fingers to my face and find it sticky with drying blood from the cut. I might have a fashionable scar. Something character building, Harry Potter–esque. Something to show that I have survived a great battle.

"Hey," I say, as the medic finishes fussing around him. "You've got a drip too. Are you on morphine? It's pretty good, isn't it?"

"It really is. You okay?"

"I'm okay," I reply.

I reach out, stretch tired fingers toward him. He takes hold of my hand, and we lie still and silent and connected as the doors are slammed shut behind us.

The engine starts and the ambulance moves, jolting our entwined fingers. I cling on—we've been through so much together, and I'm not ready to let go just yet.

"So. We've seen another beautiful sunset, and we're not in pain. No excuses. What's your name? I'm Elena."

"Nice to meet you, Elena." He smiles in a lopsided, almost-asleep way. "I'm Alex."

Chapter 9

The first thing I notice when I open my eyes is that they don't hurt. I can blink without the sting of grit and dust.

The second thing I notice is that I am lying in a bed, staring up at white ceiling tiles with my grit-free eyes, surrounded by a symphony of quietly beeping machines.

I am confused, as I emerge slowly from a sleep so deep it was like being unconscious, an out-of-body experience.

Within seconds, it comes tumbling back down, threatening to bury me in panic.

I sit up too suddenly, jarring an arm that is now set in a cast and strapped to my torso by a sling. I glance around, see that I am in a room with four other beds, all of them filled by women.

Sofia, the tour guide, has one leg in plaster. She's fast asleep, her long, straight hair a black slash across the pillowcase. One of the Australian girls is sitting up reading a magazine, with no apparent sign of damage apart from a bandaged wrist.

There is another lady I don't recognize who is tapping away at her phone, her face festooned with two black eyes and her nose clearly broken. There is the elderly lady who was on the coach, the one with her husband—the couple that seemed so sweet.

She is lying on her side, staring off into the distance, her eyes glazed and unfocused. Her silver hair is greasy and flat to her head, and her body is limp and still. She could almost be dead.

"Lost her hubby," says the Australian girl. "Hasn't spoken a word to anybody since. We've all tried, but she's switched off, you know? Her daughter's on her way from London. You okay, Sleeping Beauty?"

This makes me feel at a distinct disadvantage. I have been treated, my arm cast, and, a quick touch of my face tells me, stitched up. Yet I don't remember any of it.

I twist sideways so my feet are dangling off the side of the bed and see that I'm wearing a hospital gown. Delightful the world over. I can also feel that I am wearing both underpants and a sanitary pad, which for some reason makes me blush in humiliation. I know it's silly—medical professionals are not bothered by simple biological functions, and I've been through much worse recently. But for some reason it feels awful, like my last shred of dignity has been stripped away from me.

"How long have I been out?" I ask, shaking it off. I need to concentrate on more important things—like trying to walk. I have to move, be free. Even a hospital room feels small and constrictive. Plus, I have to go and find Harry.

"Two days, on and off. The docs said it was the best thing for you. You were on a drip until this morning, antibiotics and fluids, then they said you were out of the woods and just needed rest."

I glance at my hand, see the telltale mark where a needle once intruded, a small Band-Aid peeling half off.

I tug it away absentmindedly, consumed with questions. How many people survived? Where is Harry? Is Alex okay? Has someone told my mum and Olivia that I'm here? And when can I go home?

I try to stand and feel wobbly. I'm also hungry and weak. Like a newborn foal, testing out my legs for the first time.

"Are *you* all right?" I ask, collapsing back onto the bed, frustrated. I'm going nowhere fast, so I might as well talk to the Aussie girl. "Your friends?"

"I'm all right. I'm Janey, by the way. Sprained wrist and bruised coccyx. Fell on me arse but somehow got off light. The others . . . well. Shelley's in a coma. Marissa's in the burn unit. Greta and Beth . . . they didn't make it."

"I'm so sorry," I say, the words completely inadequate. Janey's eyes are swimming with tears and she swipes them away viciously, swearing under her breath as though she's angry with herself.

"I'll be leaving soon, hopefully," she adds. "Though I'll stay around for a bit, in case Shelley comes round. In case Marissa needs me."

I nod and sip some of the orange cordial that's been left on the cabinet by my bed. I need to find a doctor or a nurse and ask about Harry. See how Alex is doing. Maybe find a phone to talk to Mum—I've no idea where mine is, and it's probably out of charge by now, bless it.

My whole body feels sore and fragile, but this time

when I stand, I manage to stay upright. It feels good—to stretch, to move, to appreciate the overlooked glory of space.

I check that the gown isn't flashing my bottom and amble along the corridor, leaning on the wall when I need to. I stare into rooms as I pass, catching glimpses of strained faces and worried relatives and still bodies attached to coiled tubes. None of them look familiar, which is both a blessing and a curse—it might mean that Harry is fine and not even in the hospital. It might mean that Harry is dead and in the morgue.

The next room along has the door propped open, and I see the mum from that family lying in a bed in a room of her own. Her head is bandaged and her skin pale, both of her arms encased in casts from her wrists upward. Her son is asleep, crashed out on a couch with a woman who looks like she could be his grandmother, his head on her lap.

The teenage girl—the one with the red hair—is sitting on the floor in the corner of the room, her head wrapped in one arm, the other arm in a sling. There is room on the couch, and there is another chair, but she is on the floor, alone. Like she's chosen to be as far away from any physical or emotional comfort as she can possibly get.

The father is not there, of course. The father is dead. One of those mangled shadows I saw in a dreamscape that wasn't a dream.

I reach a nurses' station. The chatter is loud and buzzing, the Spanish rapid and unintelligible apart from a few snatched words. Men and women in uniforms are filling in charts, answering phones, talking and laughing.

Hospitals are strange places, I recall from when my dad was ill. For the patients the world is ending, or at least changing. For the staff, it's another day at work, to be survived with as much good humor and enthusiasm as possible.

"*Hola?*" I say, trying to attract their attention. One of the nurses—a middle-aged lady, large and motherly with huge brown eyes—looks up and sees me. She puts her hands in the air and lets out a small stream of quick-fire Spanish before dashing out from behind her counter.

I have no idea what she's saying, but from the combination of smiles and the slightly scolding tone, it goes along the lines of "What are you doing out of bed, young lady?"

She tries to guide me away, but I plant my bare feet on the linoleum and hold firm. I am small but I am mighty.

"I need to talk to someone about Harry. About my boyfriend," I say, refusing to budge.

There is some to-ing and fro-ing, and the nurse's colleagues seem to find it amusing that she is unable to budge the small English person, despite her superior size. Eventually, another woman intervenes, after making a quick phone call. She speaks first in Spanish, and then says in English, "You will see Dr. Martinez, yes? He will talk to you."

I nod and feel weak with relief. I couldn't have kept that

up much longer. I am led to a tiny room, almost entirely filled with a desk, with bookshelves, with filing cabinets. Behind it all sits a man in his thirties, so handsome he could be a movie star, with thick dark hair and a neatly trimmed beard. He looks tired but kind. He smiles and gestures for me to sit in the chair opposite him.

The nurse, obviously relieved to have me off my feet, gives me a pat on my good hand before she leaves.

"Do you speak English?" I ask immediately, hoping we're not going to have to have this entire conversation in my terrible Spanish.

"I do, yes. My name is Dr. Antonio Martinez. I was on duty here when you and your friend were brought in. How are you feeling?"

As he speaks, he moves from his side of the desk to mine and pulls the stethoscope from around his neck. I tolerate it as he listens to my heartbeat, knowing it will be easier to go along.

"I'm feeling sore but basically fine. Can you please tell me about my boyfriend? About Harry? I have no idea where he is, or . . . how he is . . ."

He nods and makes a "just one moment" gesture as he straps a blood-pressure cuff to my arm. By this stage it is entirely possible that my blood pressure is through the roof out of sheer frustration. He seems happy with the result and goes back to his side of the desk.

"He is alive, and he is here," he says. "He was brought in as soon as the rescue reached Santa Maria de Alto. You, obviously, were there a little longer."

This simple confirmation allows me to breathe again.

I didn't realize quite how much the worry was crowding my chest, squatting on my lungs, keeping me tense and terrified.

"Can I see him? How is he?" I ask, realizing after the first wave of relief that Dr. Martinez has made no mention of his condition. There was no casual "he's fine" attached to his statement. There is more to come, and I can tell from the look on his face that I'm not going to like it.

"Please tell me," I say.

He nods and picks up a pen, which he flicks backward and forward through his fingers. It looks like he's twirling a tiny baton.

"Harry suffered from severe crush injuries during the earthquake. He was placed in an induced coma, because of swelling in the brain. There is also significant swelling and damage to his spinal cord. We are hopeful that he will survive, but we cannot, at this stage, predict the level of recovery that he can expect."

I stare at the doctor, strangely disconnected from the words. From the thought of Harry—my always-confident, always-vibrant Harry—being in a coma. Being so badly hurt.

It just doesn't make any sense. I understood, even if I didn't want to, that he could have been killed. I suppose I might even have been preparing myself for that possibility, even though I thought it more likely that he'd be fine. That his sheer swagger would somehow protect him, that a force field of self-belief would pop up around him like an umbrella.

This, though? This is an unexpected in-between land.

"But he will get better, won't he?" I finally ask, frowning. "Eventually. He will get better?"

"We are not a specialist unit, which is where he should be. As soon as the brain injury is stable, we can look at those options. For now, I can't give you any firm answers. The majority of the damage is in the lumbar area of the spine, which does mean that his upper body should be fine."

"His upper body?" I echo quietly.

"Yes. As for his legs, his ability to walk, we simply don't know. He may never regain full use. He may be able to after surgery or rehabilitation. He might need a wheelchair. He might not. I understand how difficult this is, hearing so many 'mights'—I wish I could be more certain, but these types of injuries are unpredictable. Even people with exactly the same injury can recover completely differently. We just can't say at this stage.

"I've already explained that to his parents, so you might want to talk it through with them as well. They've been asking after you and did visit while you were still unconscious. Your own mother was planning to fly out as well, but we told her you were expected to recover with no side effects, so she is waiting to hear from you before she decides."

My mind is still reeling, still knocked off its axis by the news about Harry, and it takes me a while to respond. I nod numbly and mumble, "Thank you. I'll call her as soon as I can. I need to go and see Harry now."

Dr. Martinez lays down his pen and fixes me with concerned eyes. He really is extraordinarily good-looking—like one of the doctors in the telenovelas Harry and I were watching in the hotel in another lifetime, giggling at the high drama and big hair.

"Before you do that, Elena, we need to talk about you."

"Me? What about me? I know my arm is broken. I know I'll probably have a scar on my face. But I'm fine. I'm okay. I was . . . lucky?"

It doesn't feel like quite the right word, but it is. I am lucky to be alive. Lucky to not have a spinal cord injury. Lucky to be sitting here, talking. I must be thankful for it all.

"Did you know," he asks slowly, examining me carefully, waiting for a reaction, "that you were pregnant?"

Chapter 10

I stare at him as though he is mad. As though he really is one of those doctors from a telenovela, and he might also tell me that I have an evil twin.

Pregnant? Of course I wasn't pregnant! We were careful . . . most of the time. Nearly all of the time. I always assumed that I'd have kids at some point in my life, but certainly not now. And Harry . . . well, he only ever talked about them with mock horror—or maybe real horror, I was never quite sure, and it never mattered too much, because we were too young anyway.

That's why we were careful, nearly all of the time.

Except . . . well. Perhaps "nearly all of the time" isn't quite careful enough?

"Are you sure?" I ask Dr. Martinez, my hand going automatically to my stomach. He nods gravely. I'm still not sure I believe him; it seems like one layer too much of strange for me to process on top of everything else.

But then I start to remember how I felt on this holiday. How Harry was winding me up about my hormones because I was snappy with him.

I was feeling off, physically. My stomach wasn't right. I was more tired than usual. I was expecting my period any day, and I was probably late—but that wasn't unusual for me. I've never been one of those women blessed with clockwork regularity, so I didn't give it a second thought. When I was younger, I always kept pregnancy tests in the bathroom cupboard because my cycle was so messed up it made me paranoid. In recent years, I just accepted that was the way I was made. That it was no cause for alarm.

Except, of course, when it is. Or is it? Do I want a baby? Am I ready? What about me and Harry? What would he think about it all?

Even as all of those thoughts swarm through my mind, in the seconds it takes for my thoughts to catch up with reality, I start to remember something else. I remember the pains I had while I was beneath the ground—how my arm hogged the spotlight but my tummy was sore. I remember that I am wearing a sanitary pad. I remember that Dr. Martinez used the past tense.

The hand I have on my belly freezes. I have spread my fingers across my skin, as though I am striving to protect a child that I suspect no longer exists. A child I never knew existed until it didn't.

I remember, I realize, and I feel something crumple inside me.

"I was pregnant?" I ask dumbly.

"Yes. We did a routine test before we treated you. Approximately seven weeks. Elena, I'm sorry to have to tell you this, but the fetus didn't survive."

Of course it didn't, I think. I barely survived myself. The poor thing didn't have a hope. It was lost before it was found; it died inside me before I had a chance to love it. To keep it safe.

"You'll need to have a few more tests," he goes on. "But so far it looks routine—this is terrible news, I know, but there is no reason to think the worst. There is no reason that you won't be able to go on and have other children. Harry's condition . . . even if he doesn't fully recover, many men with spinal injuries successfully become fathers. It's not the end for you."

I am unsure how to react, knowing that I have a part to play here but unable to play it. I am falling to pieces, fracturing, splitting into particles that might disintegrate and float away, become nothing but fragmented specks of loss and disappointment, scattering like clouds of dust into the ether. I am empty and cold and made of nothing at all.

"Thank you," I mumble eventually, decades of training in polite behavior kicking in as he looks at me. I don't want to disappoint him, so I try to smile. It is a twisted thing, I am sure.

"Do you have any questions for me?" he asks.

Oh yes. I have a lot of questions. I want to know why this happened. Why Harry is lying in a coma, facing life in a wheelchair. I want to know why so many people died. Why my baby died. Why Alex's wife died. Why I survived, when right now I wish I hadn't.

Why the whole fucking world is so extremely cruel.

"No," I reply politely, asking him none of those questions. There is a limit to what medical school will have taught him, and none of this is his fault.

I stand up, weak and floppy, using my good hand to steady myself on the desk. I accidentally knock a pile of papers over and apologize.

"I need to go and see Harry," I say simply. "Where is he?"

Dr. Martinez is clearly concerned, worried that I might collapse, or break down, or scream. He looks on the verge of telling me I need to rest. That I need to lie down, to hydrate, to process my loss. And normally he'd be right—but there is no normal about this.

"Please," I say. "I understand what you've told me, and I know I need to deal with it. But right now it's too much. I can't let myself go there . . . I can't. I might not come back from it, and Harry needs me. I need to get through this in stages, and I can't concentrate on myself until I've seen him. So please, help me. Will you take me to him?"

The doctor reluctantly agrees, but insists that I use a wheelchair. I agree and am in fact relieved to not have to walk. To not have to concentrate on sending messages from my brain to my body, on the all-consuming task of putting one foot in front of the other.

He pushes me through busy corridors, wheels squeaking, overhead lights sizzling, people making way to let us through. Nobody meets my eyes, even the staff who say hello to him, the patients and relatives who stand to one side to give us passage. It is like I'm invisible, and I am glad.

Everything feels strange, alien, off-center—the bright colors and the signs in Spanish and the chatter in a language I don't understand. It's a hospital, but not in the way I know it. Like I've been transported into a place that is both drably familiar and utterly new. Into a life that feels like a beginning and an end, in so many ways.

I was pregnant. And now I am not. I was whole, and now I am not. There is a part of me that will be forever missing, forever left behind on a hilltop in a foreign land. And now I need to set that aside, if only for a small while. I silently apologize to myself, to my baby, to the universe, and grab hold of the doctor's sleeve as we approach a room in the intensive care unit.

"Do they know?" I ask, gazing up at him. "About the pregnancy?"

He shakes his head, and I nod in acceptance. I get to my feet and draw in some deep breaths. I need to find the strength to get through this. I need to find some strength for Harry, and for his parents, and for myself.

I will think about telling them, about telling him, later. I will think about letting myself feel the full weight of this loss later. I will do it all later. But right now it would be an extra burden that I cannot expect anybody else to help me carry. I cannot add to their distress. For the time being, I will keep it secret. I will hoard that extra sadness and deal with it when I can. When we can. I will know when the moment is right.

The doctor rubs my shoulder encouragingly, and I am momentarily gripped with a need to see my own mother, to be wrapped in her arms, to be told that everything will be all right in the end. Except even that is a false hope, a false comfort.

My mother is a good woman, and I love her—but she is not that kind of mother. She would be the one crying, she would be the one needing consolation, and even though I feel guilty at the thought, I am better off without her being here.

Dr. Martinez knocks on the door and pushes it open. One look tells me that this is not the moment—that I am right to stay quiet about the baby for the time being. There is already too much grief and pain inside this small room for me to even consider adding to it.

Harry lies in a bed. He is still and silent and pale. He looks almost asleep, almost peaceful. It is quiet, apart from the background hisses and beeps of the mechanisms keeping him alive. Plastic tubes have been inserted into his nose, and his body is covered up with white sheets. Like he is mummified. Like he is an exhibit in a museum of the damned.

The horror of it curdles my stomach, as I take a careful step toward him. Toward this man who was always painted so bright, and now seems so gray.

"Elena! Thank God!" says his mother, Linda, lurching from her chair, her usually pristine hair rumpled, her normally sleek outfit creased. She throws her arms around me and holds me tight, and for a moment, I collapse against her, allowing myself a small window of respite before we pull away from each other.

We have never really loved each other, me and Harry's parents. We have got along well enough for Harry's sake, but the only thing we have in common is him. I know it is an illusion, this moment of motherly support; an emotional mirage that perhaps we both need.

His father, John, nods at me and smiles sadly. He is always the epitome of a stiff upper lip and is trying hard to maintain it here.

Linda stands back, embarrassed at her display of emotion, and smooths down her blond hair with a shaking hand—as though another woman being in the room has reminded her that she looks bad. She looks me over, her eyes pausing at the stitches on my forehead, at my bruises, at my bare feet.

"We have your things, from the hotel," she announces. "We got them packed up and sent over. You can put some clean clothes on."

"Thank you," I say, genuinely grateful. It will feel ridiculously good to be in my own things—to encase myself in a suit of fabric armor.

I touch Harry's hand, knowing he won't respond—can't respond—but still half expecting him to. I curl my fingers around his and feel a rush of love and pity and anguish. I might not be in love with him, but he is still my Harry—still the man who has meant most to me in my adult life. He should be a force of nature, not lying here like this.

"They say the brain swelling is going down well," says Linda, standing on the other side of the bed, stroking his hair away from his face with such tenderness that it takes my breath away. "They say they're going to take him off the machines at some point in the next few days. Then they hope he'll be able to talk, and . . . well. After that, we don't know. Have they told you?"

"Yes. A spinal cord injury."

"Incomplete, whatever that means."

"It means," interjects John firmly, "that he will get better. It means that he can get better, anyway. With our help. With our support."

I feel the intensity of his gaze homing in on me. It's like he can read my mind and see all the doubts I was harboring before any of this happened. Sees them, and judges me for them.

"He'll need us now," he says firmly. "All of us."

I nod and sway slightly. I grip the metal guard at the side of the bed and hear white noise and see bright spots dashing before my eyes, swimming around my vision like tiny neon-colored tropical fish.

Dr. Martinez is right by my side, taking hold of my arm.

"Elena needs to rest now," he says, looking directly at John, daring him to disagree.

I allow myself to be steered from the room, sit passively back into the wheelchair, stare silently at the pale green paint of the walls. The doctor emerges with a suitcase on wheels behind him and looks around for someone to help. A male orderly is given the suitcase, told where to take it, and Dr. Martinez pushes me away. Away from Harry, and John and Linda, and the suffocating silence of a life on hold.

When we reach my room, I tell the doctor I will be

fine. I haven't heard a word he has said for the last few minutes, but I am convincing enough that he leaves me by the doorway.

My suitcase is already waiting at the side of my table. Someone else is waiting as well.

Alex is sitting on the bed, his leg stretched out in front of him, his ankle encased in a giant boot that under normal circumstances might have looked comical. He has been cleaned up, his hair thick and blond again, and he is wearing a bright yellow T-shirt that says *I* ♥ *Tequila* in cartoonish red writing. The heart has a smiley face inside it.

As soon as I see him, I feel better. Calmer. Like I've come home on a cold winter's night to a log fire and a glass of whiskey. Like I am safe again, in a place where nobody will ask me for more than I can give.

Our eyes meet, and he smiles.

"Hi," he says simply.

I'm delighted to see him, but for some reason I immediately burst into tears, which is totally embarrassing. He tries to get up to come to me, but I wave my hands at him and sit by his side instead.

"I'm okay," I mutter between sobs. "Ignore me, please. You'll only make it worse if you're nice to me. I'm all right, honest."

"You don't look all right," he replies. "Is it the T-shirt? There was a limited supply in the lost-and-found box . . ."

I intend to laugh, but it comes out as a disgusting half snort, like a pig sneezing.

"No, it's lovely," I say. "Very you. How are you feeling?"

"Oh, you know," he answers, gesturing at his giant foot. "Like I could walk on the moon. I have called in a few times, but you were resting. I . . . I heard about Harry. I'm sorry."

I nod and notice that Janey is watching us. I don't blame her—she must be bored rigid by now. The old lady is still staring into space, Sofia is still asleep, and the other woman appears to have left.

"Can you actually walk?" I ask, seeing crutches leaning against the wall. "I could really do with some fresh air. I feel . . . trapped. Do you know what I mean?"

"I do," he replies seriously. "I've felt like that ever since we got out, ironically. I see you have your suitcase and unlike me have not been forced to make such outrageous fashion choices. Why don't you get dressed, and if you're up to it, I know somewhere we can go."

I wheel the suitcase through to the communal bathroom, lock the door behind me. I grab fresh jeans and a top, and pause as I see my toiletries bag. The feminine hygiene products I'd brought with me, expecting to need them.

And I suppose I do. I am still bleeding, but not in the way I thought. Dr. Martinez says it's normal, after a miscarriage. Normal. Whatever that is.

I stare into the mirror and see a stranger looking back at me. My face is clean but bruised, the stitches tracing a neat five-inch line across my forehead. My hair has been brushed back and put into a ponytail, and it's odd to think of someone I don't know performing such intimate acts.

There are dark circles beneath my eyes, and I look pallid despite the holiday tan.

My hand goes again to my stomach, to what is probably a phantom pain cramping inside me. Part of me wishes I'd never known, never found out. So much has happened so quickly—my whole world has been turned upside down and inside out, emotionally and physically.

I splash my face with cold water, give myself a dirty look, and go back outside. One of the nurses has left two pills—painkillers, I presume—on the bedside cabinet, but I ignore them. The pain is distracting. Distraction is good.

Alex heaves himself up, leans on his crutches, and together we walk silently out into the corridor. He guides me to the lifts and presses a button for the top floor. We are both quiet, but it is a comfortable quiet, not one that feels as though it needs breaking.

We emerge onto yet another green-painted hallway, and I follow him to a set of double doors. All of this takes quite some time, between his broken ankle and my general inertia. He pushes the doors open, and when I walk through them I feel like I'm about to tumble off the edge of the world.

It's a balcony, but huge, wrapping most of the way around the building. There are tables and chairs and plants, and even a bird feeder, surrounded by tiny sparrow-sized creatures with bright yellow chests. They fly away briefly when we come out, but soon return, wings flapping, beaks prodding. They're so pretty they threaten to make me cry again, reminding me of that hummingbird we saw, before it all began.

We settle ourselves down on two metal-legged chairs, the only people out here apart from one nurse in the far corner, who is sneaking a cigarette and checking her phone.

"Wow," I say, taking in the view. It really is the only suitable word. The city is sprawled out beneath us in glorious Technicolor. Busy roads. Honking car horns. Music. Hills in the distance, suburbs fading out to emptiness. Dusk is falling, and lights are starting to pierce the haze, flickering on all across the horizon.

"I know," he says, smiling at my reaction. "I found it yesterday and I couldn't wait to show you. I needed to get outside, but the noise down there, in the street . . . it was too much. This is as peaceful as it gets. It's so good to see you. How are you, really?"

I look away from the cityscape and into his eyes. He is probably the only person on the face of the planet who has any clue how I feel right now—and even he doesn't know all of it.

I consider lying, faking it, claiming that all is well. Why should I drag him down with more bad news, more of my drama?

"You can trust me," he says, sensing my hesitation. "We told each other all our deep, dark secrets already. When I ask how you are, I really want to know, okay? We can pretend for other people, but not each other. Deal?"

I nod and hold out my hand. He takes it in his and

examines the mark left by the drip, kissing it gently better.

"The doctor saw me earlier," I say. "Dr. Martinez."

"Ah. The handsome one. Did you swoon?"

"Almost—he is crazy handsome, isn't he? Like he might be a part-time model when he's not saving lives. And he's nice. Kind. I might marry him."

He grins, but he knows that I am stalling. Funny how well we know each other after such a short amount of time. Between us we share a variety of functioning limbs—two short of the usual amount—and one communal brain.

"Anyway. Dr. Martinez told me that I was pregnant, and that I lost the baby. Apparently being buried beneath an earthquake isn't a good maternal habitat."

A momentary look of shock flickers across his face, replaced immediately by one of supreme sympathy. He keeps my hand held tight in his and asks, "I presume you didn't know?"

"No. And now I'm not pregnant anymore, so I don't know if it even matters."

"It matters. It does. Whatever you're feeling right now, it's fine to feel it."

"That's the thing," I say, turning away from him and looking down again at the magical city below. "I don't know what I feel. I found out about Harry, then I found out about the baby, and now I'm all over the place. I feel everything, and I feel nothing.

"I feel . . . bereaved. I feel a bit like I did when my dad died, but I also feel angry with myself about that.

There isn't anything to grieve, not really. It was only a tiny blob of cells, it wasn't really a baby; I never even knew it existed until after it was gone. If the doctor hadn't told me, I never would have known.

"There are people in this hospital who have suffered real loss. The old lady in my room hasn't spoken since her husband died. Two of the Australian girls won't be going home. Harry is . . . the way he is. So . . . I don't feel entitled to any grief. It feels . . . indulgent. Selfish."

"Grief isn't something you earn, Elena, you know that," he replies, his voice quiet but firm. "There is no hierarchy. You might not have planned it, you might not have known, but it is a loss all the same. Don't begrudge yourself the chance to feel that."

Maybe he's right, I think. Maybe in ordinary circumstances that is what I would do. I would cry, and grieve, and let the full weight of loss fall upon me. I would talk to Harry, and maybe to my mum, and perhaps to a counselor. It would make me think about children and the role they play in my life.

But these are not ordinary circumstances and my feelings are all over the place. I was considering leaving Harry, not having a baby with him. How would I have coped? Would I have really even wanted a baby, if I'm being honest? There is an unreal amount of guilt attached to that particular issue, which I don't feel quite up to shouldering.

Maybe I just need to move on. This happens to millions of women. To better women than me. Women who already loved their child. Women who desperately wanted them, yearned for them. Somehow, they carry on.

There is emptiness inside me, clawing away at me, a hollow space. There is so much to think about. Harry is in a coma. He may be paralyzed. Our lives have just become a mass of possible outcomes, a labyrinth of uncertainties. And still . . . still the pain is there, hiding amid the guilt and worry, peeking around corners. Pain I don't feel I deserve.

"I don't know why I feel like this," I say, letting the tears come, rolling slowly down my cheeks. "Who knows what was going to happen with me and Harry? I was thinking of running off into the sunset and starting a new life. A baby would have changed all of that. It would have made everything complicated. Part of me even thinks I should be relieved, but I can't find that anywhere in me. Or maybe I can, a tiny bit, and that's making me feel even worse . . ."

"Elena, there are no rules here. Just because it wasn't deliberate doesn't mean it would have been wrong. And just because it would have been complicated doesn't mean you can't be sad. It's hard. So hard. Nobody should have to deal with all of this."

"That goes for all of us, though, doesn't it? You and Anna. Harry's parents down there, worried sick, because he's their baby, isn't he? No matter how old he is, he's still their baby, and they're watching him suffer. And my mum—God, I really must phone her—she'll be in pieces as well. There is plenty of pain to go around, it seems."

He is silent, and I know he can't disagree. He has had more than his share.

"I know. The world feels very cruel sometimes. Have you told them about the baby, his parents? Will you tell him, when he's awake?"

"I'm not sure," I reply. "I've been thinking about that myself, and it's very difficult. I've really only just found out myself, and my instincts are to definitely not tell his parents. He should know first, and goodness knows when that might be. I don't know when he will wake up, or how he will feel, or if he'll be strong enough to deal with anything other than getting through each day. I don't even know if it's fair to tell him—to add to his suffering when I don't need to."

"Maybe you do need to, though," he says. "Maybe, when the time is right, you need to talk to him about it, and maybe you both need to have the chance to grieve together."

I nod, knowing that he might be right. It is—was—Harry's baby too.

"Possibly. I think this whole situation is impossible to predict. But . . . not his mum and dad. I won't tell them. They have too much to deal with already. I have to try and help them through it, no matter what happens in the long term. Neither of us is going to be the same person as we were when this is over, are we, me and Harry? This . . . just adds to an already horrible situation."

The sun is finally setting over the city, a deep orange globe; the evening air still warm, the noise from below reaching us even all these stories high. It feels oddly peaceful, despite the sound of the traffic and the wailing of sirens arriving at the hospital. Like we're held apart from it all.

We sit, our clasped hands draped between the chairs, and watch as night falls, purple and bruised.

"Just remember," he says, after a few moments' shared silence, "that I'm here. You're not alone. And I'll be here for as long as you need me."

Chapter 11

Two days later, the doctors tell us that Harry is stable enough to be taken off the drugs that are keeping him comatose. That his brain has recovered, that he is ready to come back to us. That he is ready to leave his artificial hibernation.

It is good news, but I am not sure he will see it that way, when he finds out what his new reality is.

I am sitting by his side, holding his hand, his parents behind me.

"They're doing it in the morning," says Linda, the fatigue dripping from every word. "They'll reduce the drugs and see how he reacts, but they don't think there'll be any problems."

We all stay silent, knowing that there will be problems. That there will be many problems, of different shades and stripes—and that thinking too far ahead would be foolish.

John has been busy doing things—coping the best way he knows how. Researching spinal injuries, talking to doctors in the UK, finding out what "the very best" in treatment will look like. He has found a clinic that offers hope—and that also costs thousands, over a period of time that refuses to be pinned down.

There is a maze of the mundane going on—speaking to the insurance company, looking at transport, figuring out the day-to-day issues. I even found him reading customer reviews on wheelchair ramps, as though obsessing with the practical details is somehow protecting him from the trauma of the big picture.

He has told Harry's work colleagues, and various gifts have arrived—fruit baskets and flowers and giant silver helium balloons that float, semi-inflated and inappropriate, in the corners of the room, bobbing like metallic spirits of the underworld every time the door opens.

Linda has been spending every waking moment at her son's side, as well as her sleeping ones, contorted into a chair and footstool. She looks terrible—thin and damaged, a fragment of her former self. She is a woman in her fifties, but as she reaches out to caress his face, the skin on the back of her hands is taut and pale, waxy like a piece of jaundiced fruit.

"Why don't you two go and have a rest?" I suggest, as I have done frequently over the last few days.

Linda is about to refuse again, and I add, "Please. You need a break. I'll stay with him. Tomorrow, when he's awake again, he'll need the company more than he does now. Go and eat. Go for a walk. This might be the last chance you get for a while."

John nods and says firmly, "You're right, Elena. Come on, love—we'll go to the canteen. Take a stroll. He'll be fine for half an hour."

Linda still looks as though she might argue, but in the end she folds. Her will isn't strong enough to fight right now.

She fusses around brushing her hair and "doing her face," as she calls it, and asks me several times if I'm sure. When they finally leave it feels like a relief to have that grief and pain and stress taken away. I have plenty of my own, but theirs is so tangible I could slice it like pie. They are his parents, and their love for this man is different from mine. It is primal in its intensity.

"Alone at last," I say, gazing down at Harry. At his still features and his floppy hair and his cocooned body. I push back his fringe and lean forward to kiss him quickly on the lips.

It is still so strange, seeing him like this. Trying to understand what has happened—what might happen. Days ago I was coming to the difficult decision that it was all over between us. Now, looking at him so still and vulnerable, I feel confused. It is hard to untangle love from sympathy, to decipher how much I want to protect him from how much I actually still feel for him as a partner.

This, I think, is the last time he will be at peace. The last time he will be unaware of what the world has done to him. The last time that his mind and body are able to rest, oblivious to anything other than functioning and healing.

I take his flaccid hand in mine and say, "Hi, Harry. It's me, Elena. I have been here, honest—just not as chatty as your mum. Your mum loves you so much,

Harry—she's like a tired lioness, exhausted but still protecting her cub.

"Anyway. Tomorrow, they're going to wake you up. We'll be able to talk for real. None of us has any idea what's going to happen next, but I hope it'll be all right. In the end. So . . . before you are awake, there's something I have to tell you. Something I'm not sure I'll tell you again, depending on how things work out."

I scan his face, see no response. The doctors have assured us that he is resting, that technically he cannot hear or respond. Linda has found anecdotal evidence on the internet about people who say they could hear, who felt like they were looking down on their own bodies.

The internet, of course, isn't that reliable. There isn't even the flicker of an eye beneath his blue-tinged lids.

I take a deep breath and continue. "I found out a few days ago, Harry, that I was pregnant. That I was carrying our baby."

Saying the words out loud is surprisingly hard. I have talked to Alex about it, and I have thought about it, but telling Harry—even an unconscious Harry—is more emotional than I expected. I accidentally created a baby with this man, no matter how complex our relationship was becoming.

"I lost the baby. Probably during the earthquake. Miscarriages are common. I keep telling myself that, as though something being common makes it less awful . . . Whatever the reason—I lost our baby. We hadn't planned one, not yet, and maybe we never would have, who knows? Things were a bit up in the air between us, weren't they, if we're honest? Things were changing.

"But that doesn't matter. We lost a baby, and I'm so sad about it, Harry. I lie awake at night and imagine what he or she would have looked like. Somehow I think it was a boy. I wonder if he would have had my eyes, or your sense of humor; what we might have called him.

"I imagine holding a tiny baby, safe in my arms, and I . . . I love him so much. It feels like nothing I've ever experienced. And then I remember—then I remember that he's gone. That our baby is gone and will never come back. That I didn't keep him safe. That I'll never know what he would have been like—never get the answers to all those questions, all those wonderings. He's gone, and it's over, and I need to deal with that."

I scrunch up my T-shirt to wipe away tears and look down at him. Still silent, still at peace. I feel unreasonably jealous of that peace and try to ignore a surge of anger. I can't be angry at a man lying in a medically induced coma.

"I wanted to tell you now," I say, "because I'm not sure when I'll get to tell you later. You'll have so much to deal with already. There's already been too much loss, too much suffering. I don't know if you'll be able to bear any more, if it would be fair of me to add to your pain. Maybe I will tell you. Or maybe this is one for me to carry on your behalf. I just don't know yet. I'm so sorry, Harry. For everything that's happened. Everything that is to come."

I lean back in the chair, falling silent. I can hear the

traffic outside and occasional low-level chatter in the hallway. I can hear the beep of his heart monitor and the sound of my own moist breath.

I close my eyes and switch off my mind. I mute my thoughts and put myself into my own equivalent of a medically induced coma. I have become skilled at this—at compartmentalizing, at burying pain, at finding a way to function even though every emotion I have tells me to curl up in a ball and sob.

Less than half an hour has passed before Linda and John return, Linda dashing over to touch her son immediately, as though she can reassure him that she's back now. That Mummy is back and everything will be fine.

I stand up and look at John. He pulls a face and says, "Couldn't keep her away for long. Said she didn't like the music . . ."

That actually makes me smile. The music in the canteen is terrible—at least to our ears. Muzaky Spanish-language covers of pop music hits by the likes of Dolly Parton and Duran Duran and the Spice Girls.

"I don't blame her," I reply, glancing back at Linda and her maternal communion with a more-than-sleeping son. "I'm going to get some rest myself. I'll see you tomorrow."

"Thank you, Elena," he says, sounding uncharacteristically emotional. "For this. For staying. I know you could have gone home by now, if you'd really wanted to. I know this isn't easy. Thank you for . . . standing by him."

Tammy Wynette, my brain points out. "Stand by Your Man." One of the other songs I heard in the canteen.

I nod and leave, making my way through now familiar corridors and back to the part of the hospital I now strangely think of as home. I feel empty, numb—as though my mind is self-medicating, giving me the emotional anesthetic I need to get through the day.

I pass the room where the family is—the Frazers, as I now know. The mum is recovering, but their lives—like so many—will never be the same again.

I approach the vending machine at the end of the corridor, root in my pocket for some spare pesos. I order a hot chocolate, knowing from past experience that it will be more hot than chocolate. I sense someone behind me, glance back and see the girl. The one with the red hair. She looks sullen and aggressive and sad, as usual.

"Would you like one?" I ask, without thinking.

The girl glares at me, but nods.

We stand side by side and watch the machine clank and spurt, both too broken to speak. Moments later, we grimace at burned lips, a shared pain that is more than skin-deep.

Chapter 12

It is not pretty, Harry coming out of his coma—and it is not quick.

It is a gradual process over a day or so, with the drugs in his system that have kept him under being reduced. The room always seems bustling, Dr. Martinez and several nurses always around. His vital signs are constantly monitored, and we have been warned that he might be confused, or agitated, or weak. As with everything else so far, nobody seems able to predict what will happen next.

There are signs of him coming around after a few hours—his fingers twitch, his eyes move rapidly beneath his lids, his head turns. At one stage he seems to want to pull the tubes from his body, his hands clawing at his nose and face.

Linda and I sit on either side of him, gently moving his hands away, talking to him, trying to reassure his wakening mind that he is safe.

After a while, his eyes open. He stares first at the ceiling, blinking at the bright lights, then at us. Linda immediately starts chatting to him, stroking his forehead, telling him that everything is going to be all right.

He looks from me to her and back again, eyes wide in shock and confusion. I see the panic and the fear, and realize he has no idea what has happened to him, or where he is, or why his mother is there.

"It's okay, Harry," I say quietly, holding his hand. "You're in the hospital, in Mexico. You've been injured, but you're in good hands. You've been in a coma for a few days, and that's why you have the tube down your throat. They needed to leave it there to make sure you can breathe on your own. You might feel weak, and your throat will probably be sore, but try not to get too upset. Keep calm and carry on, eh, as the saying goes?"

He nods, blinks some more, and seems less frantic. Dr. Martinez has arrived and makes his way through the small crowd, calmly talking to Harry and explaining that he's going to remove the breathing tube. That he mustn't worry; they are all there to make sure he is safe.

Linda and I back away, joining John at the side of the room. Harry's eyes follow us as we go, his skin pale beneath the yellowing remnants of his holiday tan.

Linda clutches my hand as the doctor goes to work. It feels like we all hold our breath as well, waiting to see what will happen. Harry coughs, splutters, seems to choke slightly—then his breathing settles. We all sigh with him, and Dr. Martinez starts doing some basic checks.

"Well done," he says. "I think you're going to be just fine. How do you feel?"

"Weird," says Harry, his voice croaky and quiet. "Like

I'm not me. Why am I here? What happened? Can I have a cup of tea?"

One of the nurses laughs, and it seems to break some of the tension in the room. I know he's not out of the woods yet, not by a long way, but he is here. He is breathing. He is talking. He is a reduced Harry, but he is still Harry.

I rush back to his side and lean in close to look at him better. Dark marks beneath his eyes. Bruises and cuts. Dry lips and crusted eyes.

"Are you all right?" he asks, trying to raise his hand to touch the stitches on my forehead, finding himself too weak. I hold his hand and feel his fingers grip mine as hard as they can. The grip is tentative, but I can feel the desperation in it.

"I'm fine," I reply, fighting the sting of tears. "Don't worry about me. You just need to concentrate on getting stronger."

I see John, his face grim, and know what he is thinking. That soon, Harry will discover the rest of it. Will be told that he is paralyzed. Will be told that his life has changed forever.

For now, though, all we can do is offer him comfort. Make him feel safe. Give him hope.

I kiss him on the cheek and say, "Welcome back, Harry. We missed you. We're all here, all with you, and we're going nowhere."

Linda joins us, looking exhausted but exhilarated, and adds, "Darling, it's all going to be fine. Now, let's see about getting you this tea, shall we?"

Chapter 13

The next few days are harder. Harry is in pain, of every shade, and he is lashing out.

With Dr. Martinez's help, Harry has been told about what has happened. About his prognosis. He has asked questions, been given answers that don't satisfy him, has asked them all over again. Been told once more. A cycle of bitter disbelief and denial.

It's been heartbreaking, the way he listens, hears the bad news again in different terms, looks to me or his mum and dad, as though urging us to contradict it. Needing us to say it's not true. Each time we nod, each time we tell him, in our own way, that this is all real, he sinks a little lower. His mood has ranged from tearful to furious, and everything in between.

He has screamed, and shouted, and cried. He has thrown his food tray against the walls, bright green jelly sliding down pale green paint.

We have tried to remain calm, to help him, but we are all feeling the strain of seeing him in so much anguish.

I am here every day, for as long as I can. Today, he is furious. It is late afternoon and he has not eaten, and he is so angry. With the nurses, with us, with the whole universe.

Linda fusses over him, and I try to talk to him, and John just looks helpless.

"You're all lying!" he yells, pushing his mother away as she attempts to brush his hair. "I don't know why, but you're all lying to me!"

Before any of us can stop him, he is trying to get out of bed, picking up his blanket-covered legs and swinging them to one side.

He crashes to the ground, dragging his drip stand down, his legs entangled in the sheets, his head cracking against the floor. He lies there, sobbing, screaming at us to stay away from him.

I squat by his side, hold up a hand to stop the nurses that have rushed in to see what they can do to help.

"Leave me alone," he mutters, his eyes screwed up against the tears, snot and blood running from his nose from the fall. "Just leave me alone . . ."

"I won't," I say firmly. "I'm not going anywhere. None of us blame you for feeling like this, but none of us are giving up on you either. We're here, and we're staying, and there's not a lot you can do about it."

He shouts in frustration, wrapping his arms across his face, lying in the chaos of twisted bedding, the mocking sound of the heart monitor beeping in the background. His drip has been tugged out in the fall, and a small drop of blood oozes across the dry skin of his hand. I sit beside him, silently, waiting until his breathing returns to normal.

He keeps his eyes squeezed shut, but holds out a hand in my direction. I take it, hold it tight.

"Thank you," he says softly.

"You're welcome," I reply quietly, leaning down to kiss him on the forehead.

The nurses get him sorted and settled back in bed, and once he is calmer, in fact on the verge of sleep, I slip out of the room.

I lean back against the wall and rub my sore eyes with my fingers. I am wrung out, tense and tired. Nobody can blame Harry for reacting like this. This is not a film, and he is not a superhero. He is a man, who one minute was enjoying his holiday, and the next woke up in the hospital with strangers telling him his legs don't work.

But it is draining us all. We've been with him around the clock, everyone taking shifts apart from his mother, who refuses to leave the room. We are all exhausted, Harry most of all.

I have no idea what the future holds, for me or for Harry, or for us as a couple. I have had no time to think about that, or maybe I have simply been avoiding it. He is at the lowest point of his life, and it seems unforgivable to even consider not being there for him.

I would never abandon him—but if I am honest, as I suck in some deep breaths and try to calm myself, I need a break. I need to be away from that stifling room for a while. Away from Harry's pain and need.

I need to break free, just for a little while. I need to see Alex.

Even the thought of it makes me feel guilty, and I go through my usual mental checklist: Alex and I are just friends. Alex and I are helping each other stay strong. The stronger I am, the more I can help Harry when he needs it.

I'm not sure I'm even convincing myself, and I jump slightly when John emerges from the room fifteen minutes later, as though I have been caught out.

"Elena," he says, nodding at me. "You're still here. Good."

"Why?" I ask. "Does he need me?"

"No, he's asleep. You can take a break—goodness knows you deserve it. But I wanted to talk to you about something else. About doing a press interview."

I stare at him, confused. I haven't spoken to the press, not for lack of trying on their part, and I have no desire to do so.

"We've had some offers," he says, gazing past me, as though fascinated by the corridor beyond. "From a few papers, from a TV show. Wanting to talk to you, to Harry."

"But . . . why would we do that, John? Isn't there enough to think about right now? Enough pressure?"

He smiles, but looks sad as he replies, "There is enough pressure, Elena—and some of it is going to be financial. The insurance money will only go so far. And who knows when or if Harry will be able to work again? Or you, if you're looking after him."

As he puts that thought into words I feel a flutter of panic unfurl in my chest. I have a lot of love left for

Harry—but is that my future now? Giving up my career, my own needs, to look after his? I refuse to engage with that thought. It is too much.

"So we have to think about the financials," he continues matter-of-factly, "and this could be quite lucrative. There is rehab to pay for, he might need somewhere new to live . . . there will be expenses. We can help, of course, but this is one way he can help himself, which I think would be good for him."

"Have you asked Harry about it?" I say, hopeful that he will feel the same as I do—horrified.

"Briefly, this morning. He thought it was a good idea and we were going to discuss it with you this afternoon, but . . . well, events overtook us. Anyway. You look exhausted. Why don't you go and have a rest, a nap maybe?"

I nod and force a smile onto my face as we say our goodbyes.

I don't go for a nap or a rest. I go to the canteen. I know he will be there, and I know that I will feel better for talking to him. Or being silent with him. Just being with him, really.

I scan the room, the tables full of staff and visitors and even a few patients, until I see him. He is sitting with a coffee, looking at his new phone. Even seeing him there, his blond head bent, unties knots I didn't notice developing.

We have a ritual, Alex and I. Every day, we meet here, and we go up to the balcony to watch the sunset together. Part of me feels guilty for it—for having this escape, this refuge. For having a friend. For having a world outside Harry's hospital room, if only for an hour a day.

But I need it—and I know it can't last forever. I know that eventually, Alex will leave. He will go back to his real life, and I will go back to mine, whatever that might look like. I will miss him, too much.

He is stirring his coffee into submission as I walk over to him. I lay a hand on his shoulder and apologize for being late.

"You're not late," he replies, smiling as I sink into the seat opposite him. "We don't have an appointment."

"Well, we kind of do, don't we? An unofficial one. You looked serious then. Penny for them?"

He frowns. "Individually, I understand all of those words. Together they don't make much sense."

"I mean, if I give you a penny, will you tell me what your thoughts were? It's just an English saying. You probably have an equivalent."

He ponders for a moment. "We'd probably just say *vad tänker du på*? Just what it should be—what are you thinking? There would be no financial incentives offered."

"Right," I say, fishing around in the pocket of my jeans and placing a shiny coin on the tabletop. "Well, it's this kind of mercenary attitude that made us an empire . . . maybe. Anyway. Here you go. Now I own them. Your thoughts."

He stares at it seriously, then looks into my eyes. It feels suddenly intense, suddenly a little too warm, suddenly intimate. I wonder if I really do want to know his thoughts, or if they'd just add to the chaos that is my life right now.

"Sorry, I'm not that cheap," he says eventually.

"That's not what I've read on the bathroom wall . . ."

It takes him a minute to figure that one out as well, but it's easier. He grins and raises his eyebrows.

I'm tapping my fingernails on the tabletop, loosely in time to the song of the moment—a Spanish-language production of Britney Spears's "Toxic." I feel weirdly wired, like a zoo animal staring through my bars, planning an escape.

"What are you looking at?" I ask, pointing to his phone.

"Just catching up with news from home."

"From Stockholm?"

"Yes. It's practicing for Christmas right now. Dressing up."

"Oh, I bet it's lovely at Christmas! Tell me about it!"

He smiles, and nods, and tells me. I'm not sure if I'll ever get to travel now, or even if I am brave enough anymore, and I enjoy listening to his tales almost as much as being there myself.

"It is magical, Elena. There's a market at the Kungliga Hovstallet, the royal stables. The streets of the old town in Gamla Stan come alive, and everything smells of gingerbread and mulled wine and candied almonds.

"There's usually snow, and in the middle of December there is this thing called the Lucia Procession. Little girls and boys dressed in white, with their stars and lanterns, singing to Saint Lucy and banishing darkness with candle-light and song. The decorations go up, and there's ice-skating at Kungsträdgården. People wrap up warm and sit outside to eat and drink, and there's dancing, and music, and . . . well. Yes. It is lovely."

I sigh, picturing it all.

"You probably can't wait to get back home," I say.

"Well, home isn't a place, is it? It's a feeling. And sometimes . . . sometimes, being around all that happiness, all that joy and togetherness? Well, it makes me miss Anna more than ever. Makes me realize how alone I am when I'm there . . . Apologies. I'm being miserable."

"No, you're not," I say quickly. "You're just being honest. And we made that deal, didn't we? That we didn't have to pretend for each other."

"We did. But sometimes pretending is necessary. Sometimes pretending is the only thing that gets you through the day."

"Now you are being miserable!" I answer, feeling scared of what he says. Feeling worried that he might be right. That too much honesty would upset the delicate balance that everyone is struggling to keep.

That the truth of this situation—that seeing him is the best part of my day, that being apart from him hurts, that time away from him feels wasted—would crack open the world.

"You may be right," he replies. "Roof?"

I nod, and we leave the canteen. He waves to someone on the way out, and I see it is Samantha, the redheaded teenager. She throws her hair over her face and pretends she hasn't seen us. There is a camera on the table beside her, which she seems to be trying to hide. Teenagers are weird.

We make our way to the usual spot via the lifts. It is hit and miss how many other people we find up here. Some days it is completely deserted, on others there are gaggles of staff chatting and laughing, or relatives seeking some alone time, or patients still attached to drip stands.

Today, we are alone. We pull our chairs close to the edge of the balcony, to better watch the performance that goes on at this time every day.

It is around six, and within half an hour the sun will start to set. It's like a free show at the edge of the world, the mundane and the mind-blowingly beautiful combined in one spectacular scene.

The city is always busy, always filled with traffic and noise and music and bustle, but it looks completely different at night. At night, the dust and the congestion and the choked streets become something more ethereal, a blanket of neon, an urban fairy tale.

Sunset is when it all changes, at once gradual and sudden. One moment, it's like everything is changing so slowly you can almost see the sun sinking inch by inch, a blaze of orange fire as it falls into the distant hills. The next, it's over.

"It is amazing, every single time, isn't it?" I say. "And every night, when I see those lights twinkling up in the mountains, I wonder who lives there, and what their lives are like."

"Perhaps we should get in a taxi and go and knock on their doors."

"I'm not sure that's ever likely to happen," I reply, staring off into the horizon, "but it's a nice thought. How are you anyway? Have they said you can go home yet?"

He is silent for a moment, and I don't look at his face. I don't want to see what might be there. They've already told me I could go home, medically speaking, and I'm sure they've told him the same.

I know why I'm still here—for Harry. I'm not sure I'm ready to know why he is. I'm just grateful for it.

"What?" he says, gesturing at the view. "And leave all this? Winter in Stockholm might be beautiful, but it's not the perfect place for a man on crutches. Anyway, I think I've met someone special."

I can tell from his tone that he is about to say something silly and find myself smiling in advance.

"How exciting! Who is the lucky woman?"

"Bettina. I think she likes me."

"Bettina who works in the canteen?"

"Yes, that Bettina."

"The one who is about two hundred years old and crosses herself every time anyone uses a credit card?"

"Her, yes. I think we have something. She gave me a free bag of chili nuts yesterday."

"Free chili nuts? That is romantic. I wish you both well. Let me know when I need to buy a new hat for the wedding."

We share a grin and turn back to the view. The sun is

sinking, but the air is still a warm touch against our skin.

"Have you ever . . . you know, actually considered asking someone out?" I ask, after a few moments.

"Not really," he says, sipping his coffee. "Not yet. It's strange, but I feel guilty if I even think about another woman. I even . . . I even feel guilty when I'm with you sometimes. Every time we laugh, or share a joke, or watch a sunset, I feel like I'm taking a step away from her. Betraying her somehow."

"And do you think she'd feel betrayed? By us being friends? If you did meet another woman?"

"Other than Bettina? No, of course she wouldn't. She'd want me to be happy. She'd be telling me to be brave. To be fearless. To be free."

"You are brave," I say quickly. "And nobody is fearless, are they? We're all a bit scared, all the time, of different things. Small things, big things. There's always fear. That's why I'm keeping the scar. Like a really terrible holiday souvenir. Am I mad?"

I've been told by the doctors here that the cut across my forehead will leave a mark, unless I get it treated by a plastic surgeon. As I speak, my hand goes up to trace the stitches. It doesn't hurt anymore—just itches, and looks terrible.

"Probably. Most women would be horrified. But I understand what you mean—it's a reminder. A reminder that you survived. That you might not have been fearless, but you're still here. So in the future, whenever you're going through something bad, you can look in the mirror and tell yourself it will all be fine—you've survived worse. Either that, or you just have a bride of Frankenstein fetish."

"Hey, who doesn't? She rocked that look, and her fella had a certain rough charm as well, and . . . yeah. Obviously, you do understand. It's a shame you didn't get one too. Your cuts are all babies compared to mine. You'll only ever be able to look in the mirror and be reminded that you're handsome."

"Handsome?" he echoes, laughing. "I don't think so."

"Yeah, you are," I say, reaching out and prodding him on the shoulder. "You know, in a vaguely Viking kind of way. Like that guy out of *True Blood*."

"Well, I'm not sure I trust your judgment," he responds, grinning. "You think Frankenstein is hot."

"You make a fair point," I reply, and we lapse back into a comfortable silence, both quietly smiling to ourselves as we watch the sun slide down into the mountains.

We will both always appreciate this kind of thing from now on, I think—being out, being in the fresh air, watching the sun rise and watching the sun set. Being trapped in an underground tomb will do that to you.

"Harry and his family think we should speak to the press," I say, once twilight starts to settle. "I'm not so sure I want to, but it doesn't feel entirely like it's my decision to make."

"Is that why you seemed a bit jittery when you turned up today?"

"Yup."

The media has been all over this story, of course—and I understand why the world is interested. Twenty-eight people are dead, many of them tourists. A lot more are injured, some seriously. Around eighty people in total were damaged in some way—and that doesn't even take into account the psychological toll. Even those who escaped relatively unharmed will have wounds that don't show up on an X-ray.

Then there is the cost to the villagers—losing their homes, their cars, their beautiful church, the plaza. Maybe it will be rebuilt, but it will cost time and money, and won't be easy.

I've seen pictures of villagers I recognize on the front pages of the newspapers in the hospital canteen, seen them interviewed on the TV screens. Not needing a translator to explain the tears and the pain and the sense of utter desolation.

One of the Australian girls seems to have found a place on the news most nights, and the parents of the two who died, Greta and Beth, have also been on TV. They were strangely dignified, holding it together while falling apart, thanking the emergency services and the hospital and the Mexican people for all their support.

Another local family appeared, holding a framed photo of their lost loved one, weeping. A middle-aged woman, presumably the wife, plus sons and daughters and grandchildren. When I saw the photo on a close-up, I realized it was Jorge, the coach driver. So jovial and funny and gone.

My mum's been doorstepped back at home, and I

know I've been in the papers and on screens too. The night we were rescued, I didn't even notice that pictures were being taken—but sure enough, there I was, sitting in my foil blanket, looking shocked and covered in grime, gazing up at the sky. I have become famous for that tinfoil blanket.

I know Alex has received calls too, from Scandinavian papers. Neither of us has been interested in becoming a media sensation, and so far we've both avoided the direct spotlight.

Now, though, I feel it heading in my direction.

"Right," he says, when I don't elaborate. "Well, you do have a choice, you know. It is your decision as much as theirs. Why do they want to do it?"

"I think 'want' is too strong a word. But . . . I don't know. It might be a good idea. John's only just mentioned it, so I'm still settling into the idea. It was a rough day today . . . he really struggled. Maybe doing something like this might help him—something he feels more in control of? Something to make it more real? And, as his dad's just pointed out to me, he'll get paid—and in the real world, money does come in handy.

"Rehab for spinal injuries can be long and expensive if you want what John keeps calling 'the very best.' Which he always announces in this really authoritative voice, like an army major in a black-and-white film . . . as though everyone else should just make do with substandard care, and . . . no. That's not fair of me. He's just a father, doing what he can. I'm being a bitch."

"You're being a human being," Alex replies, gently nudging my ankle with his giant boot. "And don't argue with me, or you'll feel the mighty boot of justice."

I smile and shake my head. It's all a bit of a mess, really.

"I don't see how I can refuse, Alex," I say. "For his sake."

"I understand that. It's one of the things that makes you you, the fact that you can't. But you're in pain too."

I shrug. "Not really. My arm doesn't give me that much trouble now."

"I'm not talking about your arm, Elena. I'm talking about the trauma you've been through. I'm talking about the way Harry's injuries might affect your life. I'm talking about everything that has been taken away from you. I'm talking about the baby. Ever since Harry came out of the coma, it's like you don't exist anymore—it's like all you worry about is him."

I close my eyes and sigh. He is, of course, correct. I am in pain. I have lost a lot, and I have kept that loss to myself, as though keeping it to myself might make it smaller.

At first, I did consider telling Harry about the miscarriage—but he is simply not in a place where he can hear news like that. Where he can take any additional pressure. That might change; there might be a time for that conversation—but that time is not now. I can't protect him from much, but I can protect him from that. For now at least.

I've also, though, not talked to Alex about it, even

though I know he would always listen, without judgment, without expectation.

"I know. I just . . . can't, Alex. I know this is stupid, but part of me has decided that if I try hard enough not to think about it, it will go away."

"That's not how grief works, Elena. You know that. But this is your journey, not mine, and it's not my job to tell you how to get through all of this. Just know that I'm here if you need me."

"Avoiding winter in Stockholm and wooing the fair Bettina?"

"Exactly."

"It'll be strange, won't it?" I say, reaching out to touch his fingers with mine. "When we do leave? When you're in Sweden and I'm in London and we go back to our normal lives. When we don't have this to watch every night. When we don't get to chat to each other so much?"

"We'll still talk," he says. "And . . . well. It doesn't have to be that different. We can call each other. We can meet up. It'll be okay. Anyway—you might not go back to London, or at least not stay there. What about your plans? What about traveling and seeing the world?"

"That," I say, "now seems like the very definition of wishful thinking."

"It doesn't have to be," he insists. "It just feels like that now—like your choices have narrowed."

"That's a nice way of looking at it, but I don't even feel like my choices have narrowed, to be honest. I feel like they've disappeared completely. Buried, along with everything else."

"There are always choices. It just doesn't feel like it sometimes. And they're not always good ones either."

He holds my hand in both of his and strokes the skin of my palm with his fingertips. There is a moment, when the sun finally concedes defeat and the light changes from shimmering twilight to star-strewn darkness, where we simply sit in silence, hands entwined.

There is a moment where one of us could say something—where one of us could acknowledge what is happening here, the way we feel. A moment when we could take a different path, turn a different corner, find a different future.

There is a moment, and then it is gone—neither of us quite ready to face it. When I am with him, I do not doubt it, this connection—but when we are apart, I manage to convince myself that it isn't real. That there is no way these feelings could have grown so quickly.

When I am away from him, in a more muted world, I tell myself that the fizz I feel in his company, the tremor I feel when he touches me, the comfort I feel when we huddle together and watch the sunset, isn't real. That it's only there because of what we have endured together.

That it is fleeting. That it will pass. That it will fade away, glorious but transient, like the sun sinking down into the hills. It's too complicated to accept anything else. I tell myself that my focus, my loyalty, must be with Harry, who needs me.

Sometimes, I even believe it.

"Right," I say, standing up and sighing. "Back to reality."

He nods and climbs to his feet. I pass him his crutches, and we make our way to the lifts and down to our floor of the hospital, where we will go our separate ways. He will return to his side ward and I will meander back to Harry's room.

We pause in the corridor, people flowing around us.

"What can I do?" he asks. "To cheer you up?"

I smile and stand on tippy-toes to give him a peck on the cheek.

"You're doing enough," I reply. "And I appreciate you more than I can say. More than I should say. See you tomorrow?"

"See you tomorrow. Same time, same sunset."

Chapter 14

It takes a few more days for the TV interview to be arranged. I am not delighted with it, but a glance at Harry as he gets ready tells me it is the right thing for him.

He's propped up on pillows in his bed, his hair tousled, wearing a fresh black T-shirt. It makes his pale skin stand out, giving him a broodily handsome look, as though he is a Romantic poet caught out of time. He seems to have more energy, more positivity, than I've seen in him since he woke up from the coma.

There have been no more temper tantrums, no more tears—just a quiet, grim acceptance, which in its own way has been almost as disturbing. Seeing him like this again, enthused and interested and engaged, will make this ordeal worth it.

There are cameras and lights and metal boxes and coiled wires and way too many people crammed into the room, and I can tell he is feeding off the bustle and the buzz.

"Are you okay?" he asks, reaching out for my hand. "It's exciting, isn't it?"

In truth, I feel like a mannequin in a shop window, being dressed and made up and posed in various positions. Look, Ma, no strings.

He might be feeding off the buzz—but I feel deafened by it. There are too many people. Too much noise. Not enough air. I feel stifled, and know that at least some of that comes from the trauma of being recently trapped underground. The rest of it comes from the sense that I am being swept away here, carried on a current I can't swim against.

I want to help Harry. I want to do everything I can for him. I have committed to this interview, and I will do it, but I cannot wait to escape this crowded, stuffy room. To head to the balcony. To breathe again.

"I'm fine," I reply reassuringly. "You're going to be great."

"So are you . . . and thank you. For doing this. For everything. I know it's not been easy, and I want you to know I don't take it for granted."

"Take what for granted?"

"The fact that you're here, with me. It makes all the difference. When I feel overwhelmed, just knowing you are nearby helps. So thank you. For that, and for agreeing to do this interview—because you're not fooling me, Elena—I can see you'd rather be doing anything else. I bet you'd even prefer watching *Match of the Day* . . ."

That makes me laugh, and the laughter makes me relax, and I feel a surge of deep warmth for this man—his bravery, his humor. The part he has played in my life. I have no idea what the future holds for us—but right now, I am just happy to see him smiling again.

I look around the room, see the lady who will be interviewing us studying her notes, a man with a light meter, the young nurses wearing more lipstick than usual. Harry's mum seems to be enjoying the fuss, getting her makeup done and her hair bouffed, and John is looking smart in a shirt and tie.

A cameraman comes over to us, asks to take some test shots. I have been coated in makeup, and poked and prodded, and now I am moved around and told which way to look and how loud to talk.

Harry engages with banter, a glimpse of the old him peeking out. I do everything on autopilot and try not to feel guilty.

Guilty about the fact that Harry is right, and I don't want to do this. Guilty about the fact I survived with such minor injuries and he has been left paralyzed. Guilty that I resent the fact that none of them knows about the baby, even though it was my choice to keep it a secret.

Mainly, I feel guilty about Alex. The way I can't stop thinking about the time we've spent together, both above and below ground. The way the fading sunlight as we sit on the balcony always catches the sheen of his blond hair; the way his long fingers wrap around mine. The way he smiles and makes me feel like the world could still be a wondrous place . . .

When I see Harry, I see a man I was in love with when I was someone else. Someone who showed me what love was about when I was a naive eighteen-year-old. But when I look at Alex, I see a man who makes me feel on fire as much as he makes me feel safe. Who makes me feel as excited as I do comforted. Who makes me feel known, makes me feel seen, makes me feel alive.

It's not real, I tell myself again. It is an emotional aftershock. Harry is real. Harry needs me, and maybe I need Harry. Who knows?

There is sudden laughter. Harry is making the interviewer, a lady called Wendy Chin, giggle. I recognize his flirtatious tone of voice and watch as he chats with her.

He will be good on camera; I know that already.

None of the complex thoughts whirling around in my mind bear any relevance to what is going on around me right now. To this busy room that smells of hairspray and medicine, a weird alcoholic mix that makes me fear for anyone near a naked flame. I need to get my head in the game.

"Elena? Are you okay with that?" asks Wendy Chin. I have no idea what she asked me, but I nod anyway.

Wendy has a firmly placed helmet of shining black hair and the whitest teeth I've ever seen. She seems focused and professional, but also nice—genuinely interested.

"We've already filmed with John and Linda, and with the lovely Dr. Martinez," she says.

"He should have his own TV show," replies Harry. "I'd be jealous of his good looks if I wasn't such a confident man."

I roll my eyes at his bravado, but again it makes me laugh. Wendy and Harry are both trying to calm me, I realize, as though they can sense my reluctance and are handling me carefully, like hunters tiptoeing through the forest with gentle steps so the deer in their sights doesn't bolt.

Of course, that scenario doesn't end so well for the deer.

"And as you know, I've already spent some time with Harry. So today, we're going to start with Harry, and then I'd like to talk to you, Elena—about your experiences that night."

Ugh, I think, as someone gently slides my wheeled chair back and starts to dab my face with a sponge. We've arrived at the moment I've been dreading—my "buried alive drama" moment.

I nod as Rosa, one of the young nurses, bustles around making sure Harry is comfortable, getting him juice to sip. He winks at her and she actually blushes.

He looks over, catches my eye. Gives me a big grin that it's impossible not to return, no matter how crappy I feel.

This is the thing about Harry—even in these terrible circumstances, even as battered and bruised as he is, he can find some charm. Some humor. I know he is suffering. I've seen him crying in his sleep, the tears falling silently from the sides of his eyes as his nocturnal self processes his new future.

I know he's struggling, physically and mentally. He is in pain, in every possible way—and yet he still has pretty young nurses fluttering around him. He still has Wendy Chin giggling. He still manages to make everyone in the room feel like he is just swell, thank you.

It's one of his biggest attributes—finding the plus points. Faking positivity even if he isn't really feeling it. Being willing to take unsure steps into the dark, confident that he will find his way.

He really is a great man in a lot of ways, and it's easy to see why I have loved him. It's not so easy to see why I fell out of love with him, and nothing feels certain anymore. I am confused and conflicted, and every attempt to untangle my thoughts seems to choke me.

"Ready, gorgeous?" he says, holding out a hand toward me. "You look beautiful."

Someone pushes my chair closer to his bedside without warning, and my heart races. It seems a small thing, that unexpected shove, the sudden propulsion in a direction not of my choosing, but my nerves are not as steady as they once were. Most likely because of the "buried alive drama" I'm going to have to talk about very soon, to a complete stranger, while trying hard not to just stare at her teeth in amazement.

An assistant checks the tiny microphones that are clipped to our clothing, and the man I think is the director claps his hands to get our attention. He is tall and scruffy and smells vaguely of weed, but everyone on the crew hangs on to his words. Various people tell him various things about light levels and angles. He nods at Wendy, who tilts her head in a question.

Harry gives a thumbs-up, and I manage a half smile. It's okay to look sad, I decide—it's probably even better, from a TV point of view.

There is a brief countdown, but disappointingly,

nobody cries "action!" Wendy simply turns to look at us, and magically transforms her face into something serious yet caring. She leans forward slightly, her silk blouse rustling, and introduces herself and us.

"So, Harry, in your own words, take us through that night in Santa Maria de Alto . . ."

"Well, Wendy," he says seriously. "It was just like any other night in a beautiful Mexican village—until it wasn't . . ."

He tells his tale, and even though I know this story inside out, I still listen intently. There are gaps—his head trauma has left holes in his memory—but hearing him say it all out loud has me enraptured. He is calm, and open, and articulate, not shying away from anything, answering every question. He talks about the night itself, about the shock of waking up here, the even bigger shock of finding out about his long-term condition. About the pain, about his worries, about his hopes for the future.

It is an impressive performance, and one I know I will never manage. I am more likely to clam up, or fumble my words, or cry all the mascara off my face. And that's a lot of mascara.

Harry is holding the whole room spellbound as he describes those first few days when he came out of the coma. As he says how much he's been moved by the support of his family, his friends and colleagues back home, as well as total strangers.

"It's not a future I could ever have imagined, Wendy," he says sincerely, "and I'd be lying if I said it was one I was happy about. But I have to remember that at least

I have a future. At least I have the chance to carry on with my life, even if it's on a different path. So many people weren't as lucky as me."

"Lucky?" says Wendy, leaning even closer. "I don't think many people would see themselves like that in your situation, Harry."

He shakes his head and smiles. It's a good smile. One I was first dazzled by freshman week, queuing to get into a Liverpool club and finding myself next to him in the line.

"Well, it's all a matter of perception, I suppose," he replies. "I'm here, and I'm alive. I'm surrounded by people I love, I have devoted parents, and of course Elena is here with me. The fact that we both survived is a miracle. There's actually something I want to say about Elena, if that's all right?"

Wendy nods enthusiastically, while I feel nothing but a sense of dread and borderline embarrassment. I am a fraud, sitting here playing the dutiful girlfriend, listening to these declarations of appreciation. I am an impostor, trapped in a role, typecast by circumstance.

Harry looks across at me, grins reassuringly, then continues. "Well, as you probably know, Wendy, Elena and I got separated during the quake. I left her having a drink and waiting for dinner, both of us assuming we'd be back together within minutes. It didn't turn out like that, but even though she went through hell, at least Elena is still here with us.

"She's been brilliant, supporting me, supporting my

parents, even though she's got her own injuries and her own trauma to deal with. I'm not surprised—she's always been a very kind and generous person. She couldn't do the job she does, working with children with special needs, if she wasn't."

A slow wave of heat rises up through my body, making me feel itchy and uncomfortable. Like I need to burst out of this small, crowded room and breathe real air again. Like I'm suffocating.

"Well, what Elena doesn't know," he says, "is what I was doing when I left her at the restaurant table. I was actually looking at the stalls for something very specific. I knew what I wanted, and I'd just bought it when the earth literally started to move. It was a gift, for Elena. A gift to accompany a very important question—a question I should have asked her a long time ago, and that I planned to ask her that night."

I, along with everyone else in the room, suddenly understand where this story is leading. I clasp one hand to my stomach, feeling a sudden lurch, a flood of vertigo, even though I am sitting still. I blink rapidly, my eyes blurring over, tiny crackles of light zigzagging from the corners of my peripheral vision. An emotional migraine.

Wendy is smiling so hard she might crack her face in two, and the camera crew is silent and rapt as they watch the drama unfold. This must be TV gold. A total scoop. The happy ending to beat them all. Except it's not just entertainment—it's my life.

I want to stop him. I want to tell him not to do this, that it isn't right, for either of us. That this is something to discuss in private. To think about. Not to rush into. That he's making a terrible mistake.

"Elena," he asks slowly, fumbling with a small black box he's pulled from beneath his sheets. "I'm sorry I can't get down on one knee, but will you marry me?"

I see the ring. It is silver and topaz, and I remember the same type being displayed in the stall in the village. I remember thinking how pretty the display was, even trying one on, not realizing that he noticed. That he cared. That he'd ever dream of doing this.

That he was buying this ring while I was thinking about leaving him.

There is complete silence in the room now, apart from the vague sounds drifting in from outside. The beep of a car horn. Chatter from the corridor. The squeak of a bed being wheeled across the linoleum floors of the hallway.

Everyone is looking at me, waiting for the answer they assume I am going to give. I know I must look shocked, surprised—and that that is okay. Of course I do. I only hope I don't also look horrified.

My eyes skim across Wendy, who is almost out of her chair in anticipation, and I meet the gaze of Linda, Harry's mum. She is nodding at me, misty-eyed, about to cry, twisting her fingers together.

I see John, his dad, standing proud and tall behind his wife. His hands are on the back of her chair, gripping it so hard his knuckles are white. He is begging me without even saying a word, his serious eyes wide and desperate, his nostrils flaring.

They want me to say yes. They will be crushed if I say no. They will bleed for their son, for his suffering, for this humiliation and rejection by a woman who is supposed to love him. A woman he has built a life with, a woman who should stand with him at his lowest point. A woman who would never abandon him.

I know what they want, but I'm not sure I can be that woman. Without the earthquake, I would have said no. Without meeting Alex, I would have said no. Without Harry's paralysis, I'd have said no.

I want to say no now, with all my heart. Saying no would have nothing to do with his condition. Nothing to do with what happened to us. Saying no would simply be because I don't love him, not in that way. Not now.

I pull my eyes away from the intolerable pressure of his mum and dad, across Wendy's waiting face, and finally force myself to look at Harry. All of this has only taken a matter of seconds, but to him it must feel like an eternity.

I expect him to seem annoyed. To be running out of patience. To be full of his usual confidence, steady in the unshakable belief that I will say yes. That I was always going to say yes.

Instead, what I see on his drawn features surprises me. Harry doesn't look confident. He doesn't look annoyed, or steady. He looks scared, and weak, and vulnerable. He looks, for a split second, defeated. It is a side of him that I have never seen in all our years together.

It is a look that moves me in a way that no amount of fake bravado ever could. A look that makes me realize that maybe it's not completely over between us.

"Yes," I say, finally, my voice quiet. "Yes, I'll marry you, Harry."

Chapter 15

I stagger from the room minutes later, in tears of presumed joy. I plead the need to fix my face and escape feeling nauseated, as though I am going to be physically sick. Harry catches my eye as I leave, and I try to smile, tell him I will be back later.

I close the door behind me, still hearing the cheers and the applause ringing in my ears. Still feeling the clasp of Linda's trembling arms around me. Still astonished at the sheen of moisture in John's eyes as he hugged me tight, whispered "thank you" into my ear.

Still wondering if I imagined that look of desperation on Harry's face as he asked me to marry him. Still confused at what just happened.

I manage a few steps away from the door. I hold up my hand, look at the ring shining under the strip lighting. See the shaking as I try to hold boneless digits steady.

Leaning back against the wall, I suck in some deep breaths. Ignore the strange looks I am being given. I close my eyes and ignore everything and everyone, until I am calm enough to run. I run to the lifts, and I run to the balcony, and I run to the edge of the world.

I need to be free and alone, to process what has just happened. To try to understand the mass of conflicting emotions I am feeling. To distinguish between the guilt and the genuine love and the sense of duty and the instinct to flee. Each and every one of them feels real.

I love Harry, in my own way, and I know that he needs me. Maybe I could fall in love with him all over again? Maybe this will be a fresh start for us, hope drawn from the most horrendous of circumstances?

But if that is truly the case, then why does this ring on my finger feel more like a mark of ownership than a symbol of love and happiness?

I cling on to the balcony wall, drained of all strength, and look out at the sprawling city and the winding roads and the distant hills below me. I listen to the chaos of life in the streets beneath and have no idea what I really want anymore—not even in this one single moment, never mind for the rest of my life.

No idea until I hear familiar heavy footsteps behind me. Until I smell his shower gel. Until I turn around and see him. Tall, blond, solid before me. I reach up and place my hand on his chest, feel his heart beating beneath my fingers. Stare at him, unable to speak.

I realize now why I ran here, to this place. It wasn't only to hide. It was because this is our place. Because I knew I would see him here. Because I needed to be with him, if only for a few minutes.

He glances down at my hand. Sees the ring. The smile fades from his face as our eyes meet. He frowns, looks confused, then . . . angry?

"He asked you to marry him? In there, with the cameras rolling? In front of everybody?" he says.

I nod helplessly. It wasn't fair, but it happened.

"And you said yes . . . of course you did. How could you not? Maybe . . . maybe it's for the best."

His voice is flat, empty of emotion, but his eyes tell a different story.

I want to throw my arms around him. I want to kiss him, and hold him, and tell him how I feel. I want to be brave, and selfish, and honest. I want so many things that I cannot have.

I have just agreed to marry another man. I have just been hit with the full force of my attraction to this man, just been confronted by feelings I have been trying to suppress.

I know I cannot have them both. I feel torn in so many directions I fear I will tear apart and scatter in fragments.

He smiles, sad and sweet, and says, "I understand, Elena."

It is almost sunset time, and together we sit in the usual spot. I hold my broken arm close in my lap, the pain of the physical injury seeming to echo the one in my heart. I think about all the conversations we've had here, all the magical times we have shared. I think about my baby. I think about Harry and the tragedy that has derailed him.

I think about far-off places I will never see, and I think about the life I can lead and the happiness that might still be mine one day. About Alex leaving, as I know he will do, sometime soon.

I think about everything and nothing, and for the first time since the earthquake I feel truly alone.

"Penny for them?" he says, a gentle hand on my shoulder.

"Not worth it." I lean my head to one side so my cheek rests on his fingers, then look at him from swollen eyes. "You don't happen to have a bottle of tequila secreted about your person, do you?"

"Sadly not . . . though I'm sure I can find some for you later if you need it. How do you feel?"

"I can't answer that question," I reply. "Because I don't really know. I feel everything and nothing, all at the same time. This was all a big surprise. I wasn't planning on marrying Harry, you know that. And I didn't think he was planning on marrying me. But that night, when he left to go and explore, he was going off to buy this ring—so I suppose he was. And I feel . . . guilty about that."

"Guilty?" he asks. "Why guilty?"

"Well, maybe if he'd stayed where he was—where we were—he wouldn't have been crushed. Maybe he would have been with us, below ground, and maybe he wouldn't have been as badly injured. Maybe it was only because he was off looking for a ring to give me that he ended up in the wrong place at the wrong time."

"Okay. But you know that's silly, right? Because maybe he'd have died. Maybe he would have been injured even more severely. Maybe he wouldn't have come out of it at all. We nearly didn't."

"I know. At least the rational part of me does. But I

can't quite shake it, the feeling that it's because of this bloody ring that he ended up disabled . . ."

"Is that," he says carefully, "a good enough reason to marry him? To commit to spending the rest of your life with him?"

"I don't know. Probably not. But it was certainly a good enough reason not to humiliate him in front of his family and on camera. I couldn't do that to him. And maybe we'll be okay. Maybe we'll be happy. We were once. Before . . ."

I trail off and look out at the city. There is a mild breeze, and a strand of hair breaks loose from my ponytail, floating in front of my face like a feather.

"Before what?" he prompts, reaching out to touch my hand. I twine my fingers into his and turn back to face him. My eyes are stinging, and my smile dies halfway.

"I think you know, Alex. I think we both do. We've tried to ignore it, to stay friends, to pretend we don't feel more than that. But . . . it's not quite working. Not for me at least. Am I mad? Are you wondering what the hell I'm talking about?"

"Possibly you are mad, yes. But I do know what you're talking about. I feel it too. I haven't said anything because it seemed wrong. Unfair to discuss such things when Harry was in the state he is in. But here we are . . . discussing it. Do you love him?"

"That's a big question. I do love him, in a way. And I feel like I owe him, and that I just can't abandon him now . . . what would that say about me, as a person? To leave him when he's at his absolute lowest? I don't think

I could live with myself if I did that. I don't think I could just move on from that and be happy somewhere else. With someone else."

There is a hush around us, the nurses who were on their break heading back inside, the noise of the city in a temporary lull.

"I don't want you to give up your future without really thinking about it," he says. "Not just about . . . us, whatever we are. But about what you want from life."

"I know. I could say the same to you, Alex. You need to heal as well, and I'm not talking about broken bones or cuts. I'm talking about Anna, and the way you live your life. I don't know what 'us' is either—maybe it's just as simple as us having survived a terrible ordeal together. Maybe it's more . . . or maybe it could have been more, in a different life. But we live in this one, and maybe that's the answer for both of us—to just live. To move on."

He does not answer, but he slips an arm around my shoulders, and I lean against him.

"I knew you were trouble the moment I met you," he says, kissing the top of my head. "You turn my life upside down—"

"That was an earthquake, not me!"

"You turn my life upside down, and then tell me to sort my life out?"

"I know," I reply, laughing despite everything. "The nerve of the woman . . . but please, do sort your life out. You deserve better. You deserve to be out in the world.

You deserve love and happiness and all those things you seem to have shut yourself off from."

"You may be right, but I'm not sure I should be accepting life coaching from someone who just agreed to marry a man she doesn't love . . ."

He doesn't mean to be cruel. He doesn't say it out of malice—but it hurts all the same.

"So, what happens next?" he asks, when I remain silent.

"I don't know. We go home too, I suppose. We get Harry into a good rehab center. We get him well again. We . . . build whatever life we can, after all this. And you do the same. Promise me you'll do the same."

He nods but doesn't look convinced.

"I'll try. And unless you need me, I'll go sooner instead of later."

I don't want him to go. Of course I don't. I want to freeze time and stay here forever, in his arms, watching the sun set. I don't want him to go, but it isn't fair to ask him to stay.

"I think that's for the best, Alex. The time we've spent together, all of our conversations, everything we've meant to each other . . . I'll never forget it, I won't. But I don't want either of us to hurt even more than we have to. Does that make sense?"

"It makes sense, and I hate that it does. I'll go home. You'll go home. We'll both move on," he promises. "But first—one more sunset?"

"One more sunset," I say, as we silently look on as the light drains from the world.

Chapter 16

Two days later, I am helping Alex pack his bag.

Well, to be fair, "helping" is probably an overstatement. I have only one working arm, and he has hardly any stuff. It's more accurate to say that I am lurking around his room while he packs his bag.

I knew he would be leaving. We both decided it was for the best—but it doesn't make this any easier.

I look on as he folds his few items of clothing, puts his toiletries into a wash bag, double-checks the paperwork he needs to leave the country without his passport. He doesn't have much, and it doesn't take long, and part of me wants to grab that small case and throw everything over the floor so he has to do it again.

"Do you want your tequila T-shirt?" I ask, holding it up in all its garish glory.

"No, thank you—why don't you keep it? A little gift from me to you . . ."

"Wow," I reply breathlessly. "You really know how to spoil a girl, don't you?"

He laughs, but I fold the T-shirt up into a small yellow bundle and keep it.

Once he is done, he stands and glances around the

room. At the green walls and strip lighting and small rows of beds.

"This is going to sound insane," he says, "but I've not hated it here. For a hospital, it's been quite . . . homely."

"Maybe, when you get back to your own place, you should paint it green. And put some lino down on the floors."

"Maybe not—that really would be insane. But I do need to make some changes, as a wise woman with one working arm once told me. It's not doing me much good keeping everything exactly the same as it was when Anna lived there, like some kind of museum. It's not like painting the walls will make me forget her. It's a small step, but maybe it will be fun—then maybe I'll sell it. Do something wild and crazy!"

"I'd love to see you wild and crazy," I say, looking on as he shrugs his shoulders into his jacket. He pauses, meets my gaze with eyebrows raised.

"I'm not sure you're ready for that," he replies.

"Probably not. What about you—are you ready to leave yet? Time's a-ticking . . ."

I hear the falsely perky note in my own words and hate myself for it.

"Oh no," he says, picking up one of his crutches. "You're using your 'holding it together to make everyone else feel all right' voice. That means you're about to cry . . ."

"Shut up or I'll break your other foot," I answer, grabbing his case and wheeling it behind me. He is, of course, completely right, and I stomp ahead of him toward the lifts. I usually keep my pace slow to match his afflicted stride, but this time I zoom along. I need a minute, and I know he understands that. He understands everything, damn him.

He takes his time, giving me a few precious moments to swipe tears from my eyes and arrange my hair so it hides half of my face. He pretends not to notice, for both our sakes.

As usual, the lift is crowded, and we ride down to the lobby amid a buzz of excited chatter—Spanish always seems to sound excited, somehow—and a cloud of aromas: perfume, cologne, medicines, disinfectant, coffee, cigarette smoke, sugar. En masse, we spill out into the lobby, the nurses' pink shoes squeaking on the floor.

Outside, the sun looks brutal. Outside is where he has to go next. That is where he will drag his little bag on wheels, and hoist himself and his big boot and his crutches into one of the waiting cars at the taxi stand.

Outside is where we will say our final goodbye, and where he will begin his journey to the airport. Where he will check in, and wait to board, and spend hours flying away from me. Leaving me here, alone.

I know, of course, that technically I am not alone. Technically I have Harry here—Harry, my fiancé. As well as his parents, and my mum via the phone, and the nurses and doctors I am friendly with.

Technically, I am not alone—but I know that as soon as he goes, I will still feel that way. That night we first met, when we sat and sipped wine and talked as though we weren't strangers, I felt as though we were the only people in the world. As though we had created our own little bubble.

Without him, I feel as though I could be surrounded by people and still feel alone.

He stops his slow trundle in the middle of the lobby, coming to a complete standstill. Alex is usually a very polite and courteous person, but today he seems to not care that he is inconveniencing people. He stops, and the crowds are forced to ebb and flow around him.

I stop too, looking up at him and frowning, confused. I'm propelled closer toward him by the push and shove, and he places a hand on my waist to steady me. He keeps it there, and I feel the gentle pressure of his fingers.

"Are you okay?" I ask. "Is your ankle hurting you?"

"My ankle is fine," he says. "But I'm not okay."

He looks determined, and serious, and absolutely beautiful. I look up at him, with my puffy eyes and my fear, and let go of the suitcase. It falls to the floor with a thud.

"Come with me," he says simply. "Come to Sweden. Or I'll go to the UK. Or we can go anywhere you want—the two of us."

I open my mouth slightly, and he adds quickly, "Don't say no. Just listen for a minute, and then I'll go back to pretending. We both can, if that's what you really want."

We stand there, him with one working leg, me with one working arm, buffeted and battered by a shared experience that has changed us, changed our lives. We have saved each other over and over again, and I wonder where our story might lead, if it was allowed to lead anywhere at all.

"I know you said yes to Harry, but I think you made the wrong choice. I don't care how bad a person this makes me—but leave him. Come with me. We can travel the world, have adventures, go up into those hills—watch the sun set together in a different place every night.

"We can talk and laugh and cry, and we can just . . . be free. Neither of us knows what happens next in life. Neither of us can say with certainty what we want or where we might end up—but I know how I feel about you, Elena. No, don't look away."

He gently takes hold of my chin and turns my face up toward his. I feel the sting of tears, which seems to be my default setting today.

"I want to cry too," he says. "I want to cry because I don't want to leave you here. I don't want to go home, or go anywhere without you. I can't imagine the shape of my life without you to share it with. I am falling in love with you, Elena . . . No, not falling. I've already fallen.

"I know it's only been weeks. I know you're technically engaged to another man. I know this is the most out-of-character thing I've ever done in my life—but I never expected to feel like this again. And I think you feel the same. We have something here, something I never thought I'd experience again—I've been trying to

talk myself out of it, persuade myself it's just an infatu-
ation, that it will pass . . . but it won't, and I don't even
want it to. Come with me."

It is a wonderful thing to hear, and a terrible thing
to hear. It is everything I want, and nothing I can have.
I have said yes to Harry. I have made a commitment to
him, and he deserves my loyalty at this time when he
needs me most. Even if I thought perhaps I could talk
to him more rationally about it once the cameras were
gone, his excitement, the way looking forward to a
wedding has lifted him, the way his parents are already
planning it with him, ended that. I have said yes, and
I must mean yes.

I reach up, place my hand on the side of Alex's face,
my fingers tracing his cheekbone, stroking up into his
hair. It is a light and gentle touch, but it feels intimate,
magical. He leans into it and pulls me closer to him,
wrapping his arms around me, dropping his crutches to
the floor.

My head falls against his chest, and I feel the form of
him beneath the soft fabric of his T-shirt. I want to touch
him. I want to stay here, in his arms. I want to hold on
and never let go.

I look up, force myself to meet the blue of his eyes,
and say, "Alex . . . I'm so sorry, but I just can't. He needs
me too much. He loves me, and part of me still loves
him. I can't leave him now."

He nods sadly, as though that was exactly the answer
he was expecting. He pulls me to him again and buries
his face in my hair. His fingers move to my face, one

palm on either side, holding me steady as we look at each other for what might be the last time.

He leans down, kisses me, my arm clutched around his waist.

I should push him away. I should tell him to stop. I should turn around and leave.

I should—but I can't. I can't because it is the best kiss of my entire life, and the real world falls away from us. Only we are left, tangled up in our own desire, in our own need. In our own love.

I place my hand on his chest. Push with the little resolve I have left.

"Go now," I say, forcing some space between us. "Please. This hurts too much."

"I know. My flight doesn't leave for another three hours. If you change your mind, I'll be watching the sunset from the airport . . ."

He pulls away from me. He retrieves his crutches and his bag, and hobbles away toward the automatic doors.

I struggle to see him through the blurred vision of my tears. I watch him get into the cab. I see him look back, just once. I see the car pull away, and he is gone.

It seems like minutes and a lifetime since the moment we met. And now that moment has passed.

I stand alone in the lobby and bury my face in the crumpled yellow *I ♥ Tequila* T-shirt that is all I have left of him.

II

Nine years later, Cornwall, UK

Chapter 17

Next year, it will be a whole decade since the earthquake in Santa Maria de Alto. A whole decade of life, of sleeping and rising, of sunsets and sunrises. A whole decade as the new us.

A whole decade since Harry was injured, and I met Alex, and the world fell on top of us all.

We are still together, Harry and I. We have built a life together, the two of us, a good life. We've both changed—him more than me, I feel—and we've both moved on. On the surface at least.

And now, we are here, in our quiet corner of England, living a quiet life, surrounded by natural beauty and the sound of the sea.

I like the quiet, and would be happy to ignore the ten-years-on milestone that is starting to loom ahead of us. I had my fill of publicity back when it all happened and in the year that followed. Our wedding was a media event, and Harry has certainly never shied away from the spotlight if he thought it could help us—but I would prefer to stay under the radar, safe in a cloak of invisibility. Pretend it's not happening and hope no one else notices.

It's a vain hope, I know, and I've already been contacted by a woman called Em Hoyle, who is making a documentary about the Santa Maria earthquake. She is extremely tenacious and is doing her very best to persuade me to take part.

I have no desire to time travel back to that particular place or that particular time. I have no urge to dig through the rubble of my memories, or poke the ashes of hindsight, or send out a search party to find the fragments of myself that I left behind. I am not up for playing a giant game of what-if.

When her first email landed, two weeks ago, I read it, deleted it, and tried to forget about it. It was poking away at me a little, like a tiny pebble trapped in my shoe, because I knew that it would happen again—that in the run-up to that tenth anniversary, we'd become cool and interesting again.

People reading their morning paper or flicking through their newsfeeds or leafing through magazines at the hair salon will go, "Ooh, yes, I remember that . . . wonder what happened to them?"

Maybe one of the papers will go for a "where are they now?" angle, hoping a few of us are dead so they can make it extra dramatic. Nothing sells quite like a "curse of FILL IN RANDOM EVENT" story, does it—it's been selling since Tutankhamun's tomb was raided, through the cast of *Poltergeist*, and on into *Strictly Come Dancing*.

So, while it was easy to delete that first email from Em, I knew that probably wouldn't be the end of it—no matter how hard I wanted it to be.

Part of me even wondered if it wouldn't be better to

have some control over it—play along, and at least get the "where are they now?" photos done when I've had a blowout and I'm in full makeup. The alternative is being captured unawares in my True Form: snapped leaving the liquor store clutching a bottle of wine, wearing a tracksuit, and looking like I'm on my way to a horror film convention.

Em was contacting me well ahead of the pack, because she was making a TV program—a serious one, she assured me—and that takes time.

She explained that she'd already started with the preliminaries, had spent almost a month in Mexico and the United States tracking people down, and that she was now back in Europe taking it further.

Her project, she explained, wasn't a smash and grab, the media equivalent of a quick ram raid into our lives— it was a ninety-minute documentary looking at what happened, what was learned, and, most terrifyingly of all, the impact it had on everyone involved. It would be done respectfully, without sensationalizing it. It would be *tasteful*.

She told me some of this in that first email. She told me the rest of it in the next three emails. I deleted all of them without replying, but that didn't seem to put her off at all. The fifth email arrived this morning—I saw it on my phone while I was pushing a cart around Sainsbury's. I had wine in the cart, among other things, and was indeed dressed in baggy tracksuit bottoms and looking like someone on her way to a horror film convention. Or maybe just something from a horror film.

Even seeing the email there on the screen was enough to make me glance around nervously, in case any rogue documentary makers were lurking surreptitiously in the aisle, hiding behind a mountain of toilet paper.

For some reason, I haven't deleted this one—I just left it there, like the jagged bit of a broken nail you forget to trim. The one that tears a hole in your tights when you're already late for work. I haven't deleted it because the subject title is *Survivor interviews—video*. Somehow it feels disrespectful to delete it without even having the courage to take a look.

By the time I get home, my interest has been piqued. Or maybe I'm just bored, who knows? There's nothing quite like unloading the shopping and tutting at the short date on the chicken breasts to make you realize your life may be lacking a certain sparkle.

I retreat to my office—a glorified broom cupboard—and google her. It takes only a few seconds to realize she is one of those annoyingly accomplished young people who make my own generation feel like unambitious wage slaves.

Em Hoyle, it turns out, is somewhere in her mid-twenties—maybe the same age I was that night in Mexico, but a lot more focused. She makes documentaries that would probably be described as "raw" or "gritty," on subjects as diverse as sex trafficking in the suburbs and air pollution on school playgrounds.

In her pictures, although she is often shielded by a camera, she has hair so short it might be shaved and dresses like someone from the cast of *Terminator*. She has a long list of important-sounding awards to her name and is a scarily impressive specimen of womanhood.

I spend a good fifteen minutes lost in Em's world, reading reviews of her programs, reading interviews with people who've appeared in them, reading a scant biography that is filled with her professional achievements and says very little about her life outside them. I have no idea where she is from, if she is married or has children, if she's a cat person or a dog person, if she's a vegan or a Libra or a fan of musicals.

I go back to the latest email she's sent me, realizing that although I haven't replied to any of them, I have read them all, and her tone has become familiar.

Hi Elena
It's your friendly neighborhood almost-stalker again!
I know you haven't replied, but I hope you're reading this one.

The documentary means more to me than I've ever told you. I'd like to explain why, so I hope that you'll agree to meet with me face-to-face, so I can tell you my story.

I'm sending you some of the material I've shot so far (there's a clip attached)—it's a rough cut, but it should give you a sense of how I'm doing this. It's not going to be sensationalized—I want this to be truthful, honest, and solely in the words of the survivors of that terrible night.

I hope you'll let me show you more and we can meet up. No pressure, but this won't work without you!
Em

No kisses after her name, which I kind of like. I always feel vaguely uncomfortable when people I don't know put kisses on messages.

I touch the mouse pad on my laptop with a reluctant fingertip, letting the cursor hover over the file she's sent. It's called *After the Tremor—first cut.*

I bite my lip, still not sure. And then I click.

I lean back in my chair, barely breathing, ready to slam my laptop shut if I need to.

But within seconds, the screen is filled with a grid full of faces. Some instantly familiar, some less so. And immediately, I know I'm going to watch every single second. I owe it to them.

I scan the pictures, my eyes flying over the screen, searching for one face in particular. When I don't see it, I'm not sure if I am relieved or disappointed. Whether seeing Alex again would be too much of a risk to the safe cocoon of my current life.

I recognize plenty of others, though, enough to be hit with a Taser blast of emotion that reminds me why I have repeatedly said no to every other journo request in the past. I said no because it hurts to remember. Because that wound is still open, and possibly always will be. I have just learned to live my life around it, the way you do with long-term pain.

I never even knew the names of some of the faces on the screen, but I still remember. And even worse, I still remember the faces of those I will never see again: the ones who didn't make it.

Before me, still silent, I see a reduced version of Sofia, the tour guide from the trip, and I click on her little picture.

She fills the screen then, her image enlarging as all the others disappear. I stare, drinking up every detail of her features, as though I was dying of thirst and never even realized it.

She is obviously older now, her face more lined, a few streaks of silver in her long dark hair. She sits on a wooden chair, her arms neatly folded on her lap, sunlight falling through a nearby window to cast her in partial shadow.

A voice—the mild Scottish accent I recognize as Em's from clips I've seen of her other programs—floats in off camera.

"So where were you when the first tremor shook the village? How did you feel?"

Sofia leans her head to one side and smiles sadly.

"I had just been to the ladies' room, which is not exactly a glamorous answer, is it?" she replies. "But I was lucky, as it turns out. It's the reason I'm alive today. I should have been with Jorge, the coach driver. We were planning to have dinner together, as we usually did. I was walking back to the bar when we felt the first tremor. We weren't too worried then; it happens, you know? Usually we all laugh about it and carry on with whatever we're doing. That's what we did that night as well. Everyone laughed. Everyone was relieved."

She pauses and looks down at her fingers, and I

realize that she is remembering what happened next. Remembering the second tremor, the tremor that turned into an earthquake. It is impossible to forget, and she is brave to even be discussing it like this.

The clip ends there, taking me back to the main screen. I know that Em will have asked more questions, that she's just sharing snapshots with me for now.

I look at the faces on the screen again. I recognize one of the local women who was preparing our meal that night. One of the men who was running the bar outside his home. The woman who was always fighting with her husband on our coach trip; others I don't remember. I click, and I watch.

I pause to google a phrase I hear repeated over and over again in the clips: "*Qué alivio.*" *What a relief.* I felt the same. I remember clutching Alex's hands as he reassured me that it was quite normal, that we were okay. That we were fine.

We were not fine, of course.

I shake my head to clear the memory and go back to the grid screen. I find the family who was on the coach with us and in the plaza that night; the Frazers, I later learned. Half of them, at least. The mum and her teenage son, who I last saw as a little boy. The ginger-haired daughter isn't there, and I am momentarily disappointed. I still remember her so clearly—her frustration at being forced on a holiday that clearly suited neither her temperament nor her skin tone.

I bumped into her a few times at the hospital, but the memories are blurred now—those weeks after the earthquake buried deep in my mind. Sometimes I'm not sure what is real and what is a mishmash of memory and dream sequence.

Mainly, of course, the dad is missing. The dad who died trying to protect them; the image of his limp body and open, unseeing eyes one that has haunted me ever since.

The mum and her son are sitting in a kitchen, a glimpse of a garden behind them, a pine table in front. I click on the image.

"We were at the little café in the square when the first tremor was felt," she says after Em asks her question. "I just remember this huge sense of relief, you know? When the tremor started, we were all sort of frozen in place. It only lasted a few seconds really—not long enough for anyone to panic. And when it stopped, there was this wave of laughter that rolled around the square. I remember it so clearly. It brought everyone together; it was something we'd all experienced together, those few moments of fear."

The clip ends and I quickly click on the next. Now that I've started, I don't seem to be able to stop. I listen to all their stories, all their memories of that brief moment before the unthinkable happened. Before everything changed forever. Before our relief turned to horror.

When I've finished, I close down the file and wish I could close down my brain just as easily. I feel twitchy, my mind and my body in spasm, my fingertips drumming on the desk surface and my teeth mangling my lips.

Even after those few clips, I find that I want to know more. I want to know what they have all done with their lives, what has changed for them, how they feel. I want to hear their stories. I even want to share ours. I want to find out where Alex is and if he is happy. I want to reach out to people who experienced that night, and stop feeling so isolated.

Here, in the safety of my little office, it feels possible. It feels like I could open up, like I could talk to these people. These fellow survivors. It would be fascinating, and maybe freeing, to hear what became of them all in more detail.

I wouldn't have too much to tell them, personally. My life is far from interesting, which I don't mind that much really. I have already been cursed to live through interesting times, and it was awful.

I never did go back into teaching—Harry's needs had to come first to start with, and I was a full-time carer. Later, I could have done, I'm sure—but I changed as well. The world outside seemed a more threatening place, and although I still wanted to help people, I also needed to do it on my own terms.

I didn't want to commute, or engage with workplace politics, or leave the safety of my home. During the years straight after the earthquake, life revolved around hospitals and rehabs and medical facilities. I got used to that—maybe became institutionalized by proxy. Once that phase of our lives was reduced, I found that I couldn't quite face the big bad world.

So now, I work from home, editing and creating online learning resources for children with special needs. I miss the kids, but I am good at my job, and it matters. It might not be world traveling, but it is satisfying and comfortable.

Harry, though . . . well, he's a different story. He runs a social enterprise that champions the rights of disabled people, advocating on their behalf and lobbying for wider change. He helps them find work and training, access medical care, and find innovative new treatments and equipment. He is altering the way people view those with disabilities—starting with himself. He might still use a wheelchair, but in all honesty he is one of the ablest people I know, and I can't help but feel proud of him and all he has achieved despite what happened to him. Because of it, in some ways.

I forward the email from Em to Harry, asking him to let me know what he thinks. I am confused, and it would be good to have someone to help me find my way through this maze of emotions that the videos have created.

I am unsure of what to do with myself next. I am restless, and disturbed, and akin to a hibernating animal that has been prematurely woken, finding itself in a strange land rubbing sleep from its eyes.

This tiny room is cluttered to the point of hoarding, the shelves stuffed with travel guides to places I've never visited, fossils from beach walks along the coastline, a selection of strange gifts from my sister, Olivia.

The rest of the house is sleek and functional, nothing to confuse the eye or trip the foot. It is way too perfect.

Here, I have a collection of random Christmas toys gifted to me over the years. I stand up and switch them all on—a cacophony of dancing penguins and tinny-voiced versions of "Jingle Bells."

I sit, spin in my chair for a few moments, legs held in tight so I don't breach the confines of the small room and bang my shins against the walls.

I let the noise and the color and the silliness wash over me, and spin around and around in my chair until I am dizzy. Until the physical sensations—the wobbling head, the unfocused eyes, the assaulted ears—overwhelm the emotional ones.

When Olivia walks into the room, I am holding my face in my hands, wondering if I might throw up. She pauses in the doorway, takes in the wriggling toys and the color of my skin, and pulls a "WTF" face.

"Olivia," I say. "You're here. I'd forgotten."

"You'd forgotten that I live here?"

"You've only lived here for a week. Give me a break."

She nods and starts switching off the Christmas toys. The silence is mouthwateringly good.

Olivia drops her backpack on the floor and sits on the beanbag, looking up at me. We have different fathers, and that slight tweak in genetics has resulted in us looking really very different. She has long dark hair that seems to have been stolen from a Russian princess, and deep brown eyes, and pale skin. She looks a bit like Snow White, if Snow White had a kick-ass collection of Converse sneakers.

Our mum and her dad are away on a cruise for a

month, and she's staying here with us. She's seventeen and doesn't think she needs a babysitter. But she's seventeen, and Mum thinks she might set the house on fire if left unsupervised for an extended period of time. The truth is probably somewhere in between.

"So," I ask, placing my hands on my knees in an attempt to calm myself. "How was your day? How was college?"

"It was all right," she replies, shrugging noncommittally. "I did a career test. That was interesting."

"Oh, right—what did it say then? The career test?"

"It said maybe I should be a journalist, or a psychiatrist, or join the police force, or become a private detective. Basically it said I'm really nosy and should try and give that a go."

"You are really nosy. I've noticed that. So . . . I can't imagine you in the police force. Maybe you could be a private dick?"

She tries to stop herself, but she can't help grinning—she's seventeen, after all. The word "dick" is still amusing.

"Well, better than being a public dick, I suppose . . . What have you been up to, anyway? You look like shit."

"Why thank you. I'm fine . . . just stuff. You know."

"Just stuff? What are you, twelve? What stuff? Why do you look like you're going to vom? Why are you sitting in here listening to Christmas toys? What's going on with you?"

Her eyes flicker to my laptop, and she makes one of

those intuitive leaps that mean she would probably be a fantastic detective.

"Was it that woman again? The documentary woman? Em Hoyle?"

"Yep. She sent me some clips. I watched them. It . . . freaked me out a bit."

Olivia nods and chews her lip.

"I looked her up," she says quietly. "After you mentioned her. She looks really cool. I think you should say yes."

"Why?" I ask. "So you can get tips on how to be even more nosy?"

"Maybe, yeah. And maybe it'd be good for you. She seems decent. And you . . . well, come on, sis, you never talk about it, do you? I was a kid when it happened but I still remember it. Us not knowing if you were dead or alive. Mum trying to get flights to Mexico, jumping out of her skin every time the phone rang. And then when you did come back . . . you weren't the same."

"You make it sound like something from a science-fiction story, Olivia. Like I was body-swapped or something."

"Well, it felt a bit like that. And it's been years now, and you still never talk about it. It's like you've just . . . boxed it all away. It's not healthy."

There isn't a trace of irony in her voice, and I realize that I am quite seriously being given mental-health advice by a teenager—a girl who not so long ago was crying when Zayn left One Direction.

"Well . . . I live in the present. Isn't that supposed to be good, mindfulness and all that?"

"Yes, but living in the present while completely denying the past? Not so sure about that. I'm just saying—this could be a good opportunity for you. To, you know, sort out some shit."

"It's not that straightforward, Olivia."

"Why not? You're the one making it complicated. It was a bad thing that happened to you ages ago. It shouldn't affect the rest of your life."

"But it does," I respond, trying to stay calm. It's not her fault that she doesn't understand, that I can't explain properly. "It does affect the rest of my life. It happened, and it changed me. It changed everything. And I have to be grateful—some people didn't survive to be changed at all. They never got the chance to make any more choices."

She stands up, faces me with her hands on her hips.

"You don't *have* to be grateful," she replies. "Or at least not all the time. Sometimes, you can just be pissed off—it's allowed. And that face you're pulling right now? The one that says 'but the world can't possibly understand my pain'? That's exactly why you should agree to doing the documentary. Because then you'd be explaining your pain, and maybe talking to people who share it, and then perhaps—though I know it's a long shot—you'd be out in the world again, living properly, instead of sitting in here abusing singing penguins."

She flounces out of the room in a cloud of Russian

princess hair, just as my phone rings. I glance at the screen, see that it is Harry.

"How do you feel?" he says straightaway. The new and improved Harry is a lot more empathetic than the old one. "Are you okay? I just watched some of those clips, and . . . well. Not easy, is it?"

"No. Olivia thinks I should say yes. To the documentary."

"Well, Olivia and I don't often agree on anything, but . . . maybe it's worth thinking about? I had therapy afterward. You never did. You still don't like to talk about it all, do you?"

He's right, of course. I don't—even to him. It's not just what happened that night that upsets me—it's the choices that followed. The way things were left. My memories comprise so many sore spots, so many things I need to avoid thinking about to stay calm and happy.

"Perhaps," I reply.

"Well, it's your decision. I'll support whatever you want to do. As you know, I won't object to the screen time—with a face like this, I was born to be in front of the cameras . . ."

I laugh, almost against my will. He is joking. Mostly.

"All right," I say, grateful for his words, for the break in the tension. "Thanks, Harry."

I look back at my laptop, at the email from Em. I hit reply.

Hi Em, I type. *Okay—you win. We can meet for a coffee at least.*

As I finish off and hit send before I can change my

mind, I wonder if I've done the right thing. Or if I've just triggered a whole new tremor, a chain of events that might swallow me into another gaping black hole.

I have a tall cupboard in here, so tall it just about sneaks in under the ceiling, so tall that I have to stand on a chair to reach the top. I have never suspected that Harry goes sneaking around snooping in my stuff, but if I was to have a paranoid moment, I would keep any deep, dark secrets in this cupboard. Harry has come a long way, but climbing on a spinny chair is beyond him.

I clamber up and open the door. I pull out a neatly folded bundle of faded yellow fabric.

I sit back down and gently take myself for a mild spin, tapping my foot to rotate my body in slow circles, all the while cuddling the treasure on my lap.

I stop abruptly, enjoy the tiny head rush of dizziness, and lift the T-shirt to my face. *I ♥ Tequila,* and I ♥ this T-shirt.

It's been washed quite a few times. It has not touched him for years. It has even been sneakily worn to bed by me when Harry has been away and washed some more. It could not possibly still smell of him.

And yet, it does. And still, all these years on, it comforts me.

Chapter 18

Ten days later I am sitting in a small café in South Kensington, wondering why I agreed to meet Em at all. And why I chose London, rather than a place nearer to home.

Perhaps it's because I remember coming here when I was a young teen, on trips to the Natural History Museum, oohing and aahing at the dinosaur skeletons.

The first *Jurassic Park* movies had been out for a while by then, and a lot of the other kids were unimpressed at the lack of teeth and blood and screaming. I, on the other hand, was amazed—and a tiny bit scared. I mean, if they *did* come to life, they'd be even more terrifying than the ones in the films. We'd be getting chased around by raging, rattling bones, wouldn't we?

Perhaps it's because I wanted to keep the two worlds separate—the life I have now, back at home, and the past that Em wants to discuss.

The café has an Italian-sounding name, and everything is painted in dusty shades of matte gray and black, like a giant chalkboard. The background noise is a pleasant mix of jazzy music and the hissing and spitting of a giant coffee machine. The staff are all stupidly young and stupidly beautiful, as though they are off-duty actors slumming it to gain life experience.

Outside, the sky is a relentlessly dull shroud. It looks like a lid made of dark clouds, held oppressively flat over the city in a way that says "the sun will never shine here again."

It is early November, and several shops and bars have already swathed themselves and their picture windows in pretty Christmas lights. I have a seat at a table for two right by the café window, watching the world go by.

Several groups of schoolchildren are snaking through the streets in lines as they tour the museums with tired-looking teachers. There's a busker wearing a duffel coat and a floppy red hat that makes him look like Paddington Bear, and a man who looks about a hundred and fifty years old, swathed entirely in neon-green skintight Lycra, promenading with a miniature poodle. Couriers and food-delivery people swish in and out of traffic on bikes; cars blare and bully their way along the congested roads.

Even at a quiet time of day, it is busy, alive, flowing with other people's stories. Every lit-up window, every face looking down from the top deck of a bus, every set of feet that carries its owner away into the long tunnel to the Tube, is a story. Not that I'll ever know any of them, because this is London.

Today, I am enjoying the anonymity of it all. I feel invisible, and it is liberating. With the anonymity, and perhaps simply the distance from my home and my real life, also comes a sense of recklessness that I haven't felt for years. I am nervous about meeting Em, about discussing the past, about being away from home—but it also feels delicious.

Harry would have come with me if I'd asked, but I felt like this was something I needed to do on my own. Em says she has a story of her own to tell, and I get the feeling she wants to tell it to me. She has reached out to me, not Harry, and I have to assume there is a reason for that.

I arrived an hour early, and have been casing the joint like a paranoid agent in a spy thriller. There is no reason for me to feel cornered, anxious, or like I should be planning an escape route—but I often feel all of those things whenever I am out in public, especially in big cities, or busy restaurants, or when surrounded by lots of tall buildings.

Pretty much every waking moment involves some kind of risk assessment—every action has a potential re-action, every curb can be tripped over, every full kettle can be a scald, every room below street level can be a dungeon.

I remind myself to concentrate on the here, the now. The smell of the almond croissant that sits untouched on a plate in front of me. The Christmas lights in the shops outside. The laughter of the children as they stream past. The busy crowds that I could just disappear off into and not meet Em at all . . .

As I consider doing exactly that, I see a young woman standing still on the pavement outside, staring through the clear patch I have wiped on the steamy window.

She is dressed in different clothes—smart trousers and a jacket that make her look a lot more businesslike than I expected—but it is definitely her. The cropped hair is distinctive and impossible to disguise. She makes direct eye contact with me and waves before she heads toward the door.

She makes the universal tipping-your-hand-up-and-down-by-your-mouth move that means "do you want a drink?" as she heads to the counter.

I shake my head. If I have more coffee, I will possibly be awake and energized long enough to walk home, and it's over two hundred miles away. I could make a playlist all about walking, and listen to the Proclaimers and Katrina and the Waves and Nancy Sinatra for days on end.

I am beginning to suspect that I have in fact already had way too much coffee. I am also beginning to suspect that I've made a terrible mistake coming here.

She puts her coffee down on the table, and it sloshes out over the rim of the cup and into the saucer, almost-black against bone white.

"Shit," she says, putting a briefcase on the floor by her feet and sitting. "It always does that, doesn't it? I've never yet opened one of those little biscuit wrappers without it being wet. Sorry I'm a bit late. The Tube was a nightmare today, wasn't it?"

"I wouldn't know." I smile. "I'm strictly an above-ground kind of person."

"Ah. Of course you are," she says.

I notice that although she is dressed in a very smart

and stylish way, she is still wearing a pair of battered cherry-red Dr. Martens boots with tartan laces.

"Childish rebellion," she says, noticing me notice. "Whenever I have to tart up for proper meetings with grown-ups, I have to keep something on to remind me who I really am."

"Oh," I reply, smiling slightly. "That makes sense, weirdly. Who were you meeting?"

"Funders for the documentary actually, hence the suit. When I saw you through the window, you looked like you were considering doing a runner."

"I was considering doing a runner," I say quietly, staring at her downy hair and big green eyes and pierced nose. She looks so familiar, and oddly, neither of us has introduced ourselves, or confirmed who we are. "I still am, to be honest."

"Nervous about meeting me, or being in the big bad city?"

"Maybe both. I tend to worry more than I used to . . . Olivia, my sister, thinks I am the safest person in the world to be out with. She says there's no way the law of averages would allow anything bad to happen to me again—I'm inoculated against car accidents, plane crashes, terror attacks, crush incidents during sales, fire, flood, and lightning strikes. She's suggested I hire my-self out as a bodyguard to protect people from forces of nature and acts of God."

Em laughs and sips her coffee, then unwraps her little biscuit from its soggy little wrapper.

The more I look at her, the more I start to think

that I know her. That I know her from somewhere other than the internet, and the deliberately blurred or blocked photos of her on there.

She meets my eyes and grins.

"You're wondering where you know me from, aren't you?"

"I am, yes. Or am I imagining that we've met before?"

"You're not, no," she answers. Her accent is warm and gentle, the softened-off sound of a Scot who has lived away from home for a long time.

"I've changed a bit," she continues, "since you last saw me. I'll give you a clue—add in a lot of red hair, a very red face, and a bad attitude. Actually, I've still got the bad attitude. I'm just hiding it right now so I make a good impression."

She stays very still, allowing me to examine her features: the now almost translucently pale skin, the almost-shaved hair. She does a theatrical scowl, demonstrating the bad attitude as well—and that's when it falls into place. The evil eye gives it away.

I realize who she is, and it does something strange and primeval to my stomach. I feel muscles clench and insides writhe and everything flip-flop. I realize who she is, and my mind tells my body I've just plunged down on a roller coaster.

"You were there," I say eventually, amazed at how calm my voice sounds. "With your mum and your brother and your . . . your dad. But your family isn't Hoyle, and you weren't Em."

She nods, and her eyes flicker to the window and

back, and I realize perhaps this is weird for her as well. She dunks her teeny-tiny biscuit into her coffee, and predictably enough, it crumbles and falls into the steaming liquid.

"Bollocks," she says, laughing. "That always happens too . . . and you're right. I changed my name when I was eighteen. One thing I've learned over the last few months is that everyone dealt with it in different ways. Some basically made themselves forget about it, pretended it never happened. Some are still in therapy. Some still talk about it every day. Some drink, some do worse, some are managing just fine.

"But me? Back then I really couldn't handle it. Because of Dad—because he died, and because of how he died, trying to protect us. At school, on the bus, everywhere, I was Earthquake Girl. I can see, as a professionally nosy person myself, why people were so fascinated—but I couldn't deal with all that scrutiny. With people thinking they knew me."

"So you changed your name?" I ask, feeling a familiar sense of numbness creep over me. The numbness is my friend, and it's how I cope when I have to remember this stuff. Self-applied anesthetic.

"Yes. I was worried my mum would be upset, feel like I was somehow turning my back on Dad by getting rid of his name . . . but she understood. The name came from this mad old aunt I had. Well, probably great-great-aunt; she was ancient even when I was a kid. She lived on her own in a trailer on a wild hill in wild country, with a nippy border terrier and a shotgun. She died when I was about twelve, but I always remember her—it felt like she'd inspired some major life goals, you know?"

"Living on your own with a dog and a shotgun?"

"Well, maybe, one day, when I actually grow up . . . but what I saw in her was complete independence. She'd never got married, or had kids, or bought a house, or had a fancy career, or even a bank account. She wasn't beholden to anyone, and she didn't give a flying frog what anybody thought about her. She was tough and strong and very, very funny. My heroine. So when I was eighteen, I moved away for university. I moved from Edinburgh to Brighton, which was probably as far away as I could physically get.

"I cut all my hair off—I always hated it anyway—and I changed my name from Samantha Frazer to Em Hoyle, and I decided that I wasn't going to be Earthquake Girl anymore. I loved my dad, and I never want to forget him, but I couldn't carry on living my life in the shadow of what happened that night, you know?"

I nod. I completely understand. And Samantha—Em—was only a child. She was sixteen years old, and she saw her father killed as he put his fragile human body between his family and an earthquake. Who wouldn't want to move on from that?

"I understand," I say gently. "I really do. We had way too much attention as well. I never liked it. So, bearing that in mind, what I don't understand is why you're making this film at all?"

I realize as we talk that I am feeling more relaxed by

the second. That being in Em's company is good. That I'm glad I didn't run away from this. I also can't wait to tell Harry who she is.

"Good question," she says. "No simple answer. I'll get the basics out of the way first—it'll be a great program. As a filmmaker, it's golden. I've got photos and video clips that haven't been used before, and I'm fascinated by the impact that one night, one event, can have on us as people—the way it affects who we are, who we become, how we live our lives.

"The less simple stuff has to do with me, and my dad, and our own story. Obviously I'm not ashamed of my dad, and I'm not ashamed of Samantha Frazer—I had my reasons for avoiding her, when I was younger and more vulnerable, but now I feel like the time is right for me to tell this story—and let's face it, this ten-year-anniversary thing means someone is going to. It might as well be me."

"But why do you need me or the others? It would be powerful enough if you did it alone."

She grins. "Moody shots of me gazing off into the horizon, photo album pics of Dad, an emotional pilgrimage back to the place where I lost him . . ."

"Yes. All of that. Exactly."

"It's not just my story, that's why. We all shared something that night. We shared something intense, and then we all went our separate ways. It's like we were thrown together, then torn apart, and left in a world that didn't really understand.

"It happened to dozens of us. It happened to Mexicans.

It happened to Brits, and Americans, and Australians, and Europeans. It happened to children and grandparents and everything in between. There is so much more to it than me. Earthquakes happen all the time—it's what happened to us all afterward that I'm interested in."

Earthquakes do happen all the time; she's right. Over a million a year, if you count all sizes. I have a minor-league obsession with it, and check the U.S. Geological Survey website like normal people check Facebook. I'm less about Twitter and more about tectonic plates.

Just yesterday there was a 6.4 in Puerto Rico, a 4.2 in Indonesia, a 4.5 in Kansas, and a 5.4 in Russia. That's not even counting the smaller ones that people don't even pay attention to.

We think of the world as being solid beneath our feet—but it's not. It's a giant jigsaw puzzle, and not all of the pieces fit together properly. There are earthquakes rumbling away constantly—moments when the movements in the Earth's crust cause a buildup of stress and friction; moments when that stress and friction meets a fault line, a place of weakness. Moments when all that energy bursts out, spreads in seismic waves, like ripples on a pond.

The earthquake we suffered through was a 6.1 in magnitude. That isn't so bad—there are more than a hundred of them most years.

In some places, it might only have caused limited damage—but not there, not that night.

Milder tremors, probably ongoing since before the village existed, had weakened the foundations of the buildings. There was subsidence from very old mining. There were sinkholes that had been developing for years. There were landslides, as the quake happened just after the rainy season.

A perfect storm.

"I don't know," I say carefully, sipping now-cold coffee. "I'm not sure that it won't just be . . . picking at a healed scab."

She stares at me, assessing and thoughtful. "I'm not sure it is healed, that scab, are you?"

I pull a face. She may be right, but I still don't feel at all sure. "Why do you need me? You have plenty of others to tell their tales. You can do this without me."

"Can I be blunt?" she asks.

"I can't imagine you any other way."

"True. Well, Elena, to risk sounding crass—you were the poster girl, weren't you? You were young and pretty, and you were the one everyone was praying for. When you were missing, and your mum was crying outside your house on the news. When they discovered you were alive under the rubble, you and Alex.

"It all made you, and later Harry, the public face of what had happened. Those pictures of you that night, sitting on the stretcher by the ambulance, covered in blood and gazing out at the destruction . . . they became the pictures that people remembered. The ones that made them think 'there but for the grace of God,' you know?"

Sadly, I do know. Those pictures—the ones I didn't even register being taken, I was so dazed and confused—

were syndicated all over the world. The happy ending, wrapped in tinfoil.

"It's not just that," she continues. "It's what happened afterward. In those next weeks and months, and all these years since. Do you think your life would have worked out the way it has if you hadn't been there that night?"

"My life is fine," I say eventually, realizing that I sound defensive.

"I'm not saying it isn't," she responds quickly. "I just think it's different than you'd imagined . . . I know mine is. And that's what I'm fascinated by, Elena—the way it changed our fates, destinies, whatever daft name you want to give it. We all started that night feeling normal— feeling like we knew what would happen next."

"And none of us did," I say. "None of us had a clue."

She shakes her head, and we are both silent. We are both remembering. We are both survivors, and no matter how much we try to forget, it is always there. Just beneath the surface, buried in mental rubble.

It feels good to sit here, with her, and quietly remember. It is a relief to be with another woman who understands that it wasn't exciting, like the uplifting scenes in a disaster movie, heroism bravely performed against the backdrop of a sweeping orchestral soundtrack.

It was terrifying, and painful, and some of the dust from that night has never washed off. Good as it temporarily feels to be here with Em, do I really want her, or anyone else, to go digging beneath that rubble again? Do I want to excavate the past? Will the anesthetic begin to wear off if I do?

I am scared at the thought. I am excited at the thought. I am . . . relieved, perhaps, at the thought?

"You and Harry settled in Cornwall, didn't you?" she asks. I frown, wondering how much about us she already knows, and nod.

"Don't worry!" She grins. "This is just a conversation. This is just two people talking, not an interview. I'm not secretly filming you with my spy cam . . . I just . . . well, it's a relief, isn't it, to chat with someone who was there?"

"It is," I reply firmly. "It really is."

"Did you go back in to teaching? I googled Harry and found out about him pretty quickly, but not you . . . Did you have any kids of your own?"

"No, and no." My hand creeps to my stomach. She has unintentionally touched upon a painful subject, and I see a look of concern flicker across her face.

I have never discussed the baby we lost with Harry. I vowed I would, when the time was right—but it simply never seemed to be.

To start with, we were never alone—we were always surrounded by his parents, by nurses, by doctors. Then he was in rehab, and it was beyond tough—physically and mentally. At the beginning I kept it from him because I wanted to protect him from more pain—and now, somehow, I have allowed years to pass. The longer I have left it, the harder it has become to do.

I have carried it alone for so long, and now I have a strange urge to tell Em—to share this hidden sadness with her. Of course, I don't—I can't tell her before I tell him.

"We haven't had kids, no," I reply. "It's . . . more complicated, with Harry's condition. By no means impossible; lots of paraplegic men become fathers, but . . . well, like I say, complicated."

She is clearly curious, and I understand that. I shake my head and smile, not intending to go into any more detail. It's private, it's personal, and it's complex. Sex itself is more complex, and Harry's little swimmers aren't as good at swimming after the injury.

We looked at various options, ranging from ways to increase the chances of it happening at home through to supremely romantic procedures involving sperm collection and IVF. Making a baby together would be possible—but it would also take time and determination. For whatever reason, neither of us has been that determined—so far at least. Harry's condition aside, I am older now, and I suppose it is something we need to figure out. A conversation we need to have, like so many others.

Harry, when we were younger, never seemed that keen. I assumed he would eventually mellow about it, but I also suspect his apparent lack of enthusiasm about fatherhood is one of the many reasons I've never told him about the baby at all.

What if he reacted badly and told me it was for the best? What if he just didn't care? What if he was relieved? I wouldn't be able to blame him for his reaction, but I know it would have hurt.

"You?" I ask, amused at the look of horror that crosses her face.

"Goodness no! I'm still figuring out how to look after my inner child, never mind an outer one . . . I do have someone, though. Ollie. The love of my life."

There isn't a trace of sarcasm as she says that, and it leaves me feeling oddly envious.

"I'm glad," I reply. "And . . . why are you putting so much effort into convincing me, Em? You don't really need me, poster girl or not. Harry would definitely do it, as long as I was okay with it . . ."

She smiles, and a flash of the much younger her flickers across her face, making her look like a teenager again.

"I need you because you meant so much to me back then."

"What? How? We barely crossed paths . . ."

"That's what you think. I remember you so vividly, Elena. I was miserable on that trip. It was hot, and I'm a ginger, and I was angry with my parents for making me come and at the world for existing."

"Really?" I say. "But you hid it so well!"

"No, I didn't. And joking aside, don't believe I haven't tortured myself with that—that the last few conversations I ever had with my dad were grumpy and monosyllabic."

I feel my emotions surge upward like bile, and my heart breaks a tiny bit for her. For the broken girl she was, and the patchwork woman she is.

"That's . . . that's harsh. You were a teenager. Most teenagers are grumpy and monosyllabic."

"Och, I know!" she says, waving her hand in the air in an attempt at dismissal. "And he thought it was funny anyway . . . It's just one of those things. The logical part of me understands it's no big deal, but the squishy part of me still sometimes bursts into tears about it while I'm standing in a self-service checkout queue in the supermarket, you know?"

"Yes. Those self-service checkouts make me cry as well."

She grabs hold of my lame joke and laughs at it, grateful for the diversion.

"But anyway . . . while I was busy being grumpy and monosyllabic and angry and trying not to engage with my own family, I did a lot of people-watching. I watched you, and I watched Harry, and I watched Alex."

"You do realize that sounds creepy?"

"I do. I desperately wanted to be older. I desperately wanted to be independent, and have my own life, and maybe a hot boyfriend who looked a bit like Hugh Grant. To be the sort of woman who dared speak to the mysterious, but equally hot, Swedish guy. You seemed so . . . together. I was kind of crushing on you, I think."

"That's really weird," I say, "thinking of me as together. I was anything but."

"Well, you were my hero. In the hospital, after . . . I think I wished myself invisible. I was so messed up. Dad was gone. Mum was hurt, my brother, Matt, was only a kid, and . . . I *wanted* to be invisible, you know? I did a lot of skulking around. A lot of sitting on my own in corridors, willing people to ignore me, but at the same time wishing someone would make everything better.

I wanted someone to give me a hug and reassure me, but I was so traumatized and covered in prickles that I scared everyone off."

"I'm sorry," I say quietly. "It must have been awful for you. I'm sorry I wasn't any use. I wish I'd noticed you more. I wish I'd given you that hug."

"Don't be silly—you had your own drama unfolding. And anyway, you did help, kind of. You bought me a hot chocolate one day, from the vending machine."

"I don't think I'm going to win the humanitarian-of-the-year award for that, Em. I can't imagine how lonely you must have felt."

"Don't underestimate the power of a hot chocolate." She pats my hand very briefly. "It wasn't the drink anyway . . . it was the act of kindness. So, to repay you, I basically started stalking you. I eavesdropped on conversations, and followed you and Alex around, and generally behaved like a horribly nosy brat. It might even have planted the seeds of what I do for a living now—which is get paid to be nosy."

"You probably remember more than I do, in that case," I reply, feeling slightly unnerved. Part of me is wondering how she managed to do so much creeping around and still remain hidden—especially with hair like hers.

"Were you there the whole time? At the hospital?" I frown as I try to piece it together. "Or did you leave before us?"

"We were there until you left. Mum had two broken arms and a head injury, and I had a broken elbow, and we were there for what seemed like forever. And it's okay that you don't really remember me. I know it was hard for you. Your whole life got thrown in a spin cycle."

I nod, pick up my cup, notice that my hands are trembling.

"Yes. It was, I suppose. It feels so long ago now . . . and like it happened to a different person. I remember sensations more than anything—the way the hospital air-conditioning made a funny noise at night. The pink sneakers a lot of the nurses wore. The canteen with the pop music."

"And the smell," Em replies. "That hospital smell. I've not been in one since. Not sure how I'd react if I needed my appendix out or anything. Do you remember the balcony, though, on the top floor of the tower block? That was nice."

I nod. Of course I remember. I remember the honking horns and wailing sirens and the brouhaha of urban life. I remember the highways lit up like neon rivers, the sky an indigo blanket of stars. The winking lights of distant houses and apartment buildings; a glittering vista stretched to infinity.

Mainly, I remember the time I spent there with him. With Alex.

"Are you all right?" Em asks. "Do you want another coffee?"

I had disappeared, I realize. Just a little. Retreated into a different part of my mind, one I keep safely tucked away. A bizarrely happy part of my mind, considering the circumstances.

"I'm fine, Em. It's just . . . well. You know how it is.

So. How would it work then? If I was to agree to this? What would you need from me?"

"Just time and conversation, on and off camera."

"What if I was unhappy with what you were asking? What if it was . . . too difficult?"

"Then we could stop. You don't have to do anything you don't want to. I'm not setting out to trick anyone, or deliberately dig up deep, dark secrets, or expose unpleasant truths."

"But what if they did?" I ask. "Get exposed. Secrets, truths. What if you find stuff out that isn't . . . easy. That doesn't fit. That feels . . . dangerous."

I can tell she is intrigued now, and wonder if perhaps I have said exactly the wrong thing to someone who is, by her own description, professionally nosy.

"Is there anything?" she asks, eyebrows raised. "Anything you'd be scared of revealing? Skeletons swinging in closets? I mean, we all have things we'd prefer the world not to know. But is there anything that would really damage you that you're worried about?"

I ponder the question. I poke at it, and prod it, and roll it around from all angles. There are things I have never told anybody. Feelings I have never discussed. Truths that could lead to some awkward conversations, maybe even to some changes.

That in itself sounds pretty scary, but would it be damaging? I am not sure. I don't know what to do, whether to take the risk. I like Em. And I feel like I owe Samantha. I even agree with Olivia and think it might be good for me—to talk about it after all these years.

But I am still fretful. Still wary of upsetting the people who matter to me, and of course myself—because nobody is that selfless. I have tried to be safe since that night, to make sensible choices, and this feels like it might not be sensible.

It also feels like it might not even be a choice.

I see her watching me and know that she senses a critical moment. That I am perfectly balanced and could tumble to either side of the fence.

"Look," she says, holding her hands flat on the table, as though trying to show me she has no weapons and means me no harm. "I'm making this program anyway, you know that. I'm flying out to Australia next week to do some interviews there. I'd like you to be in it, and I think you'll feel better if you have some involvement, some control over it.

"So I'll make you a promise. Not one I've ever made anyone else, all right? I can't say I'll give you control over what I use in the film, because I won't—that's my job, and I'm good at it. But I will involve you. You can work with me on it, as much or as little as you like. You can even help with questions, or research, if you want."

"Are you offering me a job?" I reply, amused. "Because I already have one."

"Call it a job if you like. Though I won't be paying you, so maybe more of an internship. Mainly what I'm offering is access—you'll know what's going on. Nothing will ever sneak up on you. If anything that falls into the deep-dark-secrets category comes out, I can't say I'll hide it—but I'll warn you. You'll know in advance at least. How does that sound? And do you have any other questions?"

I have one big question. One thing I am desperate to know, but am fighting the urge to ask—I want to know if she has seen him. Talked to him. If one of her film clips is of him, and how I would feel when I saw it. I don't ask—because this decision cannot be made on that alone. I have not seen Alex in years, and our last moments together were sad and difficult—I'm not sure I'm ready to think about seeing him again just yet.

"It sounds . . . better. But you know I need to talk to Harry about it. And I need time to think."

"Okay," she says, grinning. "Fair enough. And whatever you decide, Elena, it's been so good to see you again. I'd like to stay in touch. I realize I've already come across as obsessed enough during this conversation, but it really did help me back then—having you around. While I was focusing on you and your life, I could avoid my own, which was pretty sucky.

"I still remember how relieved I was when they brought you in—we all were. It was like you gave us hope again. I'm glad we had the chance to talk, and I hope I haven't dredged up too many unpleasant memories. Bizarrely, it wasn't all bad, was it?"

She's right. It was the worst of times, but it also holds some of my most precious memories. We are like older people who lived through the war, and still remember fondly the bright moments in a terrible era.

Dancing to the swing band before the bombs went off.

Chapter 19

It's hard not to be impressed by Harry. It's difficult not to be charmed by him. And it's impossible not to be proud of him for everything he has achieved.

It is also undeniably hard to ignore the fact that he is sometimes extremely annoying.

We are sitting in a café near the beachfront, across from a place called Barrelstock Bay near our home. We are waiting to meet Em and Ollie, her cameraman and partner, to start filming for the documentary.

Finding out who Em was, talking to her, had convinced me that taking part would be a good thing, and Harry agreed—and now we are here, about to plunge in. I am nervous, but Harry seems chock-full of his usual confidence.

"See that waitress?" he says, gesturing with his eyebrows toward the young woman who has just delivered our coffee. "She fancies me."

"Really?" I reply, stirring my drink and glancing at her. She is about twenty-one, and carelessly beautiful in the way of the surfing and sailing girls who are often to be found in this part of North Cornwall. "How can you tell?"

He winks at me. "Animal magnetism. I'm devastatingly handsome but also tragically wheelchair-bound— possibly after a freak snowboarding accident—which is a big double whammy."

Harry still uses a wheelchair for longer distances, but can walk and stand using leg braces that he claims make him look like Iron Man.

I notice that the waitress is indeed casting a few furtive looks in our direction, and tucking her blond hair behind her ears as she does. Damn. He may be right.

He notices me noticing this and grins at me smugly. I roll my eyes, but smile against my better judgment. Annoying, but amusing.

Harry has aged well, in all kinds of ways. He is still the kind of handsome that makes old ladies blush when he compliments them (which he does). He has worked hard on keeping as fit as he can and has bulked up considerably, filling the form-fitting T-shirts he favors in a way he likes to call "Chris Hemsworth lite." He does like his *Avengers* references.

He still has charm to spare, is still vain, and still has the ability to mock himself that offsets it all.

The big changes, though, are the ones you can't see on the surface. They're the ones that have added a hidden layer of humility, a greater tolerance for anyone less than perfect.

He always had the charisma, the ambition. He was always going to succeed in life—but the way he did it changed completely that night.

Initially the company he worked for said it would

do "everything it took" to make it possible for him to continue his career. In the flurry of publicity that surrounded us, our wedding, our return back to the UK, the start of Harry's rehab journey, it was always what we assumed would happen.

That somehow, by sheer determination, Harry would make it work.

But once the cameras stopped rolling, it changed. Emails from his bosses started to be copied in to the head of HR, coated in corporate arse-covering language.

Issues were raised about toilets, about his ability to take part in a fire evacuation. Questions were asked about whether he would be able to attend functions and conferences without a carer. Whether he would be able to fly for meetings abroad. How he could navigate his daily working life without experiencing "unnecessary strain, both physical and mental."

Harry is many things, but slow on the uptake is not one of them. He saw through it immediately, realized that they were placing obstacles in his path to deliberately discourage him from returning.

It was hard for him—so much of his identity and self-esteem were tied up in that job. I didn't care about the money or the posh cars, but I did care about him.

I should have known better. Harry's self-esteem was made of sterner stuff. He had a couple of very tough weeks where he was devastated—broken by what he saw as a betrayal. I know his parents were worried, his dad setting him up with interviews with golf-club buddies who'd be "lucky to have a man of his skills."

Maybe that's what finally dragged him out of it—the thought of accepting what he saw as a charity job from a middle-aged bloke in pink checkered socks.

So instead of crumpling, he worked even harder. He spent hours in the gym, on the supported treadmill, in the pool. Weeks and months of effort and pain and gruesome determination, as well as learning everything he could about his condition, helping his body learn and relearn how to function as well as it could in its new state.

He went to a wheelchair master class, and by the end of it was agile and confident—coming a long way from the early days, when he could be defeated by a cash machine. He spoke to new doctors, to new therapists, to other spinal-injury patients, to small companies that provided cutting-edge equipment. He knew he would have problems—with fatigue, with pain, with blood pressure, with sex, with maintaining his human dignity. He knew all of it, and he decided that he could deal with it.

It sounds like a training montage in a movie, doesn't it? Something that would be condensed into five minutes of heroic sweat and effort for our handsome hero.

The reality was that it took a lot longer than that, took a lot more effort than that. There were some very dark times. Times I thought he couldn't push any further.

I was wrong—and he refused to give up on himself. The part of me that had fallen in love with him all those years ago was thrilled. Thrilled to see that spirit, the drive that was always the flip side of the arrogance. Thrilled to see him parlay the issues with his former employers into a hefty settlement, to see him unafraid to embrace the challenges of his new life.

He knew that he was going to need care, going to need help and support, for some time yet. That he was going to be dependent on me—at least for a while. But he was always insistent that it wouldn't last forever.

What can I say? He was right. He is sitting opposite me now, flexing his biceps unnecessarily as he lifts his coffee mug. He has navigated his way here from the converted barn where he has his office without any assistance, driving his adapted car. He is the CEO of his enterprise, leading a staff of five. He is making a difference in the lives of the individuals he helps, and he is attempting to change the way people with disabilities are perceived by others.

I am so very, very proud of him—he has overcome so much, and has perhaps earned a quick flirtation with a now-blushing waitress.

"Are you sure about this? Are you ready?" he asks.

"Not really." I pile small packets of sugar into a higgledy-piggledy pile to distract myself. "You?"

I expect a glib reply—an "I was born ready" or such— but instead he ponders the question, sipping his coffee.

"Well, I'd be lying if I said I was one hundred percent. At the beginning, when things were . . . the way they were . . . it was helpful, the attention. And I've never exactly been a wallflower, have I? But I know you hated it, Elena. And I still don't know why you've decided now is the time to talk about it all, after almost a decade of solid English denial."

"I don't either . . . I just feel it's the right time to talk about it."

"Some might say perhaps it's a little overdue, nine years on?"

I shrug. "Maybe they'd be right. But it was hectic, wasn't it? And when we came home there was so much else to deal with. So much else to distract me."

"I know," he says, reaching out to place his hand over mine. "I know how hard it was for you then. I didn't at the time, I don't think. I was too self-obsessed, which I'll allow myself considering the circumstances. But I know what it cost you, putting me first. I know how much you gave up."

I meet his eyes and wonder if he does. I wonder if I do. I wonder if we are skirting near to a dangerous honesty. That opening up to Em, to each other, to ourselves, will change the shape of our lives and our relationship.

He lifts his hand from mine and knocks over my sugar-packet pile with a laugh.

"Don't look so scared. You don't have to do it. We don't. We could tell her we've changed our minds. Or . . . or we could accept that you need this, even if it is making you look like you're facing a firing squad. We could accept that it's okay for everything not to be perfect, and we could have a little faith that your instinct is right—that this will be a good thing. That whatever happens, we'll deal with it. We'll deal with anything."

"You think?" I ask, almost amused at his certainty. "Anything?"

"I think. Life has already thrown a few stinkers at us, Elena. And the logic of doing this is solid—there is going to be publicity around the anniversary. At least this way, we're involved; we have some control. Some good may even come of it—and if not, well . . . free therapy."

He is, of course, right. Life has thrown a few stinkers at us. I'm still not entirely sure that it's finished. I have secrets I have never shared with this man—this man whom I share a life and a home and a past with. I wonder if it is the same for him. If he also feels this unfurling of the wings of change inside him, the need to metamorphose.

But I also wonder if any marriage could survive full disclosure, and if what I am doing here is less an act of therapy and more an act of sabotage.

Luckily I am saved from too much wondering by the arrival of Em and Ollie.

They cause a subtle stir in the café. It's November, a crisp and beautiful day, the sunlight shining onto a flat gray sea, gulls wheeling and turning overhead. Still gorgeous, but a lot quieter than summer, when the whole area is awash with camper vans and surfboards and tired parents and toddlers covered in ice cream. At this time of year there are very few tourists, and any new blood attracts a second glance.

In this case, possibly a third. They make a striking couple—Em, with her short but very red hair, and Ollie, who is Black, much taller, and extremely good-looking.

"Hiya," he says, holding out his hand to shake mine,

then Harry's. "Nice to meet you both at last. I'm dying for a cuppa."

He has a broad Liverpool accent and a loud voice. Loud enough that the waitress immediately dashes over and takes his order, now far more fascinated by Ollie than Harry.

"Forgive him," says Em, slapping him on the shoulder. "He does his professional Scouser thing all the time when he's in places like this. He just likes the attention."

"I can't imagine getting attention is a problem he has," I reply, smiling.

"You're right there, love," he says with a wink.

He is funny and confident, and I immediately like him.

Their drinks are delivered, and I realize that Em is staring at Harry. He is aware of her scrutiny, and I laugh a little inside as I see him do another subtle biceps flex.

"You look a lot better than you did last time I saw you, Harry," she says eventually.

"That wouldn't be hard, Em, would it?" he responds. "As I'm guessing I was in a hospital bed coming to terms with waking up as a prisoner in my own body."

He has never said those particular words out loud to me, never expressed those feelings of being trapped, held hostage. It's interesting that he has said it, so openly and so quickly, to a virtual stranger.

Perhaps, I realize, he has always hidden as much of his own sadness from me as I have from him, either in an attempt to protect me, or out of the pride that used to so much define his character. Perhaps seeing Em, talking to someone who was there but who isn't his wife, is having the same liberating effect on him as it did me.

"You look amazing now," she says. "And I've been reading up on the work you do—also amazing."

"Do I sense some surprise there?" he asks, quirking his head to one side in a way he knows is cute. "Almost as though I was a bit of an arsehole back then?"

He's trying to catch her off guard, but the good ship Em isn't that easy to rock.

"To be fair I barely knew you, but you did seem a bit full of yourself now that you mention it. Maybe you still are, but the work you're doing is very impressive. Quite the change from what you did before."

Of course, she will have done her research already.

"Yes." He nods. "The whole experience was very humbling, in a lot of ways—not least of which was feeling like my career was over, feeling like there was nothing left for me to contribute. Realizing that I needed to expect more, and that I could help others to expect more as well."

It wasn't just the way he was treated by his former employers that inspired him—it was also experiencing the everyday difficulties of life in a chair: the frustrations and the casual prejudice; the thoughtless actions of people parking in the wrong places; the lack of ramps and facilities; the lack of understanding that just because part of his body didn't work in the same way, it didn't automatically follow that he was happy to be some kind of helpless hermit.

He is, no surprises, a master at fund-raising—if there

is a grant out there to be got, he will get it. If there is a potential donor to be charmed, he will charm them. If there is a room to be worked, he will work it. He is, himself, a shining example of why disabled people should never be discounted.

"I know you set up training schemes and work placements for people," Em says, "and we'd be glad to consider anyone you think would be interested."

I see him start to run Em's offer through his internal matrix and know he will have a plan in place within seconds.

"That's wonderful, thank you," he says simply. "I already have a few people in mind you could meet."

She nods and folds her arms down onto the table, leaning forward. She looks immediately more focused and serious, switching into work mode. I feel decidedly unprofessional in comparison to these two go-getters, but am also proud of Harry, of seeing how his dedication is paying off.

"So," she says. "Thank you again for doing this. I know it's not easy, and I know that you in particular had your doubts, Elena. It's been hard for me too, to be honest, when I've been interviewing people—harder to stay objective when their stories are all related to mine. I know I need to be interviewed myself as well, which is disconcerting. I've been getting Ollie to ask me questions on camera, and it hasn't always been straightforward."

"She threw her boot at my head," he adds conversationally.

"Yeah, well, that's the risk you run when you're in a relationship with me, Ollie."

"It's worth a million boots to the head, my love, you know that," he replies, winking again. It seems to be his thing.

She winks back and they share a smile, and they seem so very happy and so very relaxed that it almost makes me envious. Harry and I get along well enough, but it's clear that Em and Ollie adore each other in a way that makes the rest of the world disappear.

"So how will this work?" I ask. "And what have you done so far, apart from the clips you sent me? Have you spoken to a lot of people?"

"I've interviewed the people you've already seen," she answers, "plus some others. I tracked down the supremely sexy Dr. Martinez, who is now at a different hospital, and talked to him and some of the nursing staff about what it was like over those few days. I haven't been back yet . . . to the village."

"Do you plan to?" I ask, wondering how I'd feel about that. If I could even do it.

"Yes. I think so. I'll need to film there, no matter how hard that might be. I'm told it became a bit of a ghost town for a while—nobody wanted to go back there to start with, which you can understand. But I think in the last couple of years there's been some rebuilding. There's a new church, I've heard."

I let that thought settle in. New church. New homes. Maybe new tourists, who knows? Much as I like to keep an eye on earthquake activity, I've studiously avoided keeping an eye on Santa Maria.

"I don't know if you remember Janey Gregor and Shelley Dawes, two of the Australians?"

I nod, and she continues. "Well, I've met with them. Marissa . . . well, she didn't make it."

I frown in confusion, as Marissa was the one in the burn unit. She made a full recovery and went back home to Sydney to be with her boyfriend. Shelley was still in a coma when I left, but is clearly alive and well now.

"I thought Marissa recovered?" I ask, wondering if I've got the names switched around somehow.

"She did, physically. Apart from the scarring. But . . . well, according to her boyfriend, she never recovered mentally. She died a year after."

I bite my lip and dig my fingernails into the palms of my hands to stop the tears that threaten to spring up as the full weight of Em's words sink in. As I realize that she is telling us, as subtly as she can, that Marissa took her own life. I remember her as one of those carefree young girls, laughing and giggling their way around Mexico. I look at Harry, see that he is equally distraught.

Em reaches out and touches my arm briefly, united in our shared grief.

"It's one of the things I've noticed most," she says. "How the earthquake has affected us all so differently, how we're all still to some extent 'surviving' all these years later. Still learning how to process what happened that night."

I nod, understanding what she means.

"Have you talked to everyone involved?" asks Harry. "Have you talked to Alex Andersson?"

My eyes flick to Harry's, taken aback by the unexpected question. Shocked by hearing Alex's name out loud. Like a splinter trapped in the soft flesh of my heart.

He shrugs and looks at me. "I know you're wondering what's happened to him, Elena. So am I."

"I haven't spoken to him yet, but I think I might be close. Hopefully. Turns out that Andersson is pretty much as common in Sweden as Jones is here. Did you stay in touch with him?"

"Just for a little while," I reply quietly, hoping to leave it at that.

"Elena met up with him a few times, didn't you?" Harry says. He turns back to Em and adds, "I think it helped them both, having each other to talk to. Plus it gave Elena a bit of time away from me every now and then, which she thoroughly deserved. It was a lot, what we were going through, and I know her friendship with Alex helped."

He's right: it did help. For a while. A few weeks after he went back to Stockholm, Alex contacted me and apologized for the kiss. For the way we'd left things.

I didn't think he had anything to apologize for, but I think we both knew that if we were going to stay in each other's life, we needed to draw a line under it. Revert back to being friends.

So we emailed, shared stories, occasionally talked. He was trying to rebuild his life in Sweden and I encouraged him. I was trying to rebuild a life in the UK, and he supported me in a way nobody else did. Here, I was too busy being strong for Harry's sake—but with Alex, I could be weak, and sad, and myself. We were friends—the very best of friends.

When he first suggested meeting up in London I felt both excited and worried. Would it be awkward? Would it feel wrong? Would it be somehow betraying Harry?

When I discussed it with him, Harry was astonishingly understanding. He gave me his blessing, seemed to understand that we shared a bond, an experience, a friendship that I needed back then. A friendship that I still feel the loss of today.

I can feel Em's gaze on me and try to calm my breathing to a steadier pace. She seems a bit like one of those human lie detectors, and I am not quite ready to have this conversation. Not quite ready to remember when I last saw Alex.

"I haven't spoken to him in years," I reply. And it's the truth. The last time I saw him, on a cobbled street in Paris, we were both in tears. Even now the pain of that memory can take my breath away.

"Well. We'll find him, I'm sure," she says, smiling at me reassuringly. "Hard to tell your story without his, isn't it?

"Anyway, if you're both up for it, I thought we could get some footage today? The lighting is perfect here by the sea, and then we can film some more stuff back at your home. Ollie will be operating the camera, and you'll have a lavalier microphone attached to your clothing, so you don't need to worry about speaking loudly or anything. And, I promise, I'll do everything I can to make you feel comfortable. You don't even need to look at the lens, just look at me. Okay?"

I nod, but in all honesty I'm barely listening. My mind has fluttered away, to another place and another time, to Alex. To when I last saw him, and how much I miss him if I let myself think about it. To a future that might bring us into each other's lives again, if Em finds him.

"That sounds fine," says Harry. "Right, Elena?"

"Sorry, yes," I reply, dragging myself back to the present. To reality. To my husband.

"So what sort of shots do you want?" asks Harry, wheeling his chair out from under the table. "Holding hands as we look out at the sea? Gazing moodily into the sunset together, that kind of thing?"

"Not the sunset," I say quickly. "Sunrise, if we need to. But watching the sun go down makes me too sad."

I feel all three of them looking at me. Feel their curiosity, their concern, their surprise.

"Whatever you want, Elena," replies Em, smiling at me in a way that makes me wonder if she knows exactly why.

Chapter 20

The following day, we start filming in earnest. Em and Ollie have spent the morning with Harry, at his workplace.

I know he's proud of it—rightly so—and he will use the opportunity to highlight the challenges he's faced, that the people he works with and for have faced. He will be positive, but not shy away from difficult subjects. He really is at his best when he's passionate, and his career brings out the fire in him.

While they did that, I went for a walk along the beach in an attempt to clear my mind. I made friends with two Irish setters, and I rolled down a sand dune like a child rolls down a grassy hill in summer. I was hoping to gain some clarity, but all I gained was twigs in my hair and a red face.

I took a shower, and was so worried about sounding unnatural and forced in the interview that I spent a while trying to rehearse talking into a mirror—which of course did not help in the slightest. It's hard to practice being spontaneous.

It is now after lunch and I am back at home, waiting for Em and Ollie. Olivia has come home from college early and is hopping with excitement about it all, but pretending to be not at all bothered. It's hard work being a teenager.

I am nervous, because it is my turn to start filming. I am not a natural, like I know Harry will be, and I am convinced that I am going to lose all power of speech once the cameras are rolling. I am worried that I won't be able to revisit these difficult subjects with any calm or clarity. That I will cry, or clam up, or struggle to remember, or remember too much.

"They're here!" screeches Olivia, jumping up from one of the stools by the kitchen table when she hears a car pull up outside.

"OMG!" I reply, pulling a shocked face.

She flicks me the finger, and our brief spurt of mutual abuse helps to calm me down as I let them in, along with their various metal boxes and coils of wires and microphones.

Even the sight of it all makes my throat go dry. A worry flickers across my mind about electrical fires, but I am self-aware enough to understand that is not what is really worrying me. I am worried about doing this—about exposing myself, making myself vulnerable.

"Nice place," says Ollie, gazing around him. "It's very . . . minimalist. Very bright."

"I know," I say, filling the kettle. "The whole bungalow is. Harry's great with his chair, but life is a lot easier for him—for us—if there aren't too many obstacles."

"You should see her office, though," says Olivia. "It's like a thrift shop exploded."

"This is Olivia, my sister," I explain.

"Olivia . . . can I call you Liv?" asks Ollie, and I suck in a breath and await the tirade. He has immediately stumbled upon one of her pet hates.

"Only if I can punch you in the face," she replies sweetly.

"Oooh—feisty!"

"Why do men call women feisty like that?" she asks, frowning and looking genuinely interested. "It's like, women who disagree with something or have a bit of self-belief are always called 'feisty,' or 'kick-ass.' Like those are our only two choices."

Ollie seems to give it some thought, then responds, "Can't say for sure, love, but as someone who is very aware of the nuanced power of language and its ability to oppress, I shall make sure I think twice in the future."

She regally nods her acceptance and offers coffee.

Em is gazing out into the garden, at the sliver of the sea you can just about spot at the end of it. That's the one element of my dream house that made it into reality, and it is a constant solace. It's almost winter now, but on a bright and clear day the water shines shades of turquoise and blue, the most beautiful shimmer on the horizon.

"Harry said he was staying late to catch up on the work he missed today. Alison—the office manager?— was there as well," she says. "He'll be back about seven, he thinks. Impressive setup he has there, isn't it? He really has done such a good job of . . . I don't know, winning at life somehow?"

"Yep," I say, letting out a small laugh. "It's one of

his specialities, bless him. And he does a lot of good for people along the way. How did it go, the interview?"

"Good," replies Em firmly. "Really good. Harry remembers different things, as does everyone—the aim is to piece them together to get a coherent picture, like a big, gnarly jigsaw puzzle. There's a lot he's forgotten, so hopefully you can help with some of it. Would you like to see? Feels weird, but I'm sure he won't mind."

When I nod, she sets up her laptop at the table and clicks open some files. I see soundless shots of Harry at work, at his desk. Harry on the phone. Harry with Alison and the team. Finally, Harry alone, sitting in the office's meeting room.

She pauses it and says, "You know, I remember Harry a certain way. A bit cocky, good-looking and he knew it . . . even from just watching you guys on the coach trip. And after . . . well, I have to confess I had this teenage-girl idea that you and Alex would get together. As an almost-mature adult now, I know that was just my silly daydreaming, but part of me came here still thinking I might not like Harry . . ."

"And it's impossible not to like Harry, isn't it?"

"Yes, damn him!" she says, laughing as she hits play.

I look at the screen as Em, off camera, asks, "What do you mean by that? That you were sleepwalking?"

We've obviously come in midconversation, at an interesting point.

"I mean," he replies, "that I was sleepwalking through life. I thought I knew what I wanted, had it all figured out. But now, when I look back on my life then, I'm not sure I was even enjoying it. I was on autopilot. It was about ticking boxes—the career, the cars, the apartment, the money. It's like I was competing, all the time. Frankly, I think I was empty, a hollow man, trying to fill up the space with the stuff I thought I needed."

"And now you're not?"

"I don't think so—though maybe in ten years I'll look back on this stage of my life with a critical eye, who knows? I do know that I'm different. I'm not going to be glib and say something like it was the best thing that happened to me—it was horrific. I would prefer not to be in this chair, I'd prefer to be going for jogs and playing rugby and not having to think about accessible toilets. But it did have some positive effects—in some ways, some important ways, it did change me and my life for the better."

"In what ways? Give me some examples."

"Well, it made me realize how fake my world was. It gave my life, certainly my working life, more value. I lost a lot, but I gained a lot as well. Weirdly, when I look back on that night, the things I regret the most all happened in my life before the earthquake."

"Like what?"

"Ah, where would the mystery be if I told you that? Nothing life-shattering. I'm not a secret war criminal, I don't have a double life as a CIA assassin. I just . . . I did things that now make me feel ashamed of myself. I'm sure that's true for everyone who looks back with reflection on their life, at their younger selves; it's a natural part of growing up—but with me, because of what happened, it felt like I did that growing up overnight."

"Okay. So, looking at those positives—one of them must be Elena. If your life is a before and an after, then Elena has been a constant, hasn't she? The part of your old life you took with you into your new life."

Harry smiles and nods. "Yes. Elena. She has always been a constant—and I'm not so selfish as to not appreciate what all of this cost her. What sacrifices she made to be at my side when I needed her. My parents too. It didn't just happen to me—it happened to all of us."

Em presses a key that pauses the video and Harry's face freezes on the screen.

"So," she says, when I remain silent. "What do you think?"

"It was good," I reply. "He's a natural. I warn you I won't be like that. I'll stutter, and forget words, and laugh at inappropriate moments. By the end of this process the world will assume Harry was my carer, not the other way round."

As we chat, I can't stop thinking about what it was that Harry regretted so much. What mysteries he is alluding to.

When you've spent years helping a man deal with his toilet requirements and testing wheelchair ramps with him, it's easy to be absorbed by the practical—the logistics of life are all-consuming, and navigating a path through his physical needs was not easy. Converting the bungalow to make it Harry-friendly, managing the medications and appointments, sourcing equipment—it felt like a full-time job.

Everything became about that. About coping. About

adapting. About dealing with the frustrations of how people treated him—the fact that being in a wheelchair rendered him invisible, the way people would talk to me over his head as though he didn't exist.

Now, he is so strong, so independent—but I have to acknowledge that I have rarely seen him as a creature of mystery. As a deep thinker, or as someone who carries around regrets or shame. He's simply never talked to me about that—and I have never asked. I have accepted him at face value, which is perhaps unfair.

"Okay," I add, as Em continues to give me a slightly disappointed look. "It wasn't just good—it was great. Enlightening. And it was odd, hearing him talk like that. It's making me wonder if this whole project is going to be like that for us—if we'll learn more about what we both really think and feel talking to a camera than we have by being married for all these years."

"It's more common than you'd think," replies Em, shutting down the laptop as if to banish Harry from the room. "Sometimes it's cathartic and allows people to revisit things safely."

I manage a nod, but have no idea if it will be that way for me. What I will say, or what I won't say. How I will react.

Ollie walks toward us, lays a hand on Em's shoulder. She leans into it, her cheek briefly touching his skin. It is such a small gesture, but it says so much—this is a couple who are truly in love.

"Right," says Em, grinning at me. "Are you ready for your close-up?"

Chapter 21

We set up in the kitchen, at the big table, lots of natural light coming in from the garden.

There's a large camera set up on a tripod, and there are wires snaking around the floor attached to LED panels for lighting. I have a tiny microphone on my collar, which makes me feel like I'm someone important like Madonna's bodyguard, and another attached to the camera.

I have exiled Olivia to her room, as I know I won't be able to do this with her watching. I might not be able to do this anyway.

"Okay," says Em, sitting on the opposite side of the table to me and nodding reassuringly. "Are you ready to go? You look like you're really excited about this. In the same way I'd be excited about a long weekend at Guantánamo Bay."

I let out a strained laugh. "No. I'm fine, honest."

She nods and begins. It is strange, I think, that I have now watched so many video clips of this exact same scenario—interviewee sitting in camera shot, Em's voice floating in questions from the ether. Now it is my turn, and I feel like a sacrificial lamb.

"So, Elena," begins Em, her voice subtly different, more rhythmic than usual. "Tell us about that night. From your perspective."

"Well," I reply, my eyes darting nervously to hers—even though I was expecting the question, I still feel startled. "I was enjoying myself. We all were, I suppose. It was beautiful. The weather, the village. I was tired but I was fine."

I was tired—it makes me remember. Tired in a manner that I explained away to myself as being because of an action-packed tour, and the stress about ending things with Harry. Tired because, I know now, I was pregnant.

"What did you do, when you got there? Different people did different things, didn't they? Some just had a stroll or a drink. What about you, and Harry?"

"Well, we walked around. We looked at some stalls. I bought a bracelet for Olivia . . . How funny, I've only just remembered that. I never got to give her the bracelet. I lost my bag and the bracelet was in it. I suppose we lost the sombrero as well, but that's not really a loss . . . I'm sorry, I'm rambling, aren't I?"

"Not at all," she replies, her voice soothing and calm. "Take it slow, it's fine. You haven't talked about this night for a long time. You're just rusty."

I take a breath, look at Em, remind myself that I am talking to someone who understands. Someone who lived through it.

"Rusty. Yes. That's exactly it—to be honest I think I've tried to avoid even thinking about it, never mind putting it all into words. Anyway. I liked the people-watching on the trip. The different couples and families and groups, you know? The Aussie girls. That older couple . . . well, I liked that. And the village itself was magical. I love that stuff, though—old buildings, history, culture. Harry not so much. He found it pretty boring, I think."

As I say it, it feels like a small betrayal—but it is true. And at least I didn't mention his obsession with Imodium.

"He went and got us a drink and I went to the church, and then he went off to do some shopping," I continue, replaying scenes in my mind that I've left buried for years now.

"To get a ring for you?"

"Yes, though I didn't know that then. I went to the church on my own first, to look around. There was a lady in there . . . gosh, I wonder what happened to her? It doesn't seem fair, does it, to die inside a church while you're praying? At least I was outside, in the open air. And . . . well, I also didn't die. Obviously."

I peter out, and look Em straight in the eyes. "You can edit this so I don't sound like a complete idiot, can't you?"

"You don't, but yes—don't worry. I have no interest in making you or anyone else look like an idiot. I'm just interested in the truth of what happened that night."

"Don't you think," I say, "that there might be lots of different truths about what happened? Memories distorted by time and distance? I know I'm feeling weird right now, remembering little details that I'd forgotten."

"Like what?" she asks.

"Like the hummingbird. There was a hummingbird. We were sitting by the side of the restaurant, drinking wine, and there was a hummingbird. It was so beautiful, so exotic. Tiny but perfect—I don't think I've ever seen anything quite so pretty. He managed to get some photos of it, but the phone didn't live to tell the tale."

"Who? Harry?"

"Oh! No . . . Alex. I was with Alex. I'd seen him too, in the church. He was always very mysterious, wasn't he, on that trip? The Man in Black. Always so polite, but always on his own. So I saw him in the church and I'd lit a candle for my dad, and I suppose that made me feel a bit melancholy, along with some . . . other stuff, life stuff . . . and maybe I didn't want to be alone. So I asked him to sit with me and have a glass of wine. He almost said no. I could see he almost did—he was turning away, like he wanted to make a run for it.

"But for some reason he didn't. He sat down. He drank the wine. We talked . . . it was easy to talk to him. He told me about Anna, his wife."

For the first time since I've met her, Em actually looks surprised.

"His wife?" she echoes, and I realize that I am unintentionally trampling on Alex's privacy.

"That's his story to tell," I say firmly. "Hopefully you can ask him yourself."

"I will—I've had an email from him, funnily enough, just this afternoon. So weird that we were talking about him yesterday in the café—it's like he heard!"

She takes one look at my face and gestures for Ollie to stop filming.

"I've been emailing various Alex Anderssons for some time now," she continues, "and I finally found the right one. He's going to think about it, whether he's happy to be interviewed or not, and . . . are you all right?"

I realize that I am not all right. That she was right to pause, because I do not want this reaction to be filmed. I realize that I am not prepared for how all of this is affecting me. I haven't done a good enough risk assessment—even hearing her talk about Alex, even the thought of being back in touch with him, triggers so many different emotions. I never thought it was possible for one human being to make me feel so much.

"Is he all right?" I manage to ask, still dealing with the aftershock of Em's small revelation.

"Yes. He asked if you were doing this too . . . Are you? You seem a bit shaky. You knew I was going to try and find him, didn't you? Is that a problem? What's upsetting you so much, and can I help?"

I did know, of course, that she would probably track him down. But knowing it in theory and knowing it's happening are two different things.

It's not just that, though, it's not just the prospect of Alex being involved in my life again, however tangentially—it's everything. Being asked to describe that night. Being asked to feel it and remember it and relive it. Emotions I've buried for so long are coming back, and I'm starting to think I was a fool for even considering this.

I know she will want me to talk about the time I was below ground, the time I spent trapped—and even considering opening up about it, making it real again, is making me panic. I know she will want to talk to me about my time in the hospital, and that will make me think about the baby I lost. About the way I felt when Harry first proposed.

These are difficult subjects, and I am starting to think that I have fooled myself. Told myself I was ready when maybe I am not yet brave enough.

Em is gazing at me from across the table, her expression soft and worried. I think she is concerned for me as well as her footage, and there is no reason she can't be concerned for both. For a moment she looks so young, and I flash back to that teenage version of the woman she is now. To the girl who was screaming beneath a table, her father dying in his attempt to protect her.

She has been more than brave. She has been extraordinary—and this is for her as much as me. If Em can try to face the past, then I can try too.

"I'm fine," I manage, and see a visible sag of relief in her shoulders. "It's just . . . a lot."

Ollie disappears for a diplomatically timed cigarette break in the garden, and Em asks, "When did you last see him, Alex?"

"Years ago, like I said. We used to meet up once a year; it was . . . well, I suppose it was good therapy for us both. Harry used to call him Dr. Alex."

"And why don't you see him now?" she asks gently.

There is no such thing as gentle enough for this particular subject not to hurt, though, so I shake my head and say, "Stuff and things, you know."

"Stuff and things? Brilliant. Obviously a conversation for another day."

"Yes. Maybe. Shall we carry on? I feel a bit better now."

Once Ollie is back and we are filming again, she says, "One of the questions I've asked people is how it affected you—how it changed you?"

"Well, there was the break in my arm," I reply. "Bruising and cuts. This delightful scar."

I point to my forehead as I say it and wonder why I've never grown bangs, or tried to hide it. I intended to, but in the end it felt right to leave it there. To see it every morning. To have that reminder, like Alex once said, that I survived—that I will continue to survive. Battered and scarred, but still here.

"Nothing too serious," I continue, moving on swiftly, worried that Em will spot that I am hiding something about my injuries, about my scars. "Compared to lots of others, it was nothing at all."

"I always tell myself that," Em replies. "But we're allowed our own pain, aren't we? Not everything has to be compared to other people. We do that to belittle it, to make it manageable, to stop ourselves from going down the road of self-pity. But sometimes maybe it's okay to feel sorry for ourselves?"

I nod and find myself smiling. Olivia said something very similar a while back, and I am starting to see the truth in it. We're raised to be positive, to comfort our-selves by saying things like "there are people far worse off than me." Which is odd, isn't it? Taking consolation from the fact that the world is even shittier for others?

"You're right," I answer. "And it was awful. It wasn't just the broken arm, or the physical pain, or the dehydration. The way our lungs were clogged, and I never thought I'd take a relaxed breath again. It was the terror. The terror of being trapped underground, not knowing if I'd ever get out. Being down there for so long, in so much pain, in so much fear. I don't think I'd have made it alone—if he hadn't been there . . ."

"Alex?"

"Yes. Alex. We got each other through it," I say, reluctant to discuss him again, but knowing that this story—my story—is intertwined with his.

"Tell me about that," she says. "About the time underground. I know what it was like up above, but where you were . . . I can't imagine how terrible, how frightening, it must have been to be there for all those hours, not knowing if you were close to rescue or not."

I stare at her and fumble for words. My throat is dry, and even thinking about it is making me feel short of air.

"Can we come back to that?" I say. "Or do it another day, even? I'm sorry . . ."

"There's no need to apologize. And of course we can. I have some TV news footage from the aftermath and some photos, if you want to see them."

I'm not at all sure that I do, but I nod my agreement. I missed most of the live coverage because of being buried, and then I was out of it in the hospital for a while. I've seen some clips—the lights, the digging, the interviews with survivors and rescuers, faces smeared in dirt, hard hats on, clutching plastic water bottles—but none of that night. The night I rose like a supremely battered phoenix from the ashes. The night I became the "poster girl," as Em once described it.

Even thinking about it puts me on edge.

"So, since then," she rolls on, seeing how close I am to panic and moving me on to safer ground. "What did it change for you? Tell me about your life now, and how it was altered."

"Well," I reply, giving it a few minutes' thought, choosing my words carefully. "It definitely changed things. Harry was severely injured, and life got very complicated because of that. We had a lot of medical stuff to deal with: rehab, finding a new home, finding a new way to live. So, yes, it changed a lot."

"But that happened to Harry," she says, "and it had that knock-on effect on your life. But what did it change for you, personally? What did it alter, for good or bad, for you individually?"

I am momentarily stumped by this question. I have spent many years seeing my and Harry's fates as intermingled. Seeing what happened to him as something that also happened to me. Harry and I were together for a long time before that night. We looked to the world at large like a solid couple, like two people who built a life together and would continue to build a life together.

The fact that we got married, have a home, are still a couple, would surprise nobody who knew us before our trip to Mexico. The reality that other people saw was not my reality—that I never expected to still be with Harry. That I was not happy with him. That we grew so far apart that I thought it was the end. That I even told Alex I couldn't imagine my future with Harry in it.

I tap the kitchen table with my nail, and feel jittery and wired and suddenly too hot. I feel like I am treading on a minefield here, tiptoeing my way through potential explosions. Even the safer ground feels treacherous— because there is so much I could say, and so little that I can say.

I cannot say that I was unhappy with Harry already, that I was considering ending things. I cannot say that I applied for a job as a volunteer in a school in Guatemala—a job that I got, I found out, over a month later, in a bittersweet, *Congratulations, you have been successful!* letter that eventually found its way to me.

I cannot say that I wasn't in love with Harry then. I cannot say that because it would hurt him, and he has been hurt enough.

I cannot say that it derailed my entire life, left me broken in ways nobody could see, both gave me a man whom I actually could love and took him away in the same night. I cannot say that I lost a baby, a baby I never even knew existed until it didn't.

I cannot say that hearing Alex's name again has lit a small fire inside me.

There is so much that I cannot say that I am left without words. One night in Santa Maria de Alto, so many possible outcomes, so many ways my life could have changed. It was like my own living version of one of those maze puzzles I did as a child, where each pathway you follow takes you to a different dead end, escape, or perhaps even both.

"I don't think I can do any more today," I say simply, unclipping the collar microphone with shaking hands and walking from the room.

Chapter 22

Em is understanding, for which I'm grateful. They pack up their gear and she gives me a quick hug.

"I know it's hard," she says, pulling away as though embarrassed at her unprofessional show of emotion. "I've only done about half an hour myself because I keep getting angry or sad or both. I've got plenty to be getting on with, and I'm due to speak to Shelley in Australia at some ungodly hour anyway—she's been looking for some more pictures. Even has a whole film on one of those old disposable cameras she needed to get developed. So . . . I'll see you tomorrow?"

Once they've left, I check in with Olivia and tell her we're done for the day. She raises her eyebrows at me. "That didn't take long. Are you okay, sis? Want me to come for a walk with you?"

Her concern makes me smile—she hates going for walks as much as I love them. I fake a smile and tell her that I am indeed okay.

I'm actually feeling scattered, confused. One session with Em has made me realize that I need to find my footing, and to do that I think I need to see Harry. I need to talk to him about some of these feelings, some of this anxiety, some of these doubts.

I call his mobile and Alison answers, explaining that he's on another line.

"Is it urgent? Is it anything I can help with?" she asks.

Alison is a super-impressive woman—ten years or so older than me, and raising twin toddlers as a single mum after her partner abandoned ship. She's always calm and organized and well put together, and I'd quite like to be her when I grow up. But I think this is beyond even her skill set.

"Thank you, no. Can you get him to meet me at the Cooper's Arms as soon as possible, please?"

There is a pause, and I imagine she is checking schedules and assessing meeting lengths and being her usual efficient self. Then she replies, "He should be able to be there in about forty-five minutes? Are you sure I can't help?"

"No, but thanks. Just tell him I need to talk to him."

I put the phone down and rush around grabbing my coat and bag. Once I've done that, I force myself to sit still for a moment, perching on the edge of our bed, and breathe deeply.

There is no need to move so quickly. There is no need to put myself through this hectic dash. There is no need to give in to this strange sense of urgency—yet I can't deny it's there, bubbling inside me. The need to move, to run, to explode with all the emotion my conversation with Em has brought up.

I soothe myself enough to let my heart rate steady to that of someone who isn't actually about to explode, and set off to the pub. As Harry can't make it straightaway, I have time to walk—and I hope the frosty air and traipsing along clifftop ridges will get rid of some of this angsty energy I feel flowing through me. It does help, and I even break out into some little jogs along the way.

The Cooper's is midway between us and the barn where Harry works. It's also one of the easiest places for Harry to patronize, with a big car park with disabled spots right by the door and accessible toilets. Most of the rooms are large, the tables well spaced, and it's not difficult to navigate in a wheelchair. It pays to be prepared in our circumstances—in fact it's become second nature now.

It's perched on the side of a steep hill, the waves crashing into the cove down below, and looks like a picture-perfect version of a Daphne du Maurier novel. I never take views like that for granted but, like anywhere, when it's home you don't always see it through visitors' eyes.

Today, on a late afternoon midweek in autumn, it is quiet. The sea is still beautiful, but it has lost its turquoise shimmer, and the car park is less than half full. One solitary man is sitting out at one of the beer garden tables, smoking a pipe, a chunky black Lab asleep at his feet.

I walk to the bar and order myself a large glass of red wine—delighted at the foresight I displayed by not driving here—and a half pint of some hideous-looking real ale that Harry will probably like. I think perhaps this is one of the occasions when we could both use a prop.

Maybe it was the filming, maybe it was facing up to the reality of Alex being back in my life—but I feel stirred and shaken and need to know if he feels the same. If Harry is feeling as uncertain as I am as we navigate our way through this.

By the time I see him pull into the car park from my window seat, I am halfway through my wine and wondering if I will look like a terrible alcoholic if I immediately order another. I decide I don't really care and wave to the barman.

Harry takes a while to get inside—his car has been adapted for his needs, and is automatic with hand controls, but getting his chair in and out is no simple or quick process.

He waves at me through the window and within a few moments is with me. I see him chat to the manager and say hello to a few people as he passes. He was born and raised in Hertfordshire, but somehow he's become more part of the community locally than I am. Everyone knows him, everyone likes him—the Harry Effect.

"Are you all right?" he says, looking at the wineglass. I don't usually drink much either. "Alison said you sounded upset."

"No, I'm not upset," I reply, exactly as a new glass of wine is delivered to the table.

"I can see that," he comments wryly, raising an eyebrow. "What's this?"

He points at his glass and I say, "I don't know. A half of Badger's Bottom or something."

"Ah. Who doesn't love a Badger's Bottom? Look, what's wrong? You're not yourself. What's happened? Has someone said something to upset you?"

That, I think, is a weird thing to suggest—as though I am a child getting picked on at school. I shake my head. "No. It's just that I thought we should talk. You know, to each other."

"All right . . . I'm still confused. We talk to each other all the time. We're talking to each other right now."

"I mean, about real things. Not what day the recycling is due or whether you need a repeat prescription picking up or what we're going to have for dinner. I mean real things—things like the things Em is asking us about. Because I saw some of your interview today, and it intrigued me. And I did my first interview today, and I . . . well, I freaked out a bit. So. Those things."

"Ah," he says, nodding. "Those kinds of things." He takes a small sip of his beer. "Okay. I can see that it has freaked you out. And maybe you're right—maybe we should have thought this through a bit more carefully. Weighed up the pros and cons. It's bound to bring things up, hit some sore spots. So . . . I don't know . . . maybe we should pull out? Say it's just too much for us?"

I am surprised that he has suggested it, but I don't know why. It is in fact the logical thing to do. To keep the lights dim, keep the corners dark, keep our personal mythology intact. It's the easiest thing to do, for sure.

But I find that I don't want to do any of that—I don't

want to pull out. I don't want to stay hidden. In fact, I think it's time that both of us did some spring cleaning.

"No," I reply firmly. "That's not what I want to do."

"Well, what do you want to do? Just tell me, and I'll do it with you."

The words themselves are supportive, but he sounds slightly exasperated and I can't say that I blame him.

"I want to do it, but I want us to be honest with each other. Talking to Em today, seeing your interview, made me realize that we need to talk properly. That we need to be . . . more truthful with each other."

I see his eyes widen and know that I have touched one of those sore spots he mentioned. To his credit, he pauses, puffs some breath in and out, and seems to think about what I've said.

"Right. Honesty. Truth. Big stuff. Are you sure we're up to it?" he asks.

"I don't know, Harry. But if we get through this, we might be stronger, happier, more together."

"And what do you think we are now? Weak and unhappy?"

"No, I don't—and I didn't mean for you to think that. I don't think either of us is weak or unhappy. But I also think we've both been busily protecting ourselves— protecting each other sometimes—from some of what happened that night, and before, and after. I feel like we both . . . I don't know how to say this, but I feel like we both knew that we had to hide things to survive. The impact of it all, and the way it could have crushed us . . . it didn't. We got through it. And maybe one of the ways we did that was by ignoring other issues, other truths—and we needed to, back then, I think."

"But . . . you don't think we need to now?" he responds.

I smile at him over my second wineglass and feel an unexpected rush of warmth toward him. He still has the Hugh Grant hair and the fearlessness that always appealed to me. He is brave—in many ways braver than me.

"I don't think we need to anymore, Harry, no. And I don't think we need each other anymore either. You certainly don't need me. To start with, you did. But now you're doing brilliantly. You have your work, and you're pretty much independent, and . . . like I said, you don't need me anymore. So, I suppose one of the things this might help us figure out is whether we *want* each other . . ."

He takes another gulp of his beer, seems calm but has a slight flush to his face. I have one moment of fleeting worry—we have to keep an eye on his blood pressure, it's one of the risk factors he faces—but reassure myself that he is simply surprised. I have performed a small ambush here and caught him unawares. I want to apologize, but it has caught me unawares as well.

I am unbalancing our equilibrium, which feels uncomfortable—but necessary.

I lay my hand over his. "I'm not saying anything will change . . . I'm just saying that we're still young. We still have a lot of life left to live together—so let's live it well. Let's see if we can open up to each other before we bare our souls on television for millions of other people to see."

Even as I speak these words and mean these words, I also know that we will need to be careful. We will need to tread cautiously around the sinkholes of honesty and be kind to each other.

Harry is staring over my shoulder. He's thinking, assessing, preparing himself. I wonder if he is preparing to pretend, to say that everything is fine and I am worrying about nothing. Wondering whether a part of me will actually be relieved if he does—because then I can continue to pretend as well.

"Okay," he says finally, turning his eyes back to me. "I can do that. But I don't want some big emotional energy dump, you know? Life isn't black and white; it comes in many shades in between. For both of us, I think, that's especially true. And as for us needing each other—you have always been one of the most self-sufficient people I know, Elena. Maybe it's to do with your childhood, I don't know. But I don't think you've ever actually needed me—so maybe that can be truth number one.

"Even when I was earning the big money and you weren't, you paid your way. When I bought the flashy car, you'd have been happy with a Ford Fiesta. While I was climbing the greasy pole, you were getting on with helping your kids. I've never resented you for it—in fact I've always admired it, and it's one of the things that attracted me to you. You had more depth than me. You were a challenge. Still are, it seems."

He has never said that to me. I find that I quite like it. That it is a view of myself I have never seen.

I lean forward, across the table, and kiss him on the lips. It is heartfelt and goes on for longer than our usually perfunctory pecks normally last. I am on some kind of mad roller coaster right now, unsure of how I feel, unsure of when it will end.

"Well, if that's the effect that honesty is going to have on you, I'm all in favor," he quips, raising his glass in my direction.

His phone buzzes on the table and he glances at it. I see that it is Alison calling, but he just switches it off instead of answering.

"Okay. Well, there is something I need to tell you straight off," he begins. "I have been playing this one over and over in my mind for years now, whether to tell you or not. I've been worried it might come out anyway, and you're right—better for us to sort this stuff out before we get asked about it."

I feel my stomach churn and remember that I haven't eaten at all so far today. Wine, anxiety, and blistering honesty—what could possibly go wrong?

"Go on," I urge, seeing him stall. He has perhaps noticed the sudden drain of color from my face and is worried about my reaction. "It's fine. We'll deal with it, whatever it is."

"Right. Well, it's about the ring."

"The ring?" I echo, glancing down at my fingers. Seeing the plain white-gold wedding band and the silver and topaz of the one from Mexico.

"Yes. That night . . . the night of the earthquake. I was going to buy you a ring like that. I genuinely was planning on asking you to marry me, Elena."

I am confused and frown as I ask, "What do you mean? You did buy me the ring. And you did ask me to marry you . . ."

"I didn't actually buy you that particular ring on that particular night, though," he replies, pointing at it. "It's exactly the type I'd seen you looking at in the stalls, when you bought me that yin-yang bracelet, and it's what I'd planned on getting for you. I knew you'd prefer that to some big flashy thing you'd feel too embarrassed to wear."

He is right, of course, and it reminds me that despite these half-truths of our life together, we do know each other very well, this man and I.

"But on the night, I didn't buy it. I was just walking around and thinking I'd get it on the way back to you for dinner. That maybe I'd ask you that night, or maybe I'd wait until New Year and do something corny with a champagne glass or whatever. That even though you'd normally hate the corny bit with the champagne glass, once you saw it was a ring from Mexico that I'd remembered you liked, you'd forgive me and be overwhelmed with the sense of romance, in a 'he just gets me' kind of way . . ."

He pauses, and we smile at each other. I shake my head and say, "Wow. I am so predictable. And you are so manipulative."

"Thank you," he responds, grinning.

"So. Back to that night. I never did get around to buying the ring. I think I had a pretty good excuse—building collapse, coma, paralysis, et cetera."

"But," I say, "here I am, wearing the ring. Married to you, after an even more corny sick-bed proposal. So what happened?"

"I got one of the nurses to buy it for me. Rosa, you remember?"

"Young, pretty, had a crush on you?"

"Well, that describes half the nurses there, but . . . yeah. Her. I drew a little picture, gave her some cash I got from my dad, and she snuck out to get it. And I've felt pretty crappy about that ever since, but let myself off the hook because the intention was already there. I finessed the truth a little, and I suppose I convinced myself it didn't matter when I'd bought the bloody thing or where.

"What matters is that I didn't ask you to marry me because I was injured—I was going to ask you anyway. It just changed the timescale and the way it happened and . . . well. I don't know why I haven't told you, or why I even said it to start off with. It's not like it wasn't all dramatic enough as it is."

I nod and stare at my wineglass for a few moments, trying to process what he has told me and trying to figure out why it stings. I've always kind of hated the bloody ring anyway. It was a reminder of a night that was quite literally a disaster.

As for why he did it in the first place, that's a more complex issue. Why lie about the ring at all?

I think part of it is as simple as this: Harry is a born showman. He has a flair for the dramatic, he has perfect comic timing, he could in another life have been an entertainer. He knew that producing a ring that had—according to the legend he created—somehow survived in his shorts pocket was a far more enticing version of events than "the ring I meant to buy and didn't and asked someone else to get for me."

Part of it is more complicated, I suspect. I think deep down he knew that I was edging away from him. Doing it the way he did made everything feel bigger, more committed—more escape-proof.

I have such a mix of different feelings flowing through me that I can't quite identify which one is dominant. I am angry and resentful that he lied, and I feel like a fool for believing that pretty fiction. I am frustrated that I spent such a long time feeling guilty about an item of jewelry and what it represented—my ill-formed belief that if he had been at a different place at a different time, then maybe he wouldn't have ended up paralyzed.

Every time I have looked at that damn ring since, there has been a sliver of guilt: If it wasn't for this ring, he might have survived unscathed. If it wasn't for this ring, he could have been safe.

Of course, over the years, as life has settled and both shrunk and expanded, the guilt has also been mixed in with other ifs. If it wasn't for this ring, Harry might not have been injured, and I might not have felt obliged to marry him. If not for this ring, both our lives might look entirely different.

All of these thoughts are swirling through my mind, and I don't feel quite capable of expressing any of them. I asked for honesty, and I don't want to react by lashing out, by being cruel. I need to let it sit awhile, let the layers and the implications unfold. I need to not cry.

"Do you believe me?" he asks, drawing me back into reality. To a pub, where I sit across a table from my husband—a man I love, in my own way.

"About what?" I say quietly. "Do I believe you when you tell me you lied? Because yes."

"No . . . do you believe me when I say I was going to ask you anyway. I don't ever want you to think that I only proposed because I was injured. That I proposed for publicity, or for sympathy, or to trap you. I proposed because I wanted to marry you."

Harry is, as I have said, a great showman—but he is not faking this. I nod my head and murmur, "I do believe that, Harry, yes. But the ring . . . part of me always blamed myself, you see. Stupid, I know, but I had this mad idea that if you hadn't gone off to buy that ring, you might have been somewhere else. You might have been safe. You might not be in that chair."

His mouth opens silently, and I see how taken aback he is. This is a new train of thought for him, I can tell.

"Why would you ever think that? Nothing that anybody ever did that night caused anything that happened to them. And certainly not that . . . God, I can't believe you've been carrying that around all this time . . ."

We are holding hands across the table, and it feels intimate, warm. Like we are in a little bubble of our own creation. It is the closest I have felt to Harry for a very long time.

"It probably isn't just that," I say, after taking in a deep breath. He has shared, he has been honest, he has taken a risk—and now I must take some baby steps in that direction as well.

"What do you mean?" he asks gently. "And it's okay. I'll take it on the chin. I'm a big boy now."

He does a biceps pop as he speaks, in an obvious and not especially effective attempt to lighten the mood.

"I think I felt guilty because I wasn't as sure as you."

"About what?"

"About us. In fact, Harry, I was sure that I needed a break . . . you must have noticed. You must have realized, even if we never discussed it. We weren't good at this honesty business even back then, were we?"

"Maybe not," he replies, "but we're doing our best now. And yes, of course I'd noticed. I didn't want to accept it, or take it too seriously, but I had noticed. I suppose, being the arrogant young buck I was back then, I thought that as soon as I popped the question, you'd be happy."

I let out a small laugh at that. "Happy" is about as far removed from the way I felt when he proposed that it is absurd. I don't say that, though—this is about honesty, not being nasty. This is about discovering what happens next with us.

"I'd actually applied for a job," I continue. "Overseas. Teaching in Guatemala. Had this image of myself saving the world, one English lesson at a time . . ."

"And you'd have been great at it. You were always great at it. You've always been such a good person . . . I think that's why I needed you. Not afterward, when I was hurt—I needed you for different reasons then. But before, you . . . I don't know, gave me light when I knew I was dark? You balanced me out. Why did you want to leave, to take a break?"

"Lots of small things, I suppose. I'd been with you since I was so young. You were my first love, my first lover, my first everything. I didn't feel ready for you to be my last. I didn't feel ready for the rest of my life as you saw it. I wasn't sure we fitted together anymore, and I needed to find out. I felt stifled, Harry—and I hated your job, and the people you worked with, and the way it made you. You talk about light and dark, and that's not right . . . neither of us is completely one or the other. But your work was . . . well, I just didn't feel like it was good for you, or something I could live with long term."

He raises his eyebrows and smiles.

"Well, you were right, weren't you? About the job. You were right to hate it, and now it's not an issue. It's one of the blessings of the whole mess—that it made me drag myself away from the dark side. Or pushed me away, I don't know."

"I think a bit of both and, honestly, I'm so glad. I'm so proud of what you've done since. You certainly don't need my light anymore, Harry."

"I'm not so sure about that," he replies, "but thank you. So. We have shared some secrets. We are both still here, both alive and well and maybe a little bit shaken up. I feel hurt that you were considering actually leaving me. I'm sure you're upset about the ring. It's a lot for both of us, and we need time to let it all soak in."

We look into each other's eyes, and I know, with inexplicable but complete certainty, that there is more to come. That this is the beginning; these were the first steps along a road to nowhere or a road to everywhere. We have started the journey, and neither of us knows where it might lead.

I know that I need to talk to him about the baby, maybe about Alex. I know that if we are going to move on in our life together in the future that we need to be open about the past.

"Yes," I say, wiping away tears I hadn't even noticed shedding. "But for now, let's just sit, and talk about nothing, and watch the world go by."

"You were always better at that than me," he answers. "I was always on the move, always keen to be on to the next thing. All those simple pleasures I missed out on, because I was too busy rushing, too busy assessing what was useful for me and what I could skip over. Maybe, Elena, when this is all done . . . maybe we can go away somewhere. You and me. We can sit in the sunshine, and talk about nothing, and watch the world go by. Together."

I am surprised by this offer, and strangely touched. Perhaps I have always been too cynical. Perhaps we are entering a new stage. Perhaps we are evolving.

"I think I'd like that, Harry," I say.

Chapter 23

The next afternoon, I make my second attempt at being interviewed, and I manage to do it all without having a meltdown—which is amazing, considering the fact that I am still reeling from Harry's revelations the day before.

I am glad that he told me, but it will take time to accept. To think about it enough that its sharp edges are worn down, the pain of the deceit eroded.

In some ways it is even helpful, having the filming to do—a distraction. Em helps me through the interview, and we manage to cover my time with Alex beneath ground, and my time with Harry in the hospital above ground. It is not easy, but we do it.

Then we focus on me and my life now—on my work, on why I never went back to teaching, on the paranoias and anxieties I have been left with. Of my discomfort in enclosed spaces, the way I sometimes barely manage to cross a road because I'm constantly checking for traffic. The stash of bottled water and enormous first-aid kit I keep in the boot of my car.

I do not blame Harry for any of this, because it is not his fault—I chose to stay with him when he needed me to, which I cannot regret. But I also chose to keep my life small and protected in the years that followed—years when I could have spread my wings. That wasn't Harry's fault; it was my choice, and possibly entirely based on a reaction to trauma that I should have talked to someone about long before now.

I am relieved to have finished the filming, even though Em warns me we might need more—I feel like now that I have done it once, and done it properly, I can do it again.

Ollie and Olivia have gone out to get celebratory pizza, and Em and I are alone, embarking on stage two of the day's tasks. She has a vast collection of video clips and photos that people have sent to her—of the night itself, of their holidays before the earthquake, of their lives since. She wants to show them to me and to gather ours for her files.

I have assembled ones I think she might be interested in, my hands shaking slightly as I opened the wedding album before she and Ollie arrived.

It was quite the show, our wedding. Harry's dad got his golf course to do the reception at a discount, and my outfit and Harry's were donated by a rental company. We had a band that played for free in return for a mention in the publicity, and the photographer didn't charge us on the basis that he could sell some of the pictures to the media.

The only way we could have made it a more commercial enterprise would have been if we'd had Harry's wheelchair sponsored by Adidas. Years on, I still don't like looking at those pictures. There is a grand canyon of contrasts between the way we look—young, joyous, optimistic—and the way we were feeling inside. At least the way I was feeling inside—which was pretty much dead.

Things have improved vastly since then. I'm not necessarily always joyous, but I am often at least content. It is perhaps less than I expected from life when I was twenty-one, but more than I expected from life on my wedding day.

Right now, though, I am feeling tender. My conversation in the Cooper's Arms with Harry was needed, and in some ways liberating, but also difficult. As we lay in bed together last night, him sleeping like a baby and me staring at the ceiling, I couldn't help thinking about my engagement ring and the lies he told.

I understood why he did it, and it is not unforgivable—but it has unnerved me, given me the strange sensation that even the start of our marriage was based on a falsehood.

I am also going to have to figure out whether to tell Em—there is no real need to expose the lie, but I feel uncomfortable hiding it from her. Uncomfortable with so much at the moment.

Em has shown me some video clips—shaky footage of the village taken from the back of the coach as we arrived, carefree and happy, those little boys running alongside us. There is higher-quality video too, from when the coach was no more, and the village was broken, and none of us was carefree.

Now we are examining the photos that people have

given her to use, including the ones from her mum's camera, which amazingly survived intact.

"It took me ages to look at these," she says as she spreads the pictures out across the kitchen table. "I just couldn't face it. Dad is in practically all of them, frozen in time, lying in the pool on a flamingo-shaped floatie with a cocktail in his hand, grinning like an idiot."

"Not a bad way to be remembered," I reply gently. I knew the loss of my own father and have some understanding of the hole it left.

"No, not at all—he was a bit of an idiot. In a good way."

She sorts the photos out into groups according to who took them, and I spend several minutes just staring. Figuring out the angles, remembering the people and where they were sitting, trying to piece together who might have taken what. Bizarrely, spotting myself and Harry in the background of one, me wearing that stupid pink sombrero. I remember the woman running that stall, the baby in the pram.

"It's so strange, isn't it?" I say, reaching out to touch a picture of the fountain at the center of the plaza. "Seeing these? It all looks so normal. People eating and drinking and chatting. The plaza, the church. And minutes later, everything had changed."

"I know," she replies, her voice small and sad. "Like it was all on pause for just these few photos . . . all of us the way we were. When Harry could still walk, and I still had a dad. When everyone still thought they'd be getting back on the coach and driving away that night."

When I still had a baby growing inside me, I think,

my eyes seeking out the sombrero again. Without even knowing it, I was standing there in that stupid hat, about to lose what might have been my only chance at being a mother.

I have imagined it, over the years, what it would be like if I'd had that baby—a boy or girl who would be around eight now. How different my life would be: a whirl of school runs and laundry and the casual, careworn euphoria I used to see on parents' faces at the school where I worked. The look that said it was such hard work, but so worth it.

Both Em and I are quiet for a few moments, dealing with our personal losses, and I feel a sense of deep comfort being with her. Sitting here in silence, but not alone, knowing she understands what it was like. We have both survived, even though there have probably been moments for both of us where we wonder why.

"How did you meet Ollie?" I ask, after a few moments of looking. I need a break from the photos, and I am also curious as to how they found each other.

"Ah, well, I was in Liverpool," she replies, leaning back in her chair and smiling. "I was filming a piece about the impact culture can have on a city's economy, and he was a freelance cameraman a friend had recommended. So I hired him, and . . . well, I finally found my People with a capital 'P,' I guess."

"Can two of you qualify as a People with a capital 'P'?"

"I think so, in this case. We've been together for three years now—we live together, we work together, we are happiest when we are together. I know it sounds very soppy for a tough girl like myself, but I still do feel soppy about him—he's my soul mate, to use a corny phrase. I feel like I'm home when I'm with him.

"It's not all been smooth sailing. The race thing didn't bother my mum, or his—but it does seem to irritate a certain sector of our society . . . And the amount of times we get eyeballed by the police, or followed by security guards in shops, is astonishing. The way people hold a wee bit tighter to their handbags when they see him."

"Maybe that's because of you," I reply. "You do look very suspicious."

She laughs. "Well, I did single-handedly empty our local Superdrug of black mascara during my teenage shoplifting days. But it's been an eye-opener. I'm sure you've had some experiences around disability in the last few years that you couldn't have imagined before."

She is right. I worked with kids with special needs, so I had some idea—but nothing quite prepares you for the way the world works when a person is seen not only as disabled, but disposable.

"Oh yes," I reply. "Most definitely. All the small freedoms you take for granted, the massive change in the way others treat you. People were always trying to help him."

"That doesn't sound too terrible?"

"No, of course not—and he never minds someone asking if he needs help. He appreciates that. What he doesn't appreciate is people who ignore him when he says no thanks, he's fine. People who assume he is saying no just because he's brave, not because he's actually fine. Occasionally they'd even just grab hold of his chair and start wheeling him somewhere—usually somewhere he didn't want to go. We used to call them the Manic Street Pushers."

She laughs at the Manic Street Pushers. "See, I wouldn't have imagined that happening—or how annoying it could be."

As we talk, I am moving the photos around, silently disappointed at not seeing the one face I have been searching for.

"I do have a few more, if you want to see them. They were taken afterward, though."

She is grinning but also blushing.

"Why are you going red?" I ask, staring at her.

She buries her face in her hands, laughs, and emerges again with full flamingo cheeks.

"Oh no! The curse of the ginger strikes again! I'm sorry . . . I suppose it's because sitting here, being with you, is so good. It feels like such a relief. And I say that as an adult now—but back then, I was a kid. A kid who was damaged and a bit weird anyway and . . ."

"Are these photos from your stalking file?" I say, suddenly realizing why she's so flustered.

"They are! And the fact that I had a stalking file is making me feel like I'm sixteen again and undoing all my adulting skills . . ." She pulls a slimmer file from her seemingly bottomless bag. "I took these after, while we were all in the hospital. Some were of my mum, while she was in her hospital bed. Some were just of the hospital itself—the doctors and nurses, the signs in Spanish, the canteen. I slipped out into the street a few times as well, and took shots of the shops and cafés and that church on the corner?"

I flick through the pictures and realize that even at such a young age, she had an eye for composition. She has captured some amazing faces, fascinating tableaux, and has a whole series of shots taken from the balcony that show the view at every different time of day. I line them up next to each other, and it looks like a time-lapse video that's been printed out.

"These are really good," I murmur, feeling a slight restriction build up in my throat. They are so good that they are making me remember a bit too much. They are making me time travel, revisit feelings, recall sensations. The way the chairs bit into your thighs. The scraping sound they made when you pulled them around. The faint smell of tobacco and car-exhaust fumes and oranges that always hovered in the air.

Most important, Alex. I was so confused back then—drawn to him in a way that felt both comforting and dangerous. I've told myself, over the years, that I've made my choices, and made the right ones. But talking about him, talking about those days, knowing Em might be interviewing him, is reawakening all kinds of feelings. Seeing the balcony creates a tender spot in my chest, as though I have an actual ache. I knew that this process wouldn't be easy—but I didn't expect it to be physically painful.

She is laying more out in front of me, chewing her

lip so hard her mouth is all twisted to one side. I can tell from her reaction that these are the money shots. I steel myself in preparation, knowing that if she is tense about how I am going to respond, I probably should be as well.

There are lots of pictures of me, which is a little creepy but also compelling. Me in the canteen, sitting alone and staring into space. Me with Harry, sitting by his bedside, sneakily taken from outside the room. Me with his dad, again in the canteen—during a conversation I don't remember, but body language I do. Him, trying to appear strong. Me, trying to appear less than devastated.

Then come the ones I know are coming—of Alex. An early one, him in his tequila T-shirt. Later, one of him actually waving at her from his bed, and another of him waving to her in the canteen, his hand a blur of movement.

"He was always better at spotting me than you," Em says. "He had some kind of sixth sense, that man."

She lays out the last few photos, and we are both silent. We are together in all the pictures, and I blink rapidly as I take them in.

Me and Alex, in one of the hospital lounges. He's obviously just said something that's made me laugh, and I am in the process of thumping him on the arm. One of us in the canteen, where we seem to be playing rock, paper, scissors—or rock, scissors, bag, as I remember him telling me it was in Sweden.

Another is of us sitting outside the hospital on a small

wall, both holding paper cones full of churros we bought from the food truck on the corner. I get an odd tingling in my taste buds—after all this time I still don't think I've ever eaten anything quite as good as the things we bought from that truck.

I don't know why seeing pictures of him affects me so much. It's not as though I have ever forgotten him: the blue of his eyes, his smile, every thick strand of blond hair. He isn't just a memory—he is part of me. And yet it does affect me—looking at him, at me, at us together in a way I've never seen before, is like a punch to the gut.

I glance at Em. "You were good at stalking us. I . . . I think maybe I'd tried to forget how much time we'd spent together."

"You were always laughing," she says. "Or comforting each other when you were sad. I followed you around, and every time you were with Harry, or his mum and dad, you were lovely and kind and exactly as you should be. But then when you were back with Alex . . . I don't know. It's like you allowed yourself to unravel. To breathe again. There is one more picture—but I warn you, it's a bit of a heartbreaker."

"That's all right," I answer. "I think I'm beyond heartbreak, Em."

She smiles and places the last shot down on the kitchen table.

It has been taken from behind us, as we sit on the hospital balcony. We are in our usual position, just before sunset, ready to watch the theatrics. My good arm is dangling loosely between us, our fingers casually interlaced, both my feet and one of his propped up on a small table.

We are cast in shadow, the backs of our heads leaning toward each other, the orange glow of the sinking sun giving the whole scene an eerie sense of unreal beauty.

I reach out and touch the picture, as though I can somehow reach through time, right back to that moment.

And I wonder now—would I do anything differently?

I jerk myself back to the present, almost confused by it, I was so lost in that moment. Ollie and Olivia are back, and they are loud.

"You okay?" murmurs Em, reaching out to touch my hand. The hand that is still holding that photo.

"Yes, I feel fine," I reply, smiling and putting it down on the table.

I am lying. I don't feel fine. I don't feel much of anything at all, and I recognize an old and unloved friend: the Elena who simply closes down and goes numb when too much is asked of her.

It started when my dad died—when things felt too much with Mum, with school, with worrying that she might die too. It happened after Alex left the hospital, and I didn't have him to talk to, to share with, to both lean on and to support. It is happening now—the emotional version of curling up in a fetal ball.

I scurry around, getting plates, preparing drinks, listening to the banter around me. I smile at the right places, and laugh at Ollie's jokes, and manage to hopefully fool them all—for I am nothing if not a master of disguise.

"Guess who we saw in the village?" says Olivia, mid-chew.

"Lord Lucan," I reply. "And don't talk with your mouth full."

"Lord Lucan?" she says, after pointedly swallowing. "Who's he? We saw Harry, and Alison."

She says this in a vaguely scandalized way, as if she's found some hidden lascivious meaning to getting a pizza.

"Oh no!" I answer, clutching my hands to my chest. "He wasn't getting garlic bread as well, was he? The cad!"

Em hides a snigger; Ollie doesn't even try. Olivia sticks her tongue out at me. It's all very civilized.

She reaches out for a can of lager. I slap her hand away and am rewarded with another delightful tongue flash.

"I'm seventeen," she says. "Not seven. I have had a drink before, you know."

"I'm aware. But anyone who sticks their tongue out this many times an hour is not mature enough to have access to alcohol. At least not under my roof . . . ha! I always wanted to say that."

She scowls at me, and as ever our jousting bursts a bubble of tension inside me. She grounds me, Olivia—reminds me that the real world can't be bad if she is in it. Reminds me that being numb means I miss out on the good stuff as well as the bad. Allows me to drift for a while, knowing I will always come back.

I half listen as Em asks her about her A levels and what she wants to do next. I smile as Olivia tells her she plans to become Cornwall's leading female private eye. She announces, very loudly for Ollie's benefit, that she intends to be both "feisty" and "kick-ass" while she does it.

They are happy and relaxed, and all is well. Their chatter means that I can escape. That I can be with them, but not. That I can be present, but absent.

I am sitting at my kitchen table surrounded by people—but part of me is still on that balcony. Still watching that sunset. Still wondering how it would feel to hold his hand again.

Chapter 24

The next day, I go around to Em's cottage to help her with one of her projects. I am still feeling off balance, still feeling confused, but have tried to at least behave normally. It is only, I tell myself, a reaction to everything that is being dredged up. I am only human, and it is to be expected that facing a past I closed down with such brutal efficiency would have some emotional repercussions.

Harry and I have been getting on well, and we have agreed to continue to talk in the open and honest way we did when he told me about the ring. I, of course, have things I need to tell him as well—and I know I should be concentrating on that, on us, our marriage, rather than allowing myself to think about Alex.

I know it, but I am not quite there yet—I will have to settle for being a work in progress. At least I can be of use to Em, I think, for which I am grateful.

She is drawing up a map of Santa Maria de Alto, along with details of who was sitting where when the tremor first struck.

The idea, she says, is to work with a graphics animation expert on it, who will bring it to life as a virtual representation of how it all played out.

"At the moment," she says, pointing at the screen, "everyone is just a colored blob, like something from the seventies. But once it's done, it'll look really cool—there'll be avatars, and a timer that shows a countdown, and . . . well. It'll be better than this."

I am sitting with her at the dining table of the cottage she and Ollie are renting. The place is twee, decorated with chintzy floral curtains and sofa coverings, dotted with ornaments made from seashells. Every wall features a framed watercolor print of a local beach or harbor. It is a typical holiday rental—but it has been Emmed. And maybe Ollied.

There are several laptops, one of which has a screen almost as large as our TV, and wires everywhere. There are extension cables and charger plugs and USB sticks, stacks of papers and files, as well as one entire side of the large living room filled with camera and lighting gear.

There is also a battered and obviously well-loved acoustic guitar covered in rainbow stickers leaning against the sofa, several empty Jack Daniel's bottles, and the fuzzy, faded smell of a burned-out incense stick. I feel like I'm trapped between some technological future world and a backstage party at a Led Zeppelin concert.

She has the big screen up and running, and is showing me the map, pointing out various locations in a very rational and dispassionate way. At first I am surprised, wondering how she is managing to stay so calm while she points out where we were and where the "Frazer party" sat—as though they had nothing to do with her.

I soon realize, when I take a sideways glance at her face, cast in the glow of the screen, that she is barely holding it together. Her voice may sound devoid of emotion, but her fraught eyes tell a different story.

I reach out and place my hand over hers, squeezing her fingers lightly.

"Don't be nice to me," she says firmly. "Don't be nice to me or I'll crack. I need to stay professional. There is a time and a place for my inevitable meltdown, and this isn't it. So please . . . don't be nice to me."

"Okay," I reply, giving her hand one last squeeze. "You're a complete bitch and I hate you. You cow."

"That's better," she replies, forcing a smile. "Now, see how we've got you and Alex sitting there in this version? Well, we'll also have other versions that show you at earlier stages during the night—you and Harry getting off the coach, going to the stalls, the church. Not just you, obviously, but as many people as we can. I've still got people to talk to. Including Alex."

I nod and stay silent. She knows that I am reluctant to discuss him, and I am—but I am also bursting with curiosity.

"He was doing some charity work," she adds. "For a kind of Habitat for Humanity setup. Designing and building homes."

"Yes," I reply. "I knew he was considering something like that. But we've not spoken for years."

She glances away from the screen and fixes her slightly intimidating look on me.

"Why is that?" she asks. "Why did you guys lose touch? I understand the fairy-tale bit was all in my head, but . . . I don't know. I always assumed you'd be friends."

"You sound weirdly sad about it, Em."

"I know I do! I actually feel a bit like a teenager whose parents have split up, I'd built such a rich fantasy life around you. With hindsight, it was a distraction for me. From losing my dad, from feeling guilty about it all, from the fact that even though I knew my mum and my brother were suffering too, I couldn't help them because I was so messed up myself. Compared to all that, following you and Alex around was light relief."

"Well, in those circumstances, I can see that it would be. I'm glad we helped in some way, even if we didn't know it."

She laughs and turns back to her map.

"I think it'll work," she says. "We'll intercut it with footage of Santa Maria de Alto as it is now."

"And how is it now? You said there was a new church?"

"Yeah, and some houses, the plaza. Not everyone wanted to go back—I think, you know . . . the ones who lost too much."

I do know. She means the children. Three of the village youngsters were killed during the earthquake, and these are images I am unable to revisit easily: those kids, chasing alongside the coach when we arrived, running off to play football, helping their parents prepare the meal. The desperate yell of parents calling out names, the plaintive cries for mama. That crumpled stroller. The boy I saw stumble and fall.

"It took ages, apparently, because there just wasn't much money to rebuild with. Plus it needed to be designed in a way that was more earthquake-proof, just in case. They're still not finished. Guess who's been helping them rebuild?"

"How can I?"

"Alex. I know you're very carefully not asking, but he's there, of all places. He helped design the church."

She has dropped this into the conversation as though it is something casual, not a time bomb. I can tell from her sideways glance that she is wondering how I am going to react. Apart from a slight flare of my nostrils there is probably not a lot to see. On the outside at least.

Inside, I feel like a bundle of threads unraveling. All of this feels so strange. Finding out about Harry and the ring. Now finding out that Alex is still there, that our lives are still connected in such an odd way.

"Is he doing it?" I ask eventually. "The documentary? Has he agreed to take part?"

"He has. It's actually brilliant from my perspective— we can meet him there, film in the village, do the interviews in the place where it happened."

"Did you say 'we'? I'm assuming you mean you and Ollie . . ."

Em turns to look directly at me, her hands on her knees, chewing her lip.

"No. I mean as many of us as possible. You don't have to do it—nobody does. Goodness knows I understand why you wouldn't want to. I'm not entirely sure I want to. But I have an instinct that it's the right thing to do . . . not just because it'll be brilliant for the program, but because it's a way of finding . . . this is terrible, I really want to say 'closure,' but that feels too glib, you know? So not closure maybe—but a way of drawing a line. A way of saying goodbye, maybe."

"I know you mentioned it when we first met, going back. But I . . . I didn't think you meant me. I'm not sure I can. I'm not sure I'm ready to see it again . . ."

It's true that the thought of seeing the village again is difficult—but the thought of seeing the village with Alex in it is somehow even harder. Imagining him there, sitting in the plaza he helped build, by a church he designed . . . back in that place where we first met and our lives changed forever. How would that make me feel?

I don't have a time machine, and the Alex and Elena who exist now are not the same as the Alex and Elena who talked about love and loss as a hummingbird hovered behind us. We are not the same Alex and Elena as we were before we went into that hole.

We're probably not even the same Alex and Elena as we were the last time we saw each other—a time that still hurts to think about.

Seeing him again might be astonishing. It might be awful. But it definitely won't be easy.

"I know, and like I said, I do understand. You don't have to decide now. I have more work to do. A few more days here, some editing, more work on the Australian side of things. Some interviews to do in Spain. It'll be months away at least. I hope you'll come—and I say that purely as a friend, not a filmmaker. I . . . well, it would be good to have you there."

She looks, and sounds, fragile. I notice the dark marks beneath her eyes that I've attributed to late nights working. The slight tremor in her voice.

"Don't take this as me being nice to you, but are you okay, Em?"

She sighs and rubs her hands over her face, across the downy buzz cut of shaved red hair.

"No. Not really. I should already have been to Santa Maria again, and there's no way I can make this program without it. But I've been stalling. Part of me wishes I hadn't even started this, because it's much harder than I thought it would be. I keep bursting into tears at inappropriate times, and getting snappy for no reason, and basically just being a bit of an arsehole. Ollie has the patience of a saint."

I stay silent for a moment, then say, "You're doing brilliantly, Em. This is such a brave thing you're doing, and I think your dad would be so proud—you're speaking for him as well as for the rest of us. But . . . I understand. Part of me wishes I'd never started this too, if I'm honest. But I also feel like I need to do it. Like I won't ever be right with it if I don't. Like it'll make me stronger, in the end."

"Yes. That's exactly it. If it doesn't kill us first, eh? Anyway. I'd love you to come. And Harry, if he wants to. I know it'd be emotional, but it'd also be . . ."

"Good television?"

"I was going to say cathartic, but yeah, I'd be lying if I said I hadn't also considered the visuals . . . What can I say? I'm a media whore at heart."

I smile, knowing that both things are true. It could be cathartic. It would also be tremendous viewing.

"I'll think about it, Em. I hadn't ever considered going back. You know what I'm like. I haven't been abroad since . . . well, not for a few years. And I check online for earthquake activity literally every day. I'm not sure I even could go back, at least not while I was conscious."

Of course, what I don't mention is that it's not only the logistics that scare me—it is the thought of seeing Alex again. I can't imagine a world where I am back in that village, with Harry, with Alex.

"I'd happily drug you."

"That's a very kind offer, but . . . I don't know. I won't rule it out, but I need time for the idea to percolate, okay? I'll talk to Harry about it too. It'll be more complicated for him with the travel, but he could definitely do it with a bit of planning. You know Harry—he'd be wheeling around the plaza, posing for the camera, presenting his ruggedly handsome profile for the world to admire . . ."

"I bet he would. He's a massive show-off, in a good way. I need to talk to him anyway—I don't know exactly what he did after he left you at the restaurant table. Some of the timings don't match up. We know he went to one of the stalls, and we know where he was . . . found. Afterward. But what I can't figure out is what else he did, or how he got there."

"And you need to know where to put his blob?"

"Exactly. A nice shade of blue for him, I think."

I realize, as she chats on, that I need to make a decision about whether I tell her—tell her that he didn't buy the ring that night, from one of those stalls. I would be happy to leave it, to leave the pretense where it is now that I know the truth, and he has said that it is up to me—he will accept it either way.

But I feel bad hiding things from Em, lying by omission. We are becoming close, we are becoming friends, and I hate the thought of her feeling betrayed.

"He didn't go to the stall," I say abruptly, interrupting her as she talks about her positioning of the couple from Manchester, whom we have nicknamed the Fight-a-Lots. "He didn't buy the ring."

"What?" she says, frowning in confusion. "Of course he did. He bought you the ring that night and proposed when he was out of his coma. He even did it on television!"

"He did. And here I am, married to him and wearing his ring. But, actually, Em, I recently discovered—like, two days ago—that there was a slight massaging of the truth going on."

"A massage with a happy ending?"

"I suppose. He actually got one of the nurses to buy it for me, one just like the rings at the stall, but . . . but he says he was planning on asking me anyway, and I believe him."

Em is narrowing her eyes, staring at a particularly

garish pastel watercolor behind me and obviously weighing things up.

"Okay. You definitely believe him? You don't feel like there's any way he said that because of what happened . . ."

"You mean to try and trap me into marriage because he was injured and thought he'd better bag a wife while he could?"

She shrugs, refusing to be embarrassed. "Yes. That's exactly what I mean. Because that would be . . . bad."

"It would be," I reply. "But honestly? I don't think that's the case. I do believe him. I think he always had it in mind, always planned it . . . it was the next logical step as far as he was concerned."

"And you? Was it the next logical step for you?"

That, of course, is a big question. The simple answer is no—it was not the next logical step for me. Harry knows this; I have told him that I was planning to leave, to travel, but I am not willing to humiliate him like that by discussing it with anybody else. I just shrug.

"But why lie?" she says. "Why claim he bought it there, that night? What if someone like the nurse said otherwise? What if he was found out? Why would he take that kind of risk?"

"Harry always takes risks," I explain. "It's part of who he is. He works on the assumption that life is on his side, despite much evidence to the contrary. As to why . . . I think he felt vulnerable. And that was an entirely new feeling for him, and it led to him making a poor decision.

He was taking a risk asking me to marry him, and I suppose he wanted to do everything he could to stack the odds in his favor. I'm . . . I'm okay with it, Em. We've all made mistakes, haven't we? We've all made bad decisions. I didn't want to hide it from you, but I also don't want to embarrass him by including this in the program, if there's any way you can avoid it."

I realize as I say it that I am protecting Harry again—that I cannot quite shake the belief that he needs protecting. That whatever our faults as a couple, I do not want to willfully hurt him.

She pauses, and I see her professional brain kick in. The conflict between the urge to tell the truth and her loyalty to us. To me.

"I'll think about it," she replies. "And thank you for telling me. I'll have to be a bit more imaginative with the blue Harry blob . . . maybe he can tell me some of the places he did wander off to, then."

"Thank you—and we'll understand, whatever you decide. As for what he did that night, I don't think you'll have much luck. He says he basically doesn't remember anything. He says his mind is a blank from leaving me at the restaurant. Apparently a traumatic spinal injury and a coma aren't very good for the memory banks."

"Shelley said pretty much the same," Em says. "She was in a coma for longer than Harry, and it was a long road to recovery for her. She didn't have the spinal injury, but she basically had to relearn how to talk, walk, everything. She spent years living back with her parents, and even now that she's moved out, it sounds like she's a bit of a hermit. No chance at all of getting her back to the village.

"As for that night, she has no memory of any of it, even getting off the coach . . ."

"Wow," I say. "Poor Shelley. Did she get her photos developed?"

"Not sure. I don't want to push too hard. She's had that camera for years—it's a miracle it survived—but she's been too . . . I dunno, too scared to look at the pics?"

"Well, yes. I can imagine. Because not remembering that night is . . . well, it's not necessarily a bad thing, is it? Maybe it's better for her not to. Maybe her mind is trying to protect her by not remembering. Maybe seeing the photos might open up parts of her memory that she doesn't want to face."

"Exactly. I don't blame her at all. But a bit like us, she feels like now is the time to face them . . . Her whole life has been derailed. She was planning on becoming a lawyer, and now she's unemployed. She had a boyfriend and wanted kids, and now she goes weeks on end without seeing another human being. She's alive, but she's not doing much living—and we're not the only ones using this project as a form of therapy.

"I don't know, Elena. I just hope I don't end up feeling responsible for pushing her over the edge. I couldn't cope with that. Sometimes, doing this job, you push . . . you have to. It's part of it. But if I push Shelley too hard and that damages her, I'll never forgive myself, you know?"

I nod. I do know. This is a tough road for all of us, and for Shelley it didn't only leave her severely injured, it effectively took the lives of three of her friends.

Em sighs and closes down the laptop screen.

She rubs her cheeks as though she is scrubbing them. She looks so tired. Drained and exhausted and ten years older.

I realize that all of this is taking its toll on her. I'm reliving my own nightmares, but she's reliving everyone's. She is carrying my story, and Shelley's, and Harry's, and her own family's. She is retelling a night that took the life of her own father and left her traumatized.

I am carrying a part of that night's tragedy—she is carrying the whole.

"Okay," I say, breaking the silence. "I'll come."

She is momentarily confused and looks at me with raised eyebrows, waiting for me to continue.

"I'll come with you," I add. "I'll go back to Santa Maria de Alto. We'll do it together, Em."

As soon as I make this promise, my head swirls. I will go back. Back to that place, to that moment. The moment we met.

Chapter 25

When I mention the potential trip to Mexico, Harry is not overly impressed.

I'm not sure how I expected him to react, to be honest—that night, that place, was traumatic for all of us, and I'm not even sure how confident I am about returning there myself. Will it be, like Em thinks, cathartic? Liberating? Or will it simply open up old wounds, dig beneath layers of emotional rubble and leave us even more exposed?

I don't have the answers, but I know I want to ask the questions—I have an instinct, a feeling deep in my gut, that this is right. That I need to do this, even if it's not easy to do.

Harry, it seems, does not. I don't know if I am disappointed or relieved, and allow that I might be both—this is not a simple situation.

"I'm not sure, Elena," he says as he gets ready to head in to work, staring at his reflection in the mirror as he gets his hair just so. Some things, of course, never change.

"About what?" I ask, from my cozy spot beneath the duvet. I love working from home. "The program, or me going to Santa Maria, or you going there? Or about your hair?"

"My hair," he says, patting it lovingly, "is as perfect as ever. Look, let me think about it, okay? My first reaction is 'no bloody way,' but that might not be my second reaction. I don't know if it's the logistics putting me off, or if I just feel . . . worried. Worried about seeing it again. Worried about how I'll react."

"Worried there'll be another earthquake?"

He hoists himself onto the bed next to me and kisses me quickly.

"That's more your thing, Elena," he says, smiling. He is, of course, right. He knows I like to keep a close eye on the devilish ways of the tectonic plates.

"Leave it with me," he adds. "I've got a busy day, and I might be working late again, but let me give it some thought. It's not a no—it's a possibly. Will it just be us, or is Em planning on assembling all the Avengers?"

"If she can. Some have already committed. Alex has said yes."

He nods and smiles at me, and I wonder if that is part of his reluctance.

Harry never seemed possessive about me when it came to Alex. Just before I set off to London that first time to have lunch with him, I was nervous—perhaps I was looking for an excuse to cancel, to be a coward. But when I asked again, Harry just replied, "Go. I don't mind. I'm not the jealous type, and I trust you. Anyway, it'd be like being jealous of the air you need to breathe—I know it's good for you to see him, I know you need that, and you spend way too much time thinking about what I need already."

Now, though, I wonder if it was ever that simple.

"Is that the problem?" I ask. "Alex?"

"No. Should it be?"

"Not at all . . . you know I haven't seen him for years."

"Yes, and I've always wondered why, Elena. Why you stopped meeting up with him. Why it all ended. You've never told me—is that one of those things I'll have to watch a documentary to find out?"

I feel both offended and threatened, and scrunch the duvet closer around me. I don't want to talk about this. I don't want to revisit this, or even allow myself to remember. It hurts too much.

"Harry, those trips . . . those times I met him . . . I never cheated on you. I'm your wife. I'd never do anything like that."

He reaches out and strokes my face, smiling but somehow looking sad.

"I know," he says. "You're too decent a person to do anything like that. Too good. It's hard to compete with sometimes. I've always felt like I don't really deserve you . . ." He sees my expression, squeezes my hand. "Don't look so worried. It'll all be fine. I'm just being odd—I've been thinking a lot, and as you know that doesn't come naturally . . . plus I didn't sleep well. I blame Olivia. I think she sneaks in at night and whispers 'you're a wanker, Harry' in her Hagrid voice . . ."

That is, in fact, entirely possible. She's been misquoting Hagrid at him for years now.

I nod and watch as he gets himself into his chair and leaves. I hear the sound of his car doors, the rev of his engine, and lie back onto my pillow. This room, like all the other communal areas, is free of both clutter and character. Clean, white, almost like a hotel room. A hotel room I never get to check out of.

I feel the familiar tug of the black dog descending and know that I need to get up, get moving, outrun it before it has a chance to drag me down into the undergrowth. I am more frayed than I thought I was.

I feel raw and jagged, too exposed. When I am this down, this vulnerable, I feel like I need the equivalent of an emotional children's play space. A nice, safe ball pit to sit in.

I am still underneath the covers when Olivia comes into the room.

"Sis?" she says, poking me. I remain silent, and she pokes me again. "I know you're there, Elena."

"No, I'm not."

"Yes, you are. I can see your toes sticking out. You're wearing those fluffy bedsocks with the pink stars on them."

"No, that's not me. Go away."

"I can't go away. It's not in my nature to be told what to do. Are you taking me to college? I heard His Princessship leave a few minutes ago."

I reluctantly sit up, and feel slightly better when I see

that she has at least brought me a coffee. It sits wafting steam on my bedside table in a mug she bought me, one that has a picture of Russell Crowe in his *Gladiator* outfit on the side and the quote "I will have my caffeine, in this life or the next."

"Are you all right?" she asks, staring at my face as though searching for visible cracks. "You look like shit."

"Wow. Thank you. I'm just tired. Em asked me to go to Mexico with her."

She raises her eyebrows. "Okay. Is that what's freaking you out? Are you scared in case you get caught up in another natural disaster? Or in case you develop a tropical disease? Or in case you die of a rare form of hypochondria?"

"You can't die of hypochondria!"

"Yes, you can," she bites back. "I read about this girl once, on the internet, so it must be true. She was googling what it meant if you have dandruff in your eyebrows, and she died. She thought it might be a symptom of a rare brain tumor."

"Eyebrow dandruff?"

"Yeah. Exactly the kind of thing that goes on in your crazy brain."

"Maybe. But I still don't see how that killed her. Was it actually a sign of a rare brain tumor?"

I scratch my eyebrows as I say this and am relieved to see they are flake free.

"No. Don't be stupid. She was so busy googling it she walked in front of a bus. So, you see, you can die of hypochondria . . ."

I shake my head, and drink my coffee, and let her

continue to babble on. She can happily talk for hours; it's just a matter of appearing as though you're listening and nodding in the right places.

"And then," she says, obviously coming to the end of an anecdote, usually my cue to look interested, "I realized that the world really does seem like a better place when you're on heroin!"

"What?" I blurt out, realizing a moment too late that I have been played. She laughs and points at me.

"Ha! Your face! I can tell when you're not paying attention, you know. Anyway. I'm only in class for the morning; I've got study periods after that."

"Right. Doesn't that mean you should go to the library or something?"

"Nobody goes to the library anymore, Grandma. It means I'm coming home to eat cake and watch YouTube videos and plot world domination. Or—get this—I was thinking about emptying Harry's hair gel out of the bottle and filling it with Veet instead. What do you reckon?"

"Leave Harry's hair gel alone. I can't promise to protect you if you make his hair fall out. He'll kill you."

"He'd have to catch me first . . . Anyway. Can you pick me up? At about one? I wouldn't ask, but I'm too lazy to walk and the bus is full of common people."

I shake my head and puff out a breath of exhaustion. She is on a roll, and it is exactly the kick-start I needed. She has swept me along with her, infused me with some of her energy.

"I'll let you know later," I reply.

"Fair enough. See you by the door in a minute then."

Once I'm dressed and have grabbed a banana from the fruit bowl and checked that all the plugs and taps are switched off, I drive the scenic route to Olivia's college and wave her off.

Harry's comments have unsettled me, and I am not sure why. All I know is that our relationship has been the dominating force in my life, and now I feel like we are both examining it a lot more closely. We could emerge from all of this much stronger—or we could emerge from all of this apart. Both options seem wrong for different reasons.

Am I in love with Harry? Probably not, in a teenage-girl way. Do I love Harry? Yes, I do. I love him and admire him and I have made a commitment to him. We have a good life together, and that is surely worth fighting for.

But, I think, as I drive aimlessly along the coastline, there is also Alex. How do I feel about him, now, all these years later? Do I still feel a flutter in my tummy when I think about him? Do I still yearn to hear the sound of his voice? Do I still watch sunsets and think about him?

If I'm honest with myself, I do. I've tried to deny it, but I do.

I feel so confused I am almost distraught as I navigate winter-quiet roads and out-of-season ghost towns. A few hardy souls are out on surfboards in wetsuits despite the low temperatures, boats bobbing farther afield. In some ways it's one of the nicest times of year, when you can have a beach to yourself and the sea can go from angry to mellow in the space of minutes.

There is a sense of freedom you get from being on the edge of the world. A sense of space; a feeling that the planet is huge, the horizons infinite. Since the earthquake, I've appreciated the infinite horizons even more.

I consider parking and going down to the beach to borrow someone's dog to play with. I am a well-known dog botherer in the local area. Harry's not keen, so we've never had one of our own. I thought about becoming a dog walker a few years ago—frankly I'd do it for free. But the one time I mentioned it in passing, Harry had a very rare outburst of petulance.

"Right," he said, his mouth twisted into a bitter version of a smile. "So then you'd have one more way of getting away from me?"

I was shocked, and upset that I hurt him, and also had to concede that possibly he had a point. Subconsciously, perhaps that was part of it—an urge to be free, to be alone. It's not a noble urge, but it is there. Harry can do many things now, but the beach is always an issue—not exactly wheel friendly, and with uneven and unpredictable terrain that makes it unpleasant for him to try to use his leg braces on.

I reassured him that wasn't the case, knowing that neither of us was entirely convinced.

I wonder how that must have felt for him—that sense of being excluded—and it brings tears to my eyes. For him. For me. For Alex. For everything that has happened to us. For all that has been, and all that could have been. For the big pains and the small, the thousand tiny paper cuts to the heart that we all seem to have suffered.

My phone rings just as I have turned off the engine in a small car park by Barrelstock Bay. I glance at it on the seat next to me, see Em's name on the display, and answer it.

"Are you busy?" she asks.

"Not really. Just sitting on the dock of the bay. That kind of thing."

"You're not going to start whistling on the phone, are you?"

"I make no promises. What's up? I thought you were editing today?"

"I was. I am. I will be," she says, covering all the bases. "I was just phoning to see how you were. And to tell you Shelley sent the photos, and you are in the background of some of them. And to see what Harry thought about coming to Mexico."

"He . . . he wasn't sure it was a good idea. Maybe he's right. I don't feel sure about anything anymore."

There is a pause, and she asks, "Are you all right, Elena? You sound upset."

"I am, Em. I'm upset about so many things I can't even say what they are. They refuse to form an orderly queue. And I'm . . . I don't know. Sad? Just really sad."

"Come over," she says instantly. "I have scones. I have

coffee. I have time. Don't feel sad on your own—come to the cottage and do it in company."

It feels good, having Em in my life. Having someone who understands. Someone who wants to help. And I am doing a terrible job of sorting myself out—maybe talking to her will help.

"I will," I say eventually. "And thank you."

Chapter 26

Em has greeted me with coffee and cake, Ollie shooed out of the house to do some "atmosphere shots."

I am curled up on her chintzy sofa, and I am starting to relax. Starting to feel the warmth of the log fire, and the warmth of her friendship.

I am, at last, telling her about Alex. I am telling her things I have never discussed with anybody else, and I am hoping that it will lift something from my shoulders—guilt, indecision, cowardice, false hope. Maybe all of the above.

"It was seven years ago, the first time we met up," I say. "In London. Carnaby Street, near Christmas."

"Very nice," she says from the armchair opposite me.

"It was. All bright and trendy, but with character as well . . . he chose it. It was a dull day, cold, but when I got there he was sitting outside the café. I knew he would be. For a while I just hid around a corner, peeking out at him, trying to decide whether to turn around and get back on the train."

"Why?" she asks, frowning. "You weren't doing anything wrong."

"I know—and I'd told Harry; it was all fine—but,

well . . . as soon as I saw him I felt nervous, and excited, and I wasn't used to that. I think I'd convinced myself he was just another friend, but seeing him reminded me that he was also very special to me. And that felt big and a bit scary, even scarier than being in such busy crowds. I was going to have to sit there and talk to this man I was close to, about myself and my life and his life, and I wasn't sure I could pull that off.

"In the end, I did. He kept looking at his watch, and seemed sad, and there wasn't any way I could hurt his feelings like that."

I remember it so vividly: the press of people, the designer shops, the bustle. Mainly, of course, him. He had a smart coat on and his hair was longer—brushing his shoulders. I wanted to reach out and touch it, bury my fingers in it.

I walked up behind him, said, "Penny for them?"

"Sorry, I'm not that cheap," he replied, remembering his lines.

We laughed and sat, and as soon as I was in his presence again, I realized that I felt energized. That the world felt lighter, more magical. That the crowds weren't bothering me anymore. That the anxiety I felt about the train journey was worth it.

"And how did it go?" Em asks, seeing me drift away.

"Well. He'd made some changes. Simple stuff, like going through Anna's things and donating them to a thrift shop. Though he did say it took him ages, because he stopped and examined everything and remembered her wearing it. It made him sad, but he did it.

"He'd rented a desk in an office in the city, sharing a space with other people who worked in creative businesses. He'd been to see his father, who he'd lost touch with. Traveled a bit. Told me this hilarious story about signing up for a solo passengers' trip and being the only man and the only person under forty, and being chased around a dining room by an over-friendly fellow traveler. Even went on a few dates. We basically carried on doing what we'd always done—cheering each other up."

"You had been in touch before, though, hadn't you?" says Em. "This wasn't the first time you'd spoken?"

"No, but we mainly emailed. I think that was easier for us both. We could be more measured, more careful. We'd shared photos and stories, and talked about how we were. Recommended books and movies to each other, talked about everything under the sun—apart from stuff that might be too painful, anything that would be too difficult, that would jeopardize us being able to stay in each other's life."

Em nods. "I think I know what you mean. You had to keep it at a certain level or you'd have to give it up. Like an addiction."

"Exactly. And seeing him again, in person, sitting with him, laughing with him . . . it was harder to stay on the right side of that addiction. It was . . . oh, Em, it was a relief! A huge, great, big relief—like I could be myself again. Like I was home. We talked about nothing of importance at all, but it was divine."

She smiles and looks a lot happier herself.

"I always loved you two together," she says. "And I

know, I know—it never really happened. You married Harry. It was a million years ago. But you always had such fun . . . such a spark . . . Was it the same?"

"Well, yes. It was. Even when we were talking about the fact that he'd been asked out by the lifeguard at his pool, and I asked if she looked like someone from *Baywatch*, and he said 'no, he doesn't,' and we just couldn't stop laughing at it even though it was silly. It felt a bit like being high—or how I imagine that would feel anyway."

I told him about the bungalow, and he told me about a new project he was working on, and he tried to persuade me that rain barrels and solar panels were sexy, and I talked about Olivia, and everything we said and everything we did was completely harmless—but at the same time, I felt guilty. Guilty for enjoying myself so much, I think, as much as anything.

"We were only together for a couple of hours," I tell Em, "and it was strange and wonderful and over too soon. Looking back, I think I felt more in those two hours than I had in the last two years. When we were saying our goodbyes, he just . . . he reached out, and touched the scar on my forehead, and that was it. The barest of touches. Nothing naughty. But . . . it made me realize how much he meant to me, how much I'd missed him. How I needed to find a way for us to stay in each other's life, even though I was married and he was starting to get out and about in the dating world.

"I wanted us to stay friends, and so did he. So, for a while, we did. We managed it. We saw each other once a year, usually around the same time."

"So what went wrong?" says Em, leaning forward and looking at me intently. "Why did you lose touch?"

"He asked me to leave Harry."

"Oh my goodness!"

"I know. And the worst thing is, Em, I really wanted to. I never did anything with Alex that a married woman shouldn't do . . . except, if I'm honest, perhaps simply forget that I was married for a few hours.

"It was four years ago, and we'd actually met up in Paris. Harry had a meeting there, with some research doctors at a rehab center, and he promised me he'd be fine on his own for a bit, as the whole place was as wheelchair friendly as it could be. We had a room there, and I went with him and arranged to meet Alex in Paris instead—it didn't make much difference to him, coming to meet me in London or coming to meet me in Paris, and it was the same time we usually met. I don't enjoy journeys, and he knew that.

"Me and Harry went on the Eurostar, because it was easier for Harry, but I was in pieces going through that tunnel. Harry didn't even notice I was bothered, but it was the first thing Alex asked—how was the tunnel?"

We met for dinner in the Marais, a place he knew well. It's one of the city's oldest communities, and it appealed to the architect geek in him—all cobblestone streets and medieval buildings and arches that made me feel like I was wandering through monastic cloisters, even as I looked inside designer boutiques staffed by impossibly chic women.

I describe it for Em, our table outside a restaurant in

the Place des Vosges. How we ate, and drank our coffee, and watched the world go by.

How he told me about the history of the place as we sat beneath a curving stone arch, bathed in golden light on a dark December evening. I felt thrilled, like a child away from home for the first time.

"There was something about that night," I say to Em, "that was different. Maybe it was the wine. Maybe it was Paris. Maybe it was just that Harry was safe, so I wasn't so tense about being away from him. I told myself there was no harm in it, that we'd done it every year, that I wasn't being unfaithful to Harry in any way—in fact Harry encouraged me to have the time to myself.

"I suppose, and this might sound weird, but that night I realized it wasn't about being unfaithful to Harry, it was about being faithful to myself. Even if it was only for a few hours a year. And suddenly, as we were walking around that beautiful place, on that beautiful night, it didn't feel like enough."

We strolled around after dinner, slightly drunk. Happy to be together again. He was wearing a new black leather jacket and a dark cashmere scarf that I gave him the year before, his thick blond hair tucked beneath it. I remember gazing at him when I thought he wasn't looking, noting how bloody gorgeous he was.

"You okay?" he asked, looking slightly concerned.

"Me? Yes? Why?"

"You sighed. Loudly."

"Oh. Right. Well, that'll just be a delayed reaction to the crème brûlée, I think. I like your jacket."

He looked down at himself and shrugged.

"I don't often buy clothes," he said, "but I saw this yesterday in Stockholm and thought I'd dress up for the occasion. Paris, you know—you can't dress down for Paris."

I'd bought a new dress for exactly the same reason. I'd been to Paris before, but only en route to Disneyland when Olivia was younger. I loved Disneyland—but it didn't feel like Paris. That place, that night with him, felt like Paris.

As I tell this story, I see that Em is resting her face in her hands, looking enraptured. I'd never have her down as the romantic type, but I can see a wistful look in her eyes that makes me smile.

"I don't suppose we'd ever really been just friends, Em, beneath the surface of it all," I say. "And that night . . . well, it just all seemed irresistible. I wanted to touch him, and be touched by him, and to see his body un-wrapped from its winter layers. I wanted to kiss him and do all the things I'd never let myself think about. I wanted to fall asleep in his arms and wake up with him in the morning. I wanted it more than anything."

I felt about sixteen again, that night. I was blushing, and everything felt deliciously uncertain, divinely insecure. When he reached out to hold my hand as we walked, I was breathless with attraction and possibility. With the simple not knowing—not knowing what it would be like for this man to make love to me.

Somehow, without either of us saying or doing any-thing, the atmosphere between us changed. We walked back to his hotel, his arm slipping around my shoulders, me allowing myself to loop mine around his waist. It wasn't a lot, but it was enough. Enough for a simple good night to feel less than platonic.

We stopped when we reached the doorway to the hotel, a small unobtrusive sign on a picturesque street. He held my shoulders, turned me to face him. Both of us bathed in starlight.

"Stay with me," he said simply.

I wanted to, so much. Physically, emotionally, with every molecule of my being, I wanted to. I even could have gotten away with it—Harry would accept it if I told him I was tipsy, I was crashing out, I'd be home for breakfast . . . but I couldn't.

"I want to, Alex—you know I do," I said. "But . . . I can't. I just can't do that to Harry. I can't be unfaithful to him, even with you."

"I know," he replied, smiling sadly and kissing the top of my head. "I know you can't. Though every time you leave me, every time you go back to him, it feels like you're being unfaithful to me somehow . . . but I know. I understand. I understand, but I don't have to like it."

I never thought of it that way, but he was right. Whenever I went back to the house I shared with Harry after one of these meetings, I felt out of place. Out of time. Like I was trapped in somebody else's life. I never even thought of how painful it must be for him— imagining me back there, with another man.

He went on dates, but there wasn't anyone special. I

had no idea how I'd feel if there was. How would I feel if he got married? I realized I'd be heartbroken, even though I'd have absolutely no right to feel that way.

He wrapped his arms around me, and for a few minutes we just stood there, on that small street, our bodies close. I remember inhaling the scent of him, letting my fingers graze the skin of his back. He kissed the scar on my forehead, nuzzled my hair. We were so close it reminded me of being together underground, battered and bruised and trapped. A time that was terrible, but gave us each other.

I wanted nothing more than to walk into the hotel room with him. To be with him, to fall asleep and dream of sunsets, and the close of days, and the moments that change everything. Those precious moments that define all the ones that come after.

"I've been offered a new job," he said, when we pulled apart. "For a charity. Working in communities in Africa, Asia, South America. Looking at ways to develop and build homes for local people that they can afford to live in. Working with those people to actually build them. It's hands on. I'll be designing, but I'll also be wearing a hard hat."

"That sounds wonderful," I replied. "You'll be perfect at it."

"Come with me. I'll teach you how to lay bricks and build timber frames and install plumbing. Come with me—travel. Do something important and useful that you'll enjoy. Be with me."

I allowed myself a single moment of fantasy. A moment where my life took a different path, one where I worked hard all day, where I built things. Where I sat with this man and watched the sunset every night.

It was only a moment, though, and only a fantasy. Harry was so much better than he was, but he still needed me. I made a commitment. I married him. I said those words, made those vows, and I knew he would be devastated if I left him. He loved me. Needed me. We'd been through too much together for us to part ways. I simply couldn't do that to him.

"So I told him no, Em," I say, feeling tears wet on my cheeks without even noticing that I cried. "I told him I couldn't go with him and that I couldn't see him anymore. It wasn't fair to any of us. Not to Harry, not to me, and definitely not to Alex—it's like I was keeping him hanging on somehow. Holding him back without meaning to. Stopping him from leading the kind of life he deserved. I told him no, and I've not seen him since."

Em, I see, is crying too. We are a pair of emotional wrecks this morning.

"How did he react?" she asks.

"He understood. He said he thought it was probably for the best. That he'd go to the end of the world for me if there was hope, but he couldn't carry on living in suspended animation. That he'd lost Anna, and now he was waiting for me, and . . . I was right. We had to stop. It was terrible. Walking away from him, leaving him there that night, alone, was terrible . . ."

"It is terrible," she replies, wiping her face. "I feel like my heart's breaking. In a different world it could have worked for you two."

"It could—and I try hard to not regret anything. There isn't any point, is there? The moment I met him was one of the most important in my life. But it also led to the greatest pain I'd ever known . . . and since then? Well, I'd be lying if I said I never googled him. Never thought of him, or wondered how he was. Hoped he was happy. I'd never expected to see him again, and now I will. Now I'll be going back to Mexico, and he will be there, and it all feels like such a mess."

"You don't have to!" she says quickly. "You can skip it . . . or you can talk to him before . . . He has asked if you're coming, in our emails."

"Has he?" I say, and she nods. "Well. I'll think about it. Thank you for listening to all of this. Harry knows I saw Alex, but . . . well. I suppose there was more to it than met the eye, and I never told him that. I just ended it. Now I feel all churned up inside, Em, and I think maybe Harry does too. You are a bringer of chaos!"

"I know I am," she says, grinning and standing to her feet. "I can't help it—it's a gift! And yes, think about it. There is no pressure here. I want to make a good TV program—but not at the cost of destroying my friend."

Chapter 27

I am waiting for Olivia to emerge from her college building when I look at the photos Em gave me. The ones that Shelley had developed, after years of leaving them hidden in a drawer.

It sounds like such a mad thing to do, leaving the camera tucked away out of sight and out of mind for almost a decade—but I completely understand why she did. That night derailed her life, killed her friends, changed everything. It takes time to build up the heart to face the reminders of such things.

Shelley had emailed them over from the land of Oz the night before. She told Em they made her laugh and made her cry, and made her miss her friends even more after seeing them all up to various acts of no good. They didn't, though, make her remember the events of that night any more clearly.

I wonder if Shelley will find it within herself to go there, to film in Santa Maria, and what it will be like to see those people again. People who are really strangers, but whom I have so much in common with.

I let the photos spill across my lap and gaze at them.

Miraculously, they do make me smile. They were so alive, these girls. I see shots of them on the coach, pulling faces at each other. Shots of them twerking in the plaza, pints held aloft. Group shots of them hugging Jorge. More pints. More dancing.

Even now, I am staggered and impressed by how much they managed to drink without once falling over. They were wonderful, and I am shot through with regret that I didn't speak to them more.

There are a few photos of the scenery, of the stalls, of one of those hummingbirds. Some of Janey doing what appears to be a handstand in the water of the fountain. The quality isn't brilliant—Shelley was drunk and the camera was cheap—but that doesn't matter. Somehow they perfectly capture the spirit of that particular group of women on that particular night.

I move through the pile, and the backdrops change. A picture of one of the little boys playing keepy-uppy. One of the church.

I reach the ones Em mentioned, of me and Alex—I don't know why Shelley took pictures of us; perhaps we were just there by accident as she clicked. We are engrossed in conversation and it feels so strange, seeing that moment captured on film. I didn't even know his name back then.

I wonder what would have happened, if the earth-quake passed us by? If the Cocos plate ramming into the North American plate sent hell running underground all the way to some other place that night?

I liked Alex, even then. I was intrigued by him, and

I enjoyed our conversation, and I found him attractive in all kinds of ways.

Maybe we'd have stayed in touch, got together, lived happily ever after. Maybe I'd have gone traveling and he would always have been a pleasant and mysterious memory, a what-if that I could look back on and smile. Maybe I'd have stayed with Harry, had a beautiful baby, gone on to enjoy a traditional life of motherhood and suburbia and contentment.

It is impossible to say, and I push the pictures to one side and look at the rest.

The next few were all taken on the side streets that I remember snaking from the central plaza, the quiet paths I wandered with Harry. Practically abandoned, as all the inhabitants were down in the square. Bright flowers around the doorways, fruit trees, the washing lines stretched out of windows. None of the other girls are in the pictures, so I assume Shelley was exploring alone.

I pick up the next few and stare at them side by side, at first unsure of what I am seeing. It's a series of three, obviously taken one after the other.

They are of Greta, one of the girls who died that night. Big blond hair, bright pink T-shirt, short shorts. She is tangled up in a man's arms, sharing a passionate kiss. In the next shot, the man has his hands firmly placed on her Daisy Dukes—clad bottom, which makes me giggle. In the final one, Greta seems to finally realize her friend is watching and gives a jolly thumbs-up sign over her shoulder, while still snogging someone's face off. These girls were masters of multitasking.

The man is in darkness, hidden by Greta and her hair and the shadow cast by the small houses that line the narrow street.

I am about to put the pictures away, to pack them all back up for Em, when something makes me take another look at that last series.

I hold the middle one up, examine it more closely. Squint my eyes as though that will help.

I see the man's hands, grabbing Greta's backside. I see his wrists. I see the bracelet he is wearing—a string of black-and-white yin-yang symbols, chasing each other around.

Light and shade.

I find myself staring at them again.

Harry.

Chapter 28

I intend to drive somewhere quiet, or to go home. I intend to simply let this new information sink in, to allow myself time to calm, to accept, to process.

I intend all of that, but what I actually do is drive straight to the barn where Harry has his offices. I think it's fair to say that I possibly look a little steamed up as I enter the reception, as Jimbo, the young man who runs front of house, appears to be terrified of me.

Jimbo is barely into his twenties and had a leg amputated after complications from childhood meningitis. He is a lovely boy and not the sort of person you feel proud of terrifying.

"I'm so sorry," he says, eyes wide, "but he's not here, Elena."

"Well, where is he then?"

"He's with Alison. They're working on a new presentation for a potential donor."

"Right. Where are they doing that? If they're not here?"

"I think," he replies, looking at his computer screen, "that they're working from home. I don't know if that means your home or hers. Sorry. Again."

I take a deep breath and force myself to appear relaxed.

"No worries, Jimbo. I'm sure I'll catch up with him. Thanks for your help!"

He looks relieved and grateful, and I tell myself off for turning into the Wicked Witch of the West as I get back into the car. I sit still for a few moments before I start the engine, wondering what on earth I hope to achieve by all of this. By tracking him down, confronting him when I'm angry, causing a fuss. I never cause a fuss. It's not usually in my nature.

My phone beeps and I see a message from Olivia, asking where I am.

You'll have to slum it, I reply. *I've got to go and cause a fuss.*

I picture her face as she reads it, imagining how wide her eyes will go and how she'll make a little "ooooh!" sound. Frankly she'll be delighted.

She responds with an animated GIF of Wonder Woman bearing the words "You Go Girl!" at the bottom. I switch the phone off—I don't want to have to answer any questions right now—and decide what to do next.

I am so rarely angry that it actually feels quite good, like something I should savor and store up. I know that doesn't sound healthy, but maybe it's just a pleasant change from feeling borderline sad, and constantly battling with myself about it.

I never in a million years lived under the illusion that Harry was perfect. I never assumed that he never looked at another woman. But this . . . this hurts, far more than I would have imagined it could. On the night he claimed he was going to propose, he was actually snogging someone else. While I was sitting with Alex, feeling guilty about the fact that I was enjoying his company, Harry was groping another woman's bottom.

It hurts for so many reasons, not all of them obvious. It hurts because my boyfriend and now husband behaved like that. It hurts that he deceived me, not only about buying the ring that night, but about what he was doing. All these years I've believed him when he said his memory was affected, and now I suspect that was simply a convenient fiction.

It also hurts because of everything that followed. I stayed when I should have left. I married him when I should have said no. I let Alex leave my life when I should have held on tight. I feel like an idiot. An idiot who trusted him, who trusted his version of events, who trusted that I was doing the right thing.

Our entire marriage is built on lies. On sinking sand. On myths and legends.

I have felt, recently, a slight shift in those weak foundations. A shared honesty, a small and creeping sense of optimism. Nothing major, nothing life-changing, but potential—potential for me and Harry to find a fuller life together. A better life.

Now, I can't find any of that. I can't find that hope at all. If he'd told me, maybe it would have been different. Maybe I could have dealt with that, if he'd been honest, like he was about the ring. Mistakes I can accept—Lord knows I've made enough of my own—but the lies leave me feeling empty, mocked. Even further away from him than before.

I have my own secrets, things I've never told him, for reasons I have convinced myself are right. I have never told him about our baby, believing that I was protecting him. I have never been totally frank about Alex, which I think was protecting both of us. But recently, I wondered if perhaps we could start afresh. Share it all, let go of our past, and move on. Now, it feels like we are trapped in a web of lies.

Unless . . . unless, I remind myself, he wasn't lying when he said his memory had been affected. What if he actually doesn't remember? What if I'm outraged because he didn't tell me when he actually doesn't know? What if seeing those photos would be as much of a shock to him as it was to me? Shouldn't I at least give him the chance to explain that?

It is a tiny ray of sunlight, but my mind basks in it. Harry might have been with another woman that night, but that was a different Harry from the one I am married to now. That was the young, callous version of my husband—and if I look at that Harry clearly, it does not surprise me that he engaged in a quick tumble with a pretty Aussie girl while his girlfriend was only meters away.

This Harry, the new Harry . . . I don't think he would do that to me. I don't think he would be that cruel. And this Harry, I try to convince myself, would have been honest about it. He knew this thing with Em would raise some questions; he knew that whole night would be under the spotlight in a way it wasn't before. He knew that any secrets might be uncovered—that's why he told me about the ring. He didn't want it to come out any other way than from him to me directly.

Surely he would apply the same policy to this? Surely he would have told me, if he actually knew? The more I turn it over and poke it, the more I think that perhaps it is genuinely one of those memories he has lost.

Jimbo is peeking at me from the barn window, and I realize that I have been sitting here for some time now. I give him a wave and start up the car.

I need to find Harry.

I swing by our house first, but can tell he's not home from the fact that his car isn't there. I should've been a detective.

I try his phone, but it goes straight to messages, and this doesn't seem like one of those situations you can adequately sum up on voicemail. I notice more "inspirational" GIFs from Olivia. Bearing in mind she has no idea what I am causing a fuss about—I mean, it could be some out-of-date milk from the supermarket—she seems very keen on the idea.

I reply to Olivia with some perfunctory emoji winky faces and go inside. I know Alison lives on the outskirts of a small town around twenty miles away, but I'm unsure of the exact address.

I decide to break into Harry's office and snoop. When I say break in, I mean open the door, and when I say snoop, I mean check his desktop Rolodex. Neither exactly requires John le Carré–level spycraft.

His office, unlike mine, is pristine. Not a dancing Christmas penguin in sight. There is a nice picture of the two of us framed on his desk, which is sweet. Or at least it might be sweet. I don't know right now; everything still feels strange and sour and unsettling.

I flick through the Rolodex and am unsurprised to see that everything is neat, orderly, and perfectly filled in. Harry never used to be quite such a stickler for tidiness and perfection, but these days he's borderline OCD. Part of it is the fact that life is much easier for him on a logistical level if everything is in its proper place, but I suspect some of it is also about control. He can't control some of the basic functions of his own body, so I think he's learned to take it where he can.

Alison Burroughs is listed like all the others—surname, first name, landline and mobile, email address, full postal address. I carry on looking, and have to smile when I find myself listed in exactly the same way under "G" for Godwin. Just in case he ever forgets where I live, I suppose.

The drive to Alison's home takes longer than I expected, due to me getting lost several times. She lives on a newish estate that doesn't appear in the memory banks of any electronic maps, and I find it only by sheer luck.

It's nice, the estate—all the homes look slightly different, trees have been planted along the roadsides, and the signs of family life save it from that soulless quality that some new-build communities have. All the streets seem to be named after poets, and I drive through Tennyson and Byron to arrive in Keats Road. I have a brief and strange urge to vandalize the shiny street sign and make it Keats Ode—which would possibly be the most pretentious piece of graffiti ever.

Alison's house is in a corner plot, a semidetached built from dark red brick. I see Harry's car parked outside, next to her Toyota.

I am suddenly aware that this might seem a bit odd to Alison. I know her in that casual way you know work colleagues or friends of friends—enough to be cheery in passing, but not close enough to have ever visited her home.

I climb out and walk around to the front of the house. The first thing I notice is the ramp. A full wheelchair ramp, set up in a similar way to ours, leading up to the door. I pause and feel suddenly less sure of myself.

Why does Alison have a wheelchair ramp at her home? She is not disabled, and neither are her children. As far as I know, her parents are fit and active. Yet here it is, in all its confusing glory.

I walk tentatively to the front door and use the brass knocker that shines against its red wooden background. There is no answer, and I peer through the window, using my hands to shield the glare of the sun. It is cold today, almost icy, but the sun is bright and the sky a vivid blue.

Through the window I see the usual things you might expect: sofas, a TV, bookshelves, toys. The whole place looks clean but lived in. Cozy, but not cluttered. It looks like a room that gets battered by young children, but lives to tell the tale.

I wait for a few more minutes, but nobody arrives to let me in. I am unsure as to what to do next. I am unsure why there is a ramp here, at the home of one of Harry's work colleagues. I am unsure about everything—including whether Olivia's insinuations about the two of them could be true. She makes so many nasty comments about Harry, and vice versa, that I immediately discount whatever criticisms she's throwing at him.

I have always trusted him—which was, I think, knowing what I do now, possibly a mistake. But Alison . . . I wouldn't have thought she was his type. Not that I have any clue what his type is, beyond the fact that he was always very appreciative of Kate Winslet in *Titanic*. But most men were.

Alison is perhaps a decade older than us, but why would that be an issue? I certainly wouldn't be considering that a big age gap if it were an older man and a younger woman.

I am still standing on the doorstep, getting colder with every second. I walk around the side of the house, past the gardens that wrap around into the back. When I get to the back fence, I see them. I'm just about tall enough to peer over, and what I see there possibly hurts me even more than seeing the pair of them starkers in a hot tub.

The back of the house opens up onto the garden with big French windows. There is another ramp there, leading down from the house and onto a patio area. The garden is large, with a network of paved paths running through it, lawns and flower beds and shrubs at the side.

There is a small plastic slide, and a couple of bikes with training wheels abandoned near it.

The French windows are open, and everyone is outside, wrapped up warm and cozy. I see Alison in a fleece jacket that I know is Harry's, and I see the children, bundled up in knit hats and gloves, and I see Harry himself, his padded gilet fastened up over a chunky sweater. A sweater that I bought him.

He feels the cold, because he doesn't move around as much as most people, so it's important he regulates his temperature when he's outside. Even as I watch them, part of me is so used to considering his health that I take a moment to check out his feet, to make sure he has his Timberlands on and not his flimsier work shoes.

He does have his boots on. He also has one child balanced on each of his knees and is pretending to rev his wheels like the engine of a car.

"Vroom, vroom!" I hear him saying, over and over, louder and louder. With each "vroom," the little ones get more excited, giggling and squirming in delight. Alison stands behind them smiling, a mug of something hot in her hands, steam whipping up into the cold air.

"Get ready!" says Harry. "Hold on tight!"

With one final whoosh, one big scream from the children, he pushes off, wheeling as fast as he can down the path. He pushes furiously, building up speed, haring around curves, the kids yelling and laughing, knit hats flapping, their little arms clinging to his neck.

He does a complete circuit of the garden and arrives back at the French windows, looking slightly out of puff.

"Again, again!" they shout, quite obviously playing a favorite game here.

"No, I need a break," he says, kissing each one on the forehead and gently lifting them down to the floor. "You've worn me out, demon spawn."

There are a few moments of pouting and attempts at persuasion, but eventually they give up and start running around the garden instead. I am fascinated by them, as I always am with small children—the sheer energy, the way they can switch moods so quickly, their amazing capacity to be happy and thrilled with the most mundane of things.

They are adorable as well, these two—both boys, I remember, though it's hard to tell under all their layers. Blond hair, chubby faces, cherubs in duffel coats.

They run, and they shout, and eventually, one of them sees me.

"Mummy!" he shouts, pointing in my direction. "There's a strange lady looking into our garden!"

Harry looks over, sees me lurking there. I meet his gaze, see the shock in his eyes, the color drain from his skin. The smile freeze on his lips.

Chapter 29

I arrive home before him, having driven uncharacteristically fast for the whole journey. Almost as though I
couldn't even bear for his car to be close to mine.

After I was spotted by the knit-hatted child, Harry
and Alison stared at me in horror. I stared back with
even more, utterly humiliated.

"Sorry!" I said, smiling so as not to scare the twins.
"Just being silly! Harry, can you please follow me home?"

I quickly texted Olivia and told her to stay out for a
bit, and headed back. Now, I am here, in this clean, clear,
pristine environment of ours, waiting for him to return.
I have got myself a glass of wine, and I've got him a glass
of the home-brewed cider one of his clients gave him as
a gift.

I look around at the bungalow, at this house that has
never really felt like my home.

I see all the indications of a good life. A happy life.
Walls that bear framed pictures from our wedding day.
Mementos from birthdays. There is food in the kitchen,
clothes in our wardrobes, a car in the driveway. There
are bookshelves, there are coats on hooks, there are

toothbrushes sitting together in the bathroom. It is a good house, near the sea.

To the outside observer, it would appear as though we had everything—and yet I realize that I could happily walk out of this building and never come back. That I could wave goodbye to the years I have spent here and move on.

The bigger question is whether I could leave Harry and never come back.

As I sit and wait, part of me wonders if he will even come straight home, or if he will avoid me until I "calm down." It would be a classic Harry move, now that I think about it, to come up with an excuse to duck the upcoming confrontation and see if the stormy waters will still.

If he does that, I decide, I will track him down and roll him off a cliff. I will take making a fuss to a whole new level.

I am saved from my fate as a murderer by the sound of him arriving. The door opens and I hear him taking his coat off before he comes through, wheeling his chair toward me at the kitchen table. His hair is ruffled, and his cheeks are pink from the cold.

He takes one look at me, one look at the glass I pass to him, and says, "Is that the cider home brew?"

"Yes."

"I hate the cider home brew."

"I know."

He nods, accepting this act of petty revenge, and takes a deep breath.

"Elena, I don't know what you think you saw back there, what you think is going on, but—"

"That's not what I want to talk about," I say, interrupting him. "Not yet, at least. I wanted to talk to you about that night, in Santa Maria. I wanted to talk to you about what you remember."

"You know the answer to that," he says, frowning. "I don't remember much at all."

"But you remembered not buying the ring?"

"It's . . . complicated. I remember bits and pieces."

"Do you remember this bit?" I ask, laying the photos down on the table. "Or this piece?"

He seems reluctant to touch them, to pick them up, to cast his eyes over them, even. He can obviously tell that they are not the bearers of good news.

"Look at them, please," I say.

He sighs, and I see a very slight tremble in his fingers as he reaches out and takes them in his hands. I watch his face closely as he examines them, studying him as carefully as he studies the photos. Harry is, I have learned recently, a much better liar than I thought he was. I hope that I will know if he is lying this time, but I can't be sure. He is mercurial, and lightning quick, and I can't afford to take my eyes off him for a moment.

He stares at the pictures for a few more seconds, then lays them back down on the tabletop, where they seem to shimmer in the light shining in from the window behind me.

He swipes one hand over his face, as though buying a moment to steady himself, then looks at me. He is pale now, and shaken, and looks more vulnerable than I've seen him for many years.

"Where did these come from?" he asks eventually.

"Shelley. She had a camera full of photos she only just got developed."

He nods, and I wonder how he is going to play this. How he is going to react. If I can even believe his reactions anymore.

"Did you know about this?" I ask, pointing at the photos. "Is this something you remember doing? If it isn't, I understand, and we can get over it. That was then and this is now. But please, Harry, be honest—is this a shock to you? That on the night I was buried alive and you were crushed, you had your tongue down another woman's throat?"

He cringes at my crude words, or my anger. Probably both.

He doesn't reply, and I add, "Harry, answer me. I just need to know. Is this one of those things you forgot happened?"

I am, of course, giving him the perfect escape route. I know I'm doing it, and I don't know why. It's almost as though I want him to take it—as though I want him to claim ignorance, apologize for his youthful indiscretion, tell me he loves me and he'd never do that now.

Part of me wants that—although how it would fit in with the scenes of cozy domesticity at Alison's home, I don't know.

I do know that I'm scared. I'm hurt. I'm uncertain of everything and I don't like the way it feels. So I give him that escape route—but he doesn't take it. I don't know if I am relieved or dismayed.

"I knew," he says quietly. "I remember. I'm so, so sorry."

"That you did it, or that you lied?"

"Both, of course. As to why I did it . . . well, I was an idiot, wasn't I? I meant every word I said to you about how I was going to ask you to marry me. None of that was a lie, I swear. But . . . I was young. I was a fool. Maybe a bit of me even did it *because* I was going to propose—maybe it was a stupid last hurrah before I made that commitment . . . I don't know.

"I can't explain it any way that lets me off the hook. I hate myself for doing it. I hate a lot about myself back then—I was not a man with a huge amount of moral fiber. I always loved you, Elena, but back then I . . . well, I was easily tempted. Back then it seemed simple—she was pretty, she was fun, it was harmless. Just a silly kiss that meant nothing. Except . . ."

"Except it turned out to be the last thing she ever did."

"Yes. Which is a tragedy on many levels. Please believe me—I'm so sorry. I can't imagine how it must have felt to look at these . . ."

He pushes at the photos with the tip of his finger, like they are contaminated and he doesn't want to come into actual contact with them.

"Okay, Harry. You were young. You were foolish. One last hurrah. I don't like it, but I can understand it. But . . . why didn't you *tell* me? You told me about the ring. You told me that, and we worked through it, and

I thought . . . God, I feel like a gullible idiot now, but I thought we were getting closer. I imagined we were getting . . . better. That this whole honesty lark might be good for us. So why didn't you tell me? Why did you let me find out this way?"

"You weren't imagining it, Elena, and you're not an idiot. We were getting better—or at least we both seemed to want to!"

"Up until an hour ago I'd have believed that. Again, Harry—why didn't you tell me about Greta, when you were clearing the air about the ring?"

"That's . . . that's a complicated question."

"I think we're well past simple, don't you, Harry? Try and explain. I'll do my best to keep up."

"All right, that's fair," he says, taking a quick gulp of his cider. Now I know he must be desperate.

"Well, I suppose one of the reasons it's complicated," he continues, "is because I've basically tried to forget all about it. I was ashamed. Ashamed that I'd done that to you, that I'd been such an arrogant moron—that I was on holiday with a woman I loved, and I was messing around like that. It was insulting to you—and even more so later. When you . . . when you stood by me. When you supported me, and loved me, and married me, and displayed more compassion and morality than I'd ever had."

I open my mouth to reply. To dispute. To tell him that I'm not that perfect—that I have made my own mistakes too.

"No," he says, waving his hand. "Let me get this out.

It's hard, and it's going to get harder the longer I leave it. So—I also tried to forget about it because I felt guilty. Not about you—though that was bad enough—but about Greta too."

"What do you mean?" I ask, confused.

"I mean, if I hadn't flirted with her, she'd have still been with her friends when it happened. If I hadn't encouraged her, she wouldn't have been in that street. She wouldn't have been in that place, at that time, and she wouldn't be—"

"Dead? Is that what you think? If she'd only been anywhere except that particular spot, she could have survived. That if you and she hadn't snuck off down that side street, everything could have been different."

He nods and meets my eyes.

"I know," he says. "You said something similar recently, about wondering if I'd not been buying your ring, whether I'd have been okay. I felt terrible when you said that, because I knew exactly what you meant. I'm so sorry."

I feel some of the anger slither out of me, like a snake crawling off to find a new place to hide. I know how that feeling of guilt can affect you over time—even if you spend years telling yourself it's nonsense.

"I did feel that. I felt like it was somehow my fault, Harry. I thought if you'd just stayed with me, you'd have been fine. If I'd said no, don't leave me here at this restaurant on my own, please stay—you could have been fine. Truth is you were kind of getting on my nerves, and I wanted to be on my own for a bit. I've felt like crap about that for so long now. So, yes, I do understand."

"Oh God," he says, voice raw with genuine anguish. "What a fucking mess everything is!"

Harry rarely swears, but this does seem an appropriate moment to do it. He reaches out a hand across the table, and I stare at it. I am not quite ready to accept that gesture, and his fingers curl up and move away, rejected.

"I'm sorry, Elena, for so many things—but especially for that. Especially when I wasn't even buying a bloody ring! You've carried that for all this time, and it wasn't even a real thing . . ."

"None of it is, though, Harry, is it? The guilt. For either of us. If you'd stayed with me you could have been crushed by the church when it came down. If you'd stayed with me, we could both have died. If Greta had stayed by the fountain, she could have died just like her friend Beth did. She could have ended up in a coma like Shelley did. She could have been killed, like so many of the others. We both carry guilt—because we survived, and so many others didn't. But the truth is there is nothing we could have done differently that night. Nothing. It's what we do now that counts."

He nods and I see a gleam of moisture in his eyes, a sheen of tears I've not seen for so many years.

"I didn't want to hurt you," he says. "When we were talking, last time? When I told you about the ring. I considered telling you about Greta, but I didn't want to hurt you. To be brutally honest, she was dead, and I didn't think it would ever come out—so I just decided it would be cruel to hurt you like that. That I'd be doing it more to clear my conscience than anything else, that it wouldn't be fair. Sometimes we keep secrets for the best of reasons, don't we?"

I nod and chew my lip. He's right, of course. We do. Minutes ago, when I was sitting here waiting for him to turn up, I was so angry and so hurt. Hurt about Greta, hurt about the past, but also stung by what I saw at Alison's house. What shook me so much.

At Alison's house, I saw Harry as a dad. I saw Harry at the heart of a family. I saw Harry with something that I never gave him—children. I saw his warmth, and his energy, and his patience. The kind of father he could have been, even though he never showed me any signs of wanting to be one. Even though I never pushed for children of our own.

We have hurt each other so much, this man and I. We have hurt each other in a thousand tiny ways, hidden so much, and we have done it for long enough. The time for secrets has passed.

"After the earthquake," I say, taking a gulp of wine, "it was chaotic. You were in a coma, and then once you were woken up, it was . . . well, like it was."

He nods, but I see he is confused at this change of subject.

"We had to concentrate on you, and getting you home, and then on rehab. And there was something back then that I never told you, Harry. Something that I should have done—but I wanted to protect you. Wanted to keep you safe from any more pain—you were suffering enough."

"What is it, Elena?" he replies, meeting my eyes. I feel strangely nervous, wound tight, as though the words still do not want to come out of my mouth. As though I have kept this to myself for so long, I have lost the ability to talk about it.

"I was pregnant," I say simply.

"What? When? How?"

I smile gently. "The usual way, I imagine, Harry. I didn't know, at the time. I didn't know until after. I didn't know until the doctor told me I'd lost it. That the baby didn't survive."

He is silent, his forehead creased by a frown as he processes the information.

"Why didn't you tell me?" he asks.

"I couldn't, Harry, not then. You . . . you weren't well enough to handle it."

He nods. "I think you're right. I'd like to disagree and say you should have told me, that I could have helped you . . . but you're right. I was in too dark a place to deal with it, and I wouldn't have reacted in the way I should. But later—why not later? Years have passed, and you've still never told me. You've dealt with this on your own for so long!"

"Well, like you said earlier—it's complicated. There always seemed to be something else going on, for such a long time. And . . . I don't know. The longer I left it the harder it became. We settled into our life, our routine, and you were doing so well, and I was all right, and . . . I'm sorry. It was your baby as well."

He reaches across the table and takes both my hands in his. This time I let him. I need the comfort, and so does he.

"I'm sorry too, Elena. Sorry that you lost it. Sorry that I wasn't there for you. Sorry for so much . . . and I'm sad. Terribly sad. I know it's not what either of us had planned, but still . . . a baby. Our baby. Maybe everything would have been different . . ."

We are both crying now, and as I cling on to his fingers I am grateful for it—grateful for the secrets being revealed, for the truths being told, for the sharing of this emotional burden.

We sit silently and let our feelings run their course. I have had years of dealing with this loss—Harry has only just been told about it. I owe him some time.

"So," I say, when he seems recovered enough to talk. "I think perhaps we need to stop lying to each other, don't you? Stop all the secrets. Tell me about Alison."

I say this gently, to reassure him that it is okay. That it is finally all right for us to be honest—that we can do so without fear of hurting each other. We both need that honesty right now.

"It's not what you think," he replies, pulling his hands slowly from mine and wiping his tear-stained face with his sweater.

"She has a ramp at her house. Her children adore you. That was clearly not your first visit. What I think is that you are part of her family, Harry."

"It's not . . . we're not . . . we haven't slept with each other, is what I mean."

It almost makes me smile the way he says that, border-line embarrassed. As though "sex" is a dirty word he's too nice to utter.

"Maybe you should," I say. "Harry, come on, we both know you don't have to sleep with someone to be having an affair, do you? There are so many ways of being unfaithful."

Maybe it's the adrenaline of the day—goodness knows there have been enough shocks since I woke up this morning. Maybe it's the alcohol. Maybe it's simply that I have had enough of the pretense, enough of the lies. Enough of living a half-life.

He looks at me and says one word: "Alex?"

"Yes," I reply. "Alex. Nothing ever happened between us, all those times we met. But I wanted it to, Harry."

It is, perhaps, too stark, the way I say that. He looks up from his glass and replies, "You wanted to, and you denied yourself. For me. Again. So . . . what went wrong? Why did you stop seeing him? Did he find someone else?"

He says this with an edge of cruelty, as though he is hoping that was the case. Hoping that I was hurt. I let it go—I know how he feels. I was feeling it myself not that long ago, that urge to lash out, that frustration. And I have just given him news that has affected him deeply.

"I ended it because it wasn't fair, to any of us. I cut off

contact with him because I felt what we were doing was wrong. And maybe he has met someone else by now. I hope he has."

"Do you? Really?"

"I think so. I don't see the point in everyone being miserable, do you?"

"I didn't think any of us were, Elena."

"Harry," I say firmly, placing my hands down on the table. "I've kept secrets of my own, I know. But I just found out that you were with another woman on the night of the earthquake, shortly after discovering that you've been lying about my engagement ring and proposal for all these years. And I've just, this very afternoon, been confronted with the fact that you've been close enough to Alison long enough for her to have altered her home for your convenience.

"I saw the way you were together—you and her and the kids. You looked happy, for goodness' sake! Not just all right, or okay, or satisfied, or any of those half-hearted words that we could use to describe our relationship— but actually *happy*. No, we weren't miserable—but we weren't happy either, were we?"

He considers this and gives me a small smile.

"I thought we could have been, once. Back in Mexico that night—my bad behavior aside—I thought I'd ask you to marry me, you'd obviously say yes, and we'd be happy."

"If the earthquake hadn't happened, Harry, I wouldn't have said yes. Regardless of Alex, or Greta, or Alison— they are nothing to do with this. You must have known that I wasn't settled, that I didn't want to make that kind of commitment. That I was thinking that we'd run our course anyway . . ."

"Ouch. Well, part of me did, obviously. I thought you were getting restless, and I didn't want to lose you. Then afterward . . . after the accident, I convinced myself I'd imagined it. That you still loved me. That you would have said yes."

"I did say yes."

"I know. And here we are. Elena, can I be honest with you?"

"Please do."

He nods, and takes a drink, and continues. "Part of me probably suspected that you only said yes because of my injuries. You've always been such a good person. You've always been so kind and generous—you're not the kind of woman who would abandon a man who's just found out he's paralyzed. You stuck with me, you put me first—I always knew that, but until you told me about . . . the baby . . . I hadn't even realized quite how much. You were suffering yourself, and you still put me first.

"Then I ambushed you as well, with the TV cameras . . . that was a bit low, I know, but I was desperate. I needed you, and you didn't let me down. Anyway. I think, under everything else, that I've always had a bit of resentment about that."

"About me saying yes? You resented me for marrying you?"

"About the fact that you married me out of pity."

"Harry," I say, horrified. "That's not all it was. We'd been together for a long time. We've built a decent life together. It wasn't just pity . . ."

"Maybe not *just* pity—but pity was a part of it, and that's never a good motive for a relationship, is it? And it's even worse now that I know how you felt about Alex. I wanted you to marry me, desperately. But it wasn't the right thing, was it? For you definitely. You did the wrong thing for all the right reasons. You weren't in love with me then, and you're not in love with me now. You kept Alex as a friend, when he should have been more—and you married me, when we should have just been friends."

I don't know how to respond to this. There is honesty, and there is brutality—and this is hovering between the two. It is searingly painful to hear.

"Harry, I do love you. I always did. And it's natural in a marriage, isn't it, for that in-love feeling to diminish over time? The honeymoon period doesn't last forever."

"Well, we didn't have a honeymoon, did we? Literally or figuratively. I know you love me—and I love you too. You're one of the best people I've ever known. But you're right—when I'm with Alison and the kids, I'm actively happy rather than passively content."

Wow. He is really going for it now—and I am floundering in such a strange mix of emotions. Pain, and fear, and regret. Excitement, elation, relief. All of it. No wonder I'm confused. I have been with Harry—through some spectacular ups and downs—since I was a teenager. I'm not even sure who I am without him.

But is that any reason to stay with someone?

"What are you saying?" I ask, needing to hear the words.

"I'm saying that we've done our best. We've tried. I don't think either of us can try anymore, Elena, do you? Maybe . . . maybe this is the end. If you want to give it another shot, I will—I swear I will. I owe you that much. But this is a lot to come back from, and I'm not sure it's really what either of us wants . . ."

I wanted to hear the words but, when I do, they make me feel sad, even if I know he is right. Even if I know it is what is best for us both.

For years we have survived together, Harry and I. But surviving something doesn't mean you are undamaged, or whole. Some of us carry breaks and tears that nobody can see, and I think my marriage is one of them.

I don't want to survive anymore. I don't want to battle my way through the next few decades. I don't want to have to try so hard to save something that I'm not even sure I want.

I don't want Harry to have to give up Alison and her kids for me. I don't want him to have to sacrifice a potentially happy relationship just because he feels like he should. I've been there, done that, and it is such a waste—of time, of emotion, of life. Of us.

"I'll always love you, Harry," I say quietly. "But I think you're right."

Chapter 30

Three months later

The closer we get, the harder it feels to breathe. I am in the back seat of a car that Em sent to collect me, and we are driving toward the place where I was buried alive. It is a place of trauma, and terror, and too many memories.

It is also undeniably beautiful. As the car pulls up to a newly paved parking area and I climb out, I feel the force of the late-afternoon sun pressing down on me. The minute I am outside the air-conditioning it is hot—very, very hot.

I can hear birdsong and insects, and smell the pine and juniper trees of the surrounding forest. It has rained recently, and the air is alive. The wildflowers around the hills have bloomed in riots of pink and purple and orange, the mountains and valleys are lush, green, and ripe, despite the heat.

I am a long way from home, and it has taken all of my courage to get here.

After Harry and I had our heart-to-heart, I moved into my mum's house. Back into my childhood bedroom. When I left the bungalow, when I left Harry, I expected to feel sad. Melancholy. Anxious.

I actually felt none of those things. I felt strong. I felt determined. I felt damn near euphoric. It was that new sense of strength, of self-belief, that got me to the airport. Got me on the plane. Got me here, despite all my fears. I am proud of myself, and I forgive myself the jolt of nerves as I look around. I may be strong—but I am not superhuman.

I have arrived alone, but see the coach that a group of the others chose to use, re-creating another element of that night. I was not ready for that. Driving here at all was nerve-racking enough, never mind doing it in another bus, thinking of Jorge.

As I walk across to the newly built plaza, my sandals kicking up clouds of still-familiar orange dust, I feel clogged with emotion. I am about to face so much. About to enter a world of unknowns. I stop, stand still. Turn my face up to the warmth of the sun and breathe it in, letting it calm me.

I am here. I made it. I will get through this, and all the challenges it presents.

The plaza is different, as I expected. There is no fountain, and the stone paving is new, and the homes around the edge of it are in various stages of development. Some are complete and bear signs of life: fruit trees being cultivated outside them, curtains in the windows, open doors, music playing. Others are mid-construction, exposed, skin and bare bones.

It is different, but it still brings me back so vividly to

that night, to everything that happened here. I pause and look on at the group of people who are gathering there, in that central spot. By the not-fountain in the almost-plaza.

I see Sofia the tour guide, her long hair gleaming in the sun. I see Shelley, whom I've since spoken to on the phone and who found the strength to make it, and I see Janey, whom I last spoke to in a hospital bed. The Frazer family—Em's mum and brother—are there too. I spot others: local people, adults, children.

The children almost make me turn around and leave again. I know there are no forecasts of earthquakes for today. I have, of course, checked. But there wasn't a forecast last time either ...

I clutch my bag, and behind my sunglasses I close my eyes tight, willing away the anxiety. Telling myself I have managed a long plane journey, a difficult drive through mountain roads. That I have faced fears and navigated dangers to get this far. That I can do this. When I open my eyes again, I see Em running toward me.

She has been here for a couple of weeks, so she is now off-white and incredibly freckly rather than ghostly. She has a baseball cap over her shaved hair, and as soon as she reaches me she swallows me up into a hug.

"How are you?" she asks, lifting my shades up so she can look into my eyes. "It's a lot, I know. First time I walked through here I thought my head would explode."

Even now, her nostrils are flaring and her fists are slightly clenched. This is the place where her father died, along with so many others.

It is quiet here now, peaceful, but I remember the roar and the rumble, the crashing and yelling, the smell of smoke and death. The horror of waking up alone, in the dark, crushed beneath an angry world. With him, the man I may or may not see today. I don't know if he is here, and I am afraid to ask. I am afraid of so much.

I allow myself that moment of fear and nerves, then I suck in the fresh air, and feel the heat of daylight, and remind myself that I am safe. I am free. I am whole. I can breathe. I am with my friend.

I reach out for Em's hand and squeeze her fingers.

"We're okay, Em," I say. I make it a statement, not a question, and it seems to reassure us both. She nods once, briskly, and looks around her.

"What's the plan?" I ask, nodding toward the small group of people milling around. I notice that they all have drinks, and smile at the thought of the villagers yet again setting up some kind of enterprise. Life does, after all, go on.

"Well, I've interviewed all of them separately already. Now we're just . . . I don't know. 'Relaxing' doesn't seem like the right word. We're chatting. We're looking around. We're remembering. Ollie has cameras set up all over the place, full disclosure, and the idea is that we simply capture what happens. We're staying to film all night, so, you know . . ."

"We'll be here at the same time of day as it happened?"

"Yep! You got me. So, it's a shame Harry couldn't make it."

"Not for Harry. He's happy, Em. And he processed

all of this a lot better than I did after it happened—he doesn't need this."

"I'm glad he's happy," she says. "But what about you?"

"I am as well. It's strange, living at home again, but it's nice too. And the divorce is simple enough. We're both moving on, and it's past time. So thank you."

"Thank you for accidentally ruining your marriage?"

I laugh. "We were most of the way there already . . ."

It should be difficult, dismantling a marriage—but it hasn't been. Once we'd made the decision, it all just . . . folded up. Got put away like garden furniture at the end of summer.

There were logistics to sort, finances to arrange, possessions to divvy up. But beneath all of that, beneath the practical, I think perhaps there was mainly a sense of relief—on both sides. It was incredibly amicable, which I think is less of a testament to our restrained and gracious characters, and more to the fact that we were both very ready to let go. It has been an unexpectedly quiet and gentle end to what has been a major era of our lives.

I think we are both aware of the suffering of the other, of pain caused and pain received, of mistakes made and truths untold.

We have both tried very hard not to hurt each other any further, and the disentangling of our existences was a tentative and cautious thing. We have sold the bungalow, and he has moved in with Alison. I wish him well and was not at all offended at the speed with which they acted—we all know that life is too short to keep wasting chances at happiness.

We will soon be officially divorced, and in some ways that is simply a legal recognition of what was going on beneath the surface for so long—a slow and gradual parting of two people who never even should have been together. We have no children, no pets, no beating hearts to consider other than our own. It has been startlingly simple.

And now I live a different life, at home in Cornwall. I might stay there. I might not. I simply do not know. I feel like a deck of cards that has been thrown into the air, no idea where the hearts and diamonds and kings and queens might land.

It is exhilarating, in its own way, to be unsure of my future. To not know what lies ahead, to have twists and turns in front of me instead of a straight line. I could travel. I could retrain as a brain surgeon. I could become a dog walker at last. I could do everything or I could do nothing. I am rootless and restless, and have no real ties to any one place or any one person—for the first time in many years, nobody needs me.

Coming here, to this place, could prove to me that I should stay at home and play it safe. It might encourage me to embark upon an adventure. Who knows?

For now, I am concerned with not having a panic attack as we approach the plaza, and with scanning the crowds looking for one particular person.

I have spent months wondering how it might feel when we meet again. How he will look, how he will be. He might have changed. He's a human being, not a museum exhibit trapped in time just the way I remember him. He might be married, or have children, or have become a priest—though I would hope that Em would have told me, even though I have not asked.

It is not reasonable or productive to picture Alex as he was the last time I saw him, or to ponder too deeply how he might feel about me. We parted on difficult terms, both in pain. I have missed him every single day since then, but am not arrogant enough to assume that the same is true for him.

We are a few meters away from the crowds now and I realize that I am nervous, in several different ways. The natural nerves of meeting people in a social setting, the extra nerves of it being filmed. The nervousness of not seeing Alex, and the underlying fear caused by the location. By part of me wondering if I need to tread lightly, or the world might sink beneath my feet.

"I'm a bit scared," I say to Em, stopping suddenly.

She stands by my side and grips my hand. "Of course you are. We all are. Why don't you go and look inside the church before you come and say hello to everyone?"

I have already noticed the church, of course. It would be hard not to. It is newly built, but it is beautiful—mellow stone, solid steps up to a shining wooden door, one small bell tower. A cross atop it all, casting a cruciform shadow on the dust of the ground beneath. It is different from the one that came before—simpler, smaller—but still striking. Still symbolic, I think, of faith—if not in God, then in the resilience of humankind. The ability to rebuild, to return, to survive—to cling on to life in this remote and rugged land.

We walk together up those steps, and Em pushes open the vast door. Inside, it is not quite as dark as it used to be. There is more natural light flowing in through bigger windows, and walls of stained glass illuminating whitewashed walls and the dark wood of the pews. It smells of incense and candles still, as well as sawdust and stone, the newness of its construction.

I light a candle, leave it flickering in its holder after saying a quick hello to my dad. I feel odd. Displaced. Like I am floating outside my own body. The last time I was in a church here, I saw Alex, back in a world when we were strangers. Minutes later, he was shielding my body from a collapsing building and tumbling with me into a temporary tomb. The last time I was in here, I was carrying a baby that I lost.

I walk to one of the rows of pews and sit. I lean my head into my hands and close my eyes. I do not have rosary beads and I'm not sure what I believe about religion, but I know this place feels holy. Special. I say a prayer, to whoever might be listening—one of thanks, for my own life, for my family. For Em, and Harry, and Alex. For anyone who lives in fear, for anyone who has suffered loss, for anyone who is lonely and yearns to feel the kind touch of a loving hand.

I hear the movement of someone near to me and wait for Em to either sit or speak.

"Penny for them?" says a voice from my side. A voice I know so well.

My eyes snap open, and I look up. It is him. It is Alex.

"This is the bit where you say 'I'm not that cheap,' and I make a comment about a bathroom wall."

This, I think, is actually the bit where I stare at him, unsure of how to deal with the rush of emotion that I am feeling. I knew he might be here. I knew I might see him again. But knowing it has not prepared me for feeling it.

I reach up and touch his face, run my fingers across his cheekbones, his jaw, his lips. I stroke his hair, and let my hand come to rest on his shoulder, and continue to stare.

"It's real. It's me," he says, smiling gently, sitting by my side. "God, I've missed you. I don't think I even realized how much until right now. I didn't even dare hope that you'd actually come, that you'd turn up. I thought perhaps you would be too afraid."

"I was. I am. But I couldn't stay away . . . How are you, Alex? I've missed you so much as well."

"I'm better now," he replies, "now that you're here. Do you like the church?"

I tear my eyes away from his face and gaze around the building.

"It's beautiful," I say. "You've built a place for magic to happen."

"Look," he says, pointing to a quiet corner of the building. "The stained-glass panel in the middle."

I follow his gesture, and I see it—sunlit, glowing in shades of green and gold. A hummingbird, filtering the light amid a small sea of similar windows all showing birds and flowers and natural wonders.

"That was for you," he explains. "For us. A memory we shared, on that first night."

"It's wonderful," I say. "It's perfect."

We gaze at each other, both clearly catching up on what we might have missed. I kiss him lightly and place my hands in his. I do not seem capable of removing them. It is entirely possible that I will want to feel my skin touching his for the rest of my days. I have let him go too many times. I have, as Harry said, done the wrong thing for the right reasons. I will never make those mistakes again.

"We split up," I say. "Me and Harry."

"Em told me," he replies gently. "I can't pretend to be sad about it. I'm just grateful to have you with me again. To have a second chance, if that's what you want?"

Our fingers intertwine, and I say, "It is what I want. I didn't know exactly how much until I saw you, and now, I don't think I'll ever let you go. I'm scared that if I let go, you'll disappear. That I'll never find you again. That all of this might be some kind of hallucination. If it is, I never want to leave it."

"It's not a hallucination. It's me, and you, and it's happening. I never stopped loving you, Elena. I never stopped wanting you, or thinking about you. And I never want you to let go of me again."

We are silent then, bathed in the glow of the stained glass. We are together—we are home.

"Come outside," he says eventually. "Come and see another sunset. We can talk, we can laugh—we can plan all the sunrises we will get to see."

He leads me by the hand and we walk out, into the big sky and the shimmering air and the village that both broke us and made us whole.

We walk out into the unknown. Into a future that is new to us. Into a life that we will build together.

I do not know where we will live. I don't know what we will do. I don't know if we will have children, or travel, or get married.

I don't know what the rest of my life will look like— but I embrace that uncertainty. I embrace it because I am certain of one thing: Alex and me.

This is where we spent those first moments together, as strangers.

And now we have more than moments. We have forever.

Acknowledgments

Cor blimey—what a year, eh? My last book, *Maybe One Day*, came out in April 2020—days after the UK went into national lockdown. As I type this note, we are in our third national lockdown. And somehow, in between all of this, I wrote *The Moment I Met You*.

Reader, I will not lie—at times it felt like I'd never finish. I was struggling to read a book, never mind write one. The combination of fear, anxiety, communal grief, crushing boredom, and moments of almost supersonic gratitude for all my blessings was very nearly overwhelming.

I know I am not alone when I say I have struggled—and knowing you are not alone is sometimes the very best thing for a poor, battered brain. All books are something of a team effort, but this one in particular has benefited from a lot of helping hands.

I couldn't have written it without the patience, insight, and kindness of my editor Charlotte Mursell, who managed to get me to basically rewrite the whole thing while simultaneously making me feel like triumph was within touching distance. Thank you, Charlotte. Thanks also to the whole Orion team, including but not limited to Harriet Bourton, Alainna Hadjigeorgiou,

Acknowledgments

and Folayemi Adebayo, and to Rachel Kahan and the team at William Morrow in the United States.

Also on the professional front, my deepest thanks to Hayley Steed, Liane-Louise Smith, Hannah Ladds, and the whole gang at the powerhouse that is the Madeleine Milburn Agency. It's been a challenging year for everyone, and I appreciate your continued hard work on my behalf.

Talking to other authors is always a joy, but especially so over the last year. Our typical conversations go along these lines: "How much have you written today?" "Ten words, and they were all crap." "Me too—have you seen the latest episode of *Vikings/Last Kingdom/This Is Us?*"

I've had versions of this conversation with so many of you—so thank you to Jane Linfoot, Carmel Harrington, Cathy Bramley, and many others. Extra special hugs to Catherine Isaac, who has had a year filled with floods, homeschooling, and pandemic-related chaos, and still managed to write lovely books, be a lovely person, and have lovely hair as well.

Milly Johnson—what can I say that I haven't already said? Love you loads, thank you for helping me stay sane(ish).

Thanks to John Quinn, a man who not only uses a wheelchair, but is also Scottish and very ginger, and assures me he gets more stick for the last two than the first. John helped me understand some of the challenges and frustrations faced by wheelchair users and allowed me to steal the phrase "Manic Street Pushers." Thank you, my copper-topped Jock.

Acknowledgments

Like many of us, I've had to accept that my social life is now often contained within small square boxes on a computer screen. Thank you to everyone who comes to the quiz nights I randomly stage to distract myself, and thanks also to John Mitchell for the quiz nights he continues to host as amusingly online as he did in real life. Virtual hugs also to Rachael Tinniswood, Pamela Hoey, Paula Woosey, Ade Blackburn, the Shennans, and everyone else I've forgotten. I'm getting old you know.

Insights,
Interviews
& More...

About the author

About the book

Read on

Meet Debbie Johnson

DEBBIE JOHNSON is an award-winning author who has sold more than a million copies of her books. She writes uplifting and emotional women's fiction and is published around the world in a variety of languages.

She began writing seriously after she turned forty and had three young children—which for some reason seemed like the perfect time to start. She lives in Liverpool, England, where she divides her time between writing, caring for a small tribe of people and animals, and not doing the housework.

Her bestselling books include *Maybe One Day*, the Comfort Food Café series, and *The A–Z of Everything*. ∿

Reading Group Guide

1. At the start of the book, Elena tells the reader "We all have our own versions of 'good things,' I suppose. . . . The bright spots that shine in a sometimes gray world." What are your "good things"? Have they evolved over time?

2. How did you find Elena and Harry's relationship at the start of the novel? Do you think they were on the verge of marriage or a breakup?

3. As Elena and Alex lie in the rubble, waiting to be rescued, she tells him, "When I get out of here, I need to make some changes." Does she follow through? Are the changes she makes the right ones? What changes do you think Alex needs to make?

4. As Elena and Alex contemplate going their separate ways, she thinks: "There is a moment where one of us could say something— where one of us could acknowledge what is happening here, the way

we feel. A moment when we could take a different path, turn a different corner, find a different future." Why don't they in that moment? Does their choice foreshadow events later in the novel?

5. Elena is shocked when Harry proposes to her on TV, but she accepts. Do you think that was the right decision? What would you have done in her situation?

6. When we meet Elena years later, she has become a virtual shut-in—working from home, caring for Harry, because "I found that I couldn't quite face the big bad world." But she thinks of Harry, on the other hand, as "one of the ablest people I know," and despite his disability, he is active and engaged with the world. Why did this happen? How did you feel seeing Elena so changed?

7. When her sister, Olivia, challenges Elena to open up about her experience, Olivia says, "It's been years now, and you still never talk about it. It's like you've just . . . boxed it all away. It's not ▶

healthy." Elena defends herself, saying, "I live in the present. Isn't that supposed to be good, mindfulness and all that?" Who is right? What does "living in the present" mean to Elena? What does it cost her?

8. After Elena sees Harry with Alison's children, she thinks: "To the outside observer, it would appear as though we had everything—and yet I realize that I could happily walk out of this building and never come back. That I could wave goodbye to the years I have spent here and move on. The bigger question is whether I could leave Harry and never come back." Do you think she should? What would you do?

9. Harry and Elena both chose not to reveal certain important truths to each other: her pregnancy, his moment with Greta, her feelings for Alex. Would their lives have been different if they'd confessed those things before they'd gotten married?

10. Harry says to Elena, "You did the wrong thing for all the right

reasons." He's talking about their marriage, but are there other decisions Elena made for which this is also true?

11. What do you think will happen to these characters in the years after the novel ends? Where will Harry, Elena, and Alex wind up? ∾

An Excerpt from
Maybe One Day

Chapter 1

Thousands of songs and poems and stories have been written about love. Millions of pages have been filled with trillions of words; countless sad songs have been sung in countless sad bars by countless battered men with battered guitars. Endless nights have been fevered with the search for the perfect match that will make everything all right. For the "one" that will make everything—*everything*—feel better.

It starts early, if you're lucky. With parents who adore you, with attention and kindness and indulgence. With books filled with pictures of cartoon hares challenging you to guess how much they love you. With friends or siblings or aunties or granddads, a whole world of love surrounding you like a sheltering, cocooning bubble.

Before long, though, it's not cartoon hares or Mum and Dad. It's a whole different world of love. It's that boy who sits in front of you in geography; the one with the gorgeous hair and the cocky smile and the cool trainers. The one who makes you giddy when he smiles, and whose name you doodle surreptitiously on your pencil case, trying out his surname for size in advance of the inevitable wedding.

You talk to your friends about him, all the time, and you think about literally Nothing Else At All. You analyze every word, every movement, every casual chew of every gunked-up wad of gum. He is the only thing that matters, the only thing that feels real. It might not be the same for everyone. It might be a girl pining for a boy, a boy pining for a girl, or any combination of the above. It might happen when you're fourteen, or when you're forty. But at some point, it probably will happen—the search for love will begin.

You won't be alone in your obsession. In fact, rarely has a subject been so well discussed and yet so badly understood— because it seems to me that nobody has a clue what love is all about. We've all experienced it, but we all have a different version of it.

The voices on the radios and the iPods and the record players all around the world; the words on the pages of books in libraries and stores and on ▶

dusty shelves; the names and heart shapes carved into tree trunks—they all have a viewpoint. They just don't seem able to agree what it is.

Is it a many-splendored thing, or a crazy little thing? Is it a battlefield, or is it a drug? A red red rose, an unchained melody, a labor lost? And is it really all you need, like the Beatles would have us believe?

I'll be buggered if I know—it's confused me since the beginning.

But I do know this one thing, with complete certainty: I have lived with love. I have felt its touch, and blossomed beneath it, and been transformed by it. I have been blessed by it, and burned by it. I've felt the scars it leaves when it's snatched away, the pain that lives in the void of its absence. I've seen it packed up, in a small white box, and wheeled down the aisle of a church.

I've lived my life with love, and for so many years now I've lived my life without it—and I know which I prefer. It's what the kids might call a no-brainer.

So tonight, as I lie here beneath a too-familiar duvet in a too-familiar house surrounded by too-familiar noises, I've decided that I need to be brave. I need to find my courage, and look for love again. I need to reach out, and see which way my story ends. To find him, and hold him, and tell him how much I regret the terrible things that happened between us. The terrible things that happened to both of us.

Nothing so far in my life has led me to believe in fairy tales or happy endings. I am not a Disney princess, and my world is completely devoid of picture-perfect moments and moving speeches and passionate yearning.

But tonight, I have stayed up late, reading by the light of a full, silvered moon shining through my open curtains. And tonight I have made my decision— to reach for that happy ending, even if I never find it.

The sun crept over the trees about ten minutes ago, gold usurping the silver. It's a fresh dawn. A new beginning. The start of rediscovering everything I thought I'd lost.

Only twenty-four hours ago, I was getting up, brushing my teeth, drinking tea alone in a silent kitchen as I was preparing for a funeral. Preparing to say my final goodbyes to a woman I loved. Hard to believe that was only a day gone by.

A day that started with a funeral— but ended with hope. Hope that I discovered wrapped in tissue paper, ▶

An Excerpt from *Maybe One Day*
(continued)

hidden in a box among the forgotten
clothes and broken sewing machines
and decaying cobwebs of a long-
untouched attic. Hope that I never
knew existed, and that now illuminates
my being like sunlight filtered through
lemon-washed linen.

Hope. How did I ever live without
it? ⤳